THE MOST DIFFICULT QUESTION

For a space of time, Max watched her in silence. When he spoke, his words were measured and slow.

"So you're saying it's not that you can't love another man, but that you won't."

She hesitated briefly. "I suppose that's what I'm saying, yes."

"It seems you were right. You do lack courage."

"Do I?" she asked, making the words a challenge. She didn't disagree, but she had liked it better when he had thought she possessed that quality.

"I fear so. Last night I could have sworn your reaction to me was that of a woman in love. And when I declared myself to you and you failed to respond, I thought it meant I was mistaken. But now it occurs that you never *denied* loving me, and I'm wondering if perhaps I was right the first time, only you're too afraid to admit it."

Gwendolyn's pulse pounded in her neck, her temples, her wrists. She longed to rip the door from the coach and run away, but it was impossible to move, impossible to tear her eyes from his.

"Do you love me, Gwendolyn?"

There was too much warring within her for her to give in to what she wanted, which was to fall into his arms and declare, *Yes! Yes, I do love you, more than I have loved anyone in my life!* For therein lay a greater danger than any she had faced before. Yes, she was afraid. Terrified!

"One of the most innovative voices in the genre."
—*Romantic Times*

Also by Marcy Stewart from Zebra Books:

CHARITY'S GAMBIT
MY LORD FOOTMAN
LORD MERLYN'S MAGIC
DARBY'S ANGEL
THE VISCOUNT TAKES A WIFE

Novellas in Anthologies:

"An Indefinite Wedding" in *FLOWERS FOR THE BRIDE*
"Lady Constance Wins" in *LORDS AND LADIES*
"A Halo for Mr. Devlin" in *SEDUCTIVE AND SCANDALOUS*

LADY
SCANDAL

Marcy Stewart

Zebra Books
Kensington Publishing Corp.

http://www.zebrabooks.com

ZEBRA BOOKS are published by

Kensington Publishing Corp.
850 Third Avenue
New York, NY 10022

First Printing: August, 1998
10 9 8 7 6 5 4 3 2 1

Printed in the United States of America

For my dad,
Gordon Ray Stewart,
with love

You were my first hero.

Chapter One

Thunder growled to the west. Over the Irish Sea, a summer storm was brewing its way toward Blackpool, but inside the stout walls of Vaughan Manor, candlelight danced shadows on the ceiling and warmed deeper reds into the wineglasses scattered upon the dining table. Though the guests around that table bore for the most part an air of repleteness, of hungers satisfied, the striking gentleman seated at the host's right appeared the exception. His emerald eyes, so often expressive of boredom, now sparked with suppressed excitement. Over and over, he traced a finger along the contours of his glass and paid only vague attention to comments directed at him. Beneath the table, his boots tapped a discreet staccato. When a second, nearer roar of thunder sounded, prompting a giggling exclamation of fear from the lady seated next to him, he responded with a wolfish grin that froze into a pointed look at his host, communicating without the possibility of misunderstanding, *Let us proceed.*

Harold Vaughan, the white-haired gentleman at the table's head, gradually showed awareness of that glance, and curiosity bloomed in his eyes. But he acceded to the unspoken demand, albeit unhurriedly, and tapped his wineglass with a spoon. When all had fallen quiet, he stood and raised his glass.

"Family and friends," he said, his voice resonating with quiet dignity, "we are gathered this evening not only to enjoy congenial company, though that is sufficient reason of itself, but to celebrate the thirtieth birthday of one who is nephew to me by blood though a son to my heart." Faded blue eyes met green. "Max, may you live to enjoy your years twice over."

Chairs scraped backward as the gentlemen rose for the toast, and all lifted their glasses and drank. Sir Maxim Aurelius Hastings, baronet of nothing save a pile of decaying stones in Herefordshire, felt his eyes grow dangerously wet and lowered his gaze to the ivory tablecloth.

One of the guests began to pound the table insistently, and others took up the rhythm. They were demanding his response, and Max was ready to give it. For half a lifetime he'd struggled to repay his uncle's generosity and affection. At last he had something worthwhile to return, something more meaningful than designing glassware for Vaughan Glassworks—a thing anyone with a small degree of talent and craft could do, and at a quarter the salary Uncle Harry gave him. Tonight he would restore a small measure of what had been bestowed upon his mother and himself by giving his uncle something the older man had sought for decades.

The thought drew him to his feet. He scanned the twenty or more faces attending him, faces softened by four silver candelabra spaced at equal intervals along the table. Among the attendees he saw his mother, Anne, who smiled encouragingly though she knew nothing of his secret; Uncle Harry's wife, Rebecca, and their ward, Felicity Warren; several other friends and neighbors, and the most important guests for this evening's purpose, Allen Devereaux and Terrence Wilkey, local businessmen and, if the next moments went as he hoped, future investors.

For an instant he wished his cousin, Roderick Vaughan, were here for his triumph; it would be interesting to see that mocking look of his face fade for once. He dismissed the thought as unworthy; he was long past boyhood with its petty emotions. Yet old rivalries died hard.

His thoughts were running like mice from a cat, and the eyes watching him were expectant. Smiling gravely, he began, "If Uncle Harry thinks of me as a son, I am honored beyond all I could hope." He cast a warm look upon his relative, who responded with a gracious nod. "He has been more than a father to me."

Max dared not look at his mother, fearing the pain this comment might cause. He kept his gaze centered on his uncle, whose lips were pressed quiveringly together. Slowly the older man rose to embrace his nephew. The emotion-fraught moment spawned another scratching back of chairs and a round of toasting.

While the gentlemen settled to their seats again with spots of conversation beginning to grow, Max kept to his feet. "Tonight you have seen my uncle give me the gift of a handsome bay for my birthday. Now it is my turn to present him with something I hope he'll find as pleasing."

As Mr. Vaughan stirred in surprise, Max's eyes lifted to the alcove that led to the butler's pantry. Taking his cue, a short, thin man dressed in black livery emerged. Arms extended importantly, he carried a cloth-covered object upon a silver serving plate. There was an air of enforced dignity about him; only his incessantly darting eyes gave hint of his nervousness. Max watched his valet with disquiet and prayed he would not stumble.

"Thank you, Carleton." He took the servant's burden, waited impatiently while the man made a hasty retreat, then set the tray before his uncle. "Do the honors, sir," Max whispered. "Have a look."

With questions brimming in his eyes, Mr. Vaughan whisked the cloth away, exposing a large, ruby goblet braced with golden filigree. A sudden hush fell over the guests as the old gentleman's expression grew thick with bewilderment. "But Max, this is—"

"The goblet from the hall?" Max could scarce contain the

edges of his grin. "Indeed it is." He lifted the glass high for everyone to see plainly, then placed it on the table. "If there is anyone present who hasn't noticed, the Guinevere Chalice is the prize object in my uncle's display case. It is an expensive treasure; I don't think I exaggerate if I say it's priceless in Uncle Harry's eyes."

When the older man nodded, still puzzled, Max said, "As it is in mine. And not because we believe the legend that accompanies the glass, that Arthur's wife drank from it. No, it's not the legend that is so precious, but its color. Or rather, the secret of its color."

Now Mr. Vaughan's interest quickened tenfold. Unwilling to miss a second of his reaction, Max kept his gaze fastened to his elder's. "Those of you who are acquainted with glassmaking know we've had many improvements in our craft in the past few decades. But in one area we are more backward than our ancestors. We could not make this goblet today, for with all our advances in cutting and engraving and making larger cast plates, we have lost the knowledge to make the color of a true red like this one."

A soft smile played at his lips. "For many years, my uncle has experimented to find the forgotten combination of metals that will produce this rich color you see before you. Although I'm no alchemist, I've been searching as well. For some time I've secretly engaged others more able than I to work on the problem."

His voice lowered to a hush, causing a few of the ladies to shiver with anticipation, though they appeared more struck by the speaker than his message. "My search has led me to someone whose family never lost the secret, but kept it hidden for more than a century. Don't despair when I say the owner of the formula is French, for he has no more taste for Napoleon than anyone in this room. The war and its aftermath have caused the destruction of his family's business, a thing that is leading him to seek a better life elsewhere; and you know there are no finer glassmakers than the French. Excepting the inhabitants of this room, of course."

He paused, hopeful of a chuckle or two, but the intensity of their attention did not allow for levity.

"You're telling us a Frenchie gave you that formula?" Mr. Devereaux inquired, his fat features stamped with disbelief.

"Not *gave,* precisely," Max said, with a dry laugh. It had cost him almost all of his savings. Quickly he inserted his fingers into his waistcoat pocket and pulled out a shard of glass. "Compare this to the ruby of the chalice; there is no difference as to quality. Here; pass it among yourselves and examine it. The edges are beveled, so don't worry about being nicked, ladies."

Uncle Harry leaned forward to take the sample. "And this is new glass, made by the formula?"

"Yes, sir. Imagine the potential for the business." He cut a look at Mr. Wilkey, the most well-heeled manufacturer among them. "We could become the only makers of true red glassware in England. It would be possible again to craft such glorious objects as this chalice."

"I prefer colorless for my crystal," Aunt Rebecca said from across the table, the characteristic whine in her voice damping him as always. "How else will I know if I am drinking milk or wine?"

"Or blood," threw in Felicity, a remark that drew a squeak from Mr. Wilkey's wife, Irene.

"And not only glassware." Max pressed on, with a brief frown for Felicity, who appeared to be enjoying herself at his expense as she often did, "but bottles. Are not we all tired of black and green bottles? And think of the added enrichment and variety that will become available for stained glass."

The shard had reached Mr. Deveraux, and he turned it round and round in his fingers, his frown growing by the moment. "You'll pardon me for saying, but you don't know the ins and outs of this business like some of us. How do we know this is new glass and not old?"

Max looked from one face to another. He had not expected so much doubt, and perspiration began to trickle down his temples. "Because I have the formula in my possession."

"Let's see it, then," Devereaux said.

"You don't seriously expect me to show it to you," he stated with an incredulous smile.

"What? Don't trust me?"

Before Devereaux could grow more belligerent, Mr. Vaughan said, "Do you respect my judgment, Allen?" Receiving a grudging nod, he ordered Max, "Bring the receipt to me. I'll see if it looks workable."

Max gave a stiff nod, rang for Carleton, and sent him on the errand. During the paralyzing few minutes he waited, little bursts of conversation sprang up around the table. He met his mother's worried stare and sent her a reassuring smile he didn't feel. The room seemed to be growing hotter.

At last his valet returned bearing a rectangular oak box. Max had him place it on the table, then pulled the key from his pocket.

"I keep it with me at all times," he said, answering his uncle's unspoken question. "Just to be certain."

A sense of foreboding shuddered through him as he turned the key in the lock. He'd not anticipated a public examination of the formula. But all would be well. It had to be. The Frenchman, Jules Soufrière, had seemed trustworthy and knowledgeable.

It won't be here. Someone will have stolen it.

He opened the lid.

A single piece of stationery, thick as vellum, rested upon the red velvet lining. Black penstrokes written in an elegant script covered its surface. Air rushed back into Max's lungs. He lifted the paper toward Uncle Harry's trembling hand and said softly, "Sir, I give you the color red."

But as the older gentleman clasped it between thumb and forefinger, Max's own fingers suddenly gripped harder. "Wait," he said hoarsely, his gaze locked on the black markings. He felt a flush spreading upward. A high-pitched keening sounded in his ears. The scent of the candles became overpowering, nauseating; he would suffocate in a moment.

For an instant, a gentle tug-of-war ensued. With an exasperated burst of laughter, Mr. Vaughan said, "Max, let go, will you?"

The force of long habit prompted mindless obedience, and he released the note, searching for words but finding none. The eager look on his uncle's face, the curious eyes watching him, stunned him to muteness.

Uncle Harry's lips moved prayerfully as he scanned the paper's contents. "Manganese oxide, alloy of copper and zinc—" He broke off, frowning, incredulous, his gaze piercing his nephew to the core. "These proportions—this is the receipt for purple! How could you make such an error, Max?"

"That's not it," Max said, his voice sounding cold and dead. "That's not what I purchased. Someone has stolen the formula and replaced it with that."

He listened to the cries of disbelief erupting from the guests, and knew he would hear them for the rest of his life. Overhead, thunder cracked, as if echoing the rending of his heart. And then on the heels of shame came roaring anger. *Roderick!*

There were no rumblings of thunder in the city of Bath that evening, but Gwendolyn Devane was not concerned with the weather. Her large brown eyes were soft upon her daughter, Camille. Both ladies were ensconced in a box seat at one of the city's newest theatres, and the girl was sitting on the edge of her chair, her expression rapt, her attention only for the players below.

Gwendolyn's gaze shifted to the stage, where a handsome couple was seated upon a bench. Behind the pair, a colorful backdrop was painted with flowers and groves of fruit trees and a road that appeared to wind into infinity. A pile of gold and brown leaves surrounded the bench.

"You cannot mean it, Lydia," pled the handsome actor, his dark eyes full of agony as he looked at the maiden, then the audience. A few feminine sighs could be heard as the full force of his devastation reached them.

"But I do," shouted his lady mournfully. "I cannot marry you, Nevin." She moved languidly to her feet, her hands clasped modestly at her waist. "Papa has promised me to another. Now that our family has a fortune, we must have a title to accompany it."

"But *why?*" cried her suitor, enough pain in his voice for a millennium's worth of rejections.

The actress moved to center stage front. Gwendolyn's eyes sharpened. This was the turning point of the first act: if Miss Sturbridge failed to produce the irony needed, the audience would not grasp the connection and all would be lost. *Now,* Gwendolyn thought, making it a prayer.

The actress pressed an overly limp hand to her forehead. "Papa says"—she sniffed pitifully—"Papa says we have made our wealth in sheep's wool; now our descendants must wear it upon their heads in the House of Lords!"

A few titters from the audience. Gwendolyn scanned the faces below. Some of the ladies appeared intent on the drama, absorbing it literally. But on the whole she sensed an air of expectation, an avid looking for the message beneath.

"But I love you!" declared handsome Nevin, falling to his knees.

"Do not say so!" answered Lydia. "I cannot return your affection, for you are only a tutor. Papa says it is a female's duty to bring either honor or wealth to her family, and preferably both! Therefore, my heart—my heart belongs to Count *Oregano!*"

Healthy chuckles rippled through the audience, and Gwendolyn relaxed. They had caught the reference to the very real Lord Pepper; from now on it would be easy to hold their attention. She returned her gaze to her daughter, whose golden eyes shone with excitement, her delicately curved mouth moving silently . . .

Gwendolyn, features displaying her usual mild amusement and goodwill, leaned forward. "Darling," she whispered. "You are betraying us."

Camille's eyes drifted to hers as if from a great distance, and Gwendolyn felt anew the strength of her daughter's beauty, which seemed to unfold brighter with every passing day. Her child's hair was an even lighter blond than her own; in the candlelight it appeared almost white and framed Camille's sweet face to perfection. The fashionable pink gown, though inset with a modest tucker, could not hide a maturing figure that would draw the interest of any man, even had she the visage of Medusa. Such beauty spelled danger for a young girl, and Gwendolyn's heart trembled with resolve. Her own disastrous past would not be repeated by her daughter. Not so long as she had breath in her body.

"Betraying us?" mumbled the girl.

"You are repeating the words with the actors," Gwendolyn whispered. "How shall we explain that, since tonight is the play's opening?"

"I can't help it, Mama; we have gone over it so many times. Besides, no one will notice."

"You cannot say that of the gentleman seated directly across from us. His attention is only for you."

Camille lifted her gaze accordingly. The person in question, an attractive man with wiry auburn hair, acknowledged her notice with an incline of his head and a slight smile. He wore a dove-colored coat over a richly embroidered black vest and black breeches. The lady at his side, a russet beauty dressed in Naples yellow, saw the exchange and lifted her chin in annoyance. Camille flushed and directed a questioning look at her mother.

"Simply do not look his way again," she advised. "He will lose interest."

But in that she was wrong. At the intermission, Gwendolyn saw him guide his lady from her seat. She almost forgot them in the next few moments as a flurry of visitors, both male and female, paid the ladies their compliments. But when an usher pulled open the curtains sheltering their box to deliver a small bouquet of roses, her senses instantly became alert. An instinct told her the flowers were from the stranger across the way, and she had not liked the intent look in his eye.

While Camille exclaimed over the flowers, Gwendolyn read the enclosed card with a wry twist to her lips: *Beauty to the beauties.* She was not surprised when the unknown gentleman entered their box immediately after the usher's leave-taking. His hat was in one hand, his personal card in the other, and he extended the latter to her with an apologetic air, charm dripping from every pore as he begged her to forgive his presumptuousness, but he was so caught by them he could not resist.

Gwendolyn permitted none of her thoughts to rise to her face. She smiled warmly and read his name aloud, a question in her voice. "Roderick Vaughan?"

"The same, ma'am. And if I may make so bold, you are . . . ?" When she introduced herself and her daughter, his expression became one of amazement. "Your *daughter?* Miss Devane, to have such a youthful-appearing mother bodes well for your own future. I had thought you to be sisters or friends, nothing more."

"Mama wed very young," Camille said. "She is only—"

"Thank you, darling," Gwendolyn interrupted with a twinkle. "You needn't speak in numbers."

Vaughan laughed. "No, there are two things one must never ask: a woman's age and a man's worth."

"How true, Mr. Vaughan, and I have often told my daughter so. You must listen to your elders, Camille."

Vaughan gave a pained chuckle. "Stop, Mrs. Devane. You're making me feel as if I'm sprouting grey hairs as we speak."

"Sir, I should be devastated to make such an impression," she said through a smile. "It is not that you are ancient, but my daughter so young. She only passed her sixteenth birthday a few weeks ago."

The light died in Vaughan's face. "Sixteenth, you say?"

She nodded once, merrily.

"I thought we weren't going to speak in numbers," Camille complained.

Gwendolyn pressed her daughter's hand apologetically, but kept her gaze on Mr. Vaughan. She could see he was shaken, but she had not come near finishing with him yet. "It was so thoughtful of you to bring flowers, sir. Why did you not bring your lady to meet us as well?"

"My lady?"

"The one sitting with you during the first act."

He appeared to collect himself. "Oh, you must mean my cousin. She was feeling unwell and had to leave." His gaze grew speculative, then deepened with interest. "How flattered I am that you noticed us."

So he meant to transfer his attentions to her now, did he? Almost as bad. "I could hardly fail to do so, since your box falls within the line of my vision when I'm observing the stage."

"Well, your box does not fall in my sight as easily, but with such blazing beauty available to admire, who could waste time watching that ridiculous play? Which leads me to ask, how is it your husband does not accompany his ladies tonight? Surely it is a risk to leave such fetching beauties alone."

"I am a widow, Mr. Vaughan," she said tightly. And then, because she could not help herself: "Are you not enjoying the play?"

"My condolences, ma'am," he said lightly. "Though from the lovely gold color of your gown, I should think you are in mourning no longer . . . ?"

"Mr. Devane expired years ago. What is wrong with the play? Most of the audience seems amused."

Roderick looked from one intent face to the other, obviously perplexed at their interest in his review. "Truth, I don't understand why they laugh. I find the acting forced and the plot tired."

"Oh," Gwendolyn said in relief. "You haven't been in Bath long, have you? If you had, you would understand that the play is a parody of a young woman who actually resided here. She was forced by her father to wed a viscount, Lord Pepper, though she loved another young man. After the marriage, she ran away to Greece with her first suitor, though not before stealing the family diamonds!"

"I see," he said with a grin. "And all of this will be played out on stage?"

"Yes, sir," Camille answered. As she noted her mother's

sharp glance, she added, "That is, I imagine it will." And then, rushing on proudly, before Gwendolyn could stop her: "Madame Rose wrote it. Have you not heard of her? Many call her Lady Scandal, for her works are always about the latest gossip in society. Both names are secret ones, though, for no one knows who she is. She pens many such plays, and everyone likes them!"

"How intriguing," he said, though his tone betrayed he was less interested in the words than the one who spoke them. "I imagine the lord you mention will not receive the play so well, though."

"That's one reason she keeps her identity hidden." Camille wrinkled her nose charmingly and dashed a mischievous glance at her mother. "The other is that ladies should not earn their livings. Or so it is often said."

"Now, Camille," Gwendolyn warned, "you are boring our visitor, and he must be tired of standing. Besides, everyone knows only a gentleman has the ability to write such a play. The pretense that the author is a female is merely a ploy to increase ticket sales. Oh, look, Mr. Vaughan. The second act is about to begin, and you still must walk the entire span of the theatre to reclaim your seat."

No gentleman could ignore so direct an invitation to leave, and he bowed. "I'm not concerned about that; my only regret is that I must leave such fair company. The last few moments have been the high point of my evening; it can only be downhill from now, and I refuse to fight it; I'm going to my inn. But you could make me happy again if you say I may call on you tomorrow morning."

The curtain was rising, and she pretended to affix her attention on the stage. "I beg you to forgive us, Mr. Vaughan, but my daughter and I always sleep late following a night at the theatre."

"Of course. What about the afternoon?"

"I'm so sorry. We have made other plans."

"The next day, then," he persisted.

She offered him a regretful, though pointed, stare. "We are often busy. It is impossible to know."

"I see." For an instant he looked offended; then he smiled, and the smile was full of challenge and interest. "We will make it another time then, Mrs. Devane. You'll find I'm a determined man."

Not so determined as I, she thought, but only inclined her head in reply, her eyes distant.

On the evening following his birthday disaster, Max burst through the front door of Vaughan Manor, bounded up the stairs, turned down the corridor leading to Felicity's room, and blindly bumped into the upstairs maid, who shrieked and dropped an armload of bedding. Apologies bled from him as he bent to help her retrieve the items, wadding one sheet atop the other until the stack looked twice as high as it had in the beginning. Patting her shoulder to relieve the wild look in her eye, he rushed onward to pound on Felicity's door.

"My goodness, Max," she complained when she opened it, the oddly shaped lines branded into her cheek betraying an afternoon nap. "You could be less noisy and still wake the dead. What is it?"

"I've been to Liverpool," he said, brushing past her to enter the sitting-room portion of her bedroom suite. "He's not there."

Sleepily, she pressed her hands against her cheeks and rubbed the outer corners of her eyes. "Who? Roderick?" she asked through a yawn.

"Of course, Roderick; who else?" He threw himself onto her loveseat at a half-sprawl, his long legs bracing his weight. Felicity stepped over them and sat beside him, her eyes still bleary. As she did, he became aware of her perfume, a powerful smell of roses. She had worn that scent since adolescence, which was precisely the length of time he'd hated it. It was harder to hate the young woman wearing it, however, especially when she was attired in a soft, flowing thing as now. An apricot or peach color it was, something that went well with her brown hair and lightly freckled skin.

She caught his eyes moving over her and grinned slyly. "Well, what do you expect me to do about it?"

He pinned his gaze to the overly sentimental portrait of Felicity's mother on the opposite wall. "I expect you to tell me where he is."

"Why should I know that? Do you think Roderick informs me of his comings and goings?"

"Not necessarily, but you've always had a way of finding out."

She looked miffed. "You make me sound like a spy."

"You must admit you're the first one to know things."

"Is that why you gave up your pursuit of me?" she asked with an arch look. "You thought I'd discover your secrets? I suppose no man likes that."

He snorted. "Aren't you remembering things backwards, Felicity?"

"Am I? Then why did you and Roderick fight so hard to win my attention? There was a time when I could not so much as take a walk without one of you at each side." Her eyes glowed at the memory.

"Ancient history. Besides, we fought over everything. You know that." He dropped all pretense at hiding his irritability. "Now, where is he?"

Her lips turning downward, Felicity removed herself to sit in a nearby armchair. "Why don't you ask your Uncle Harry? He's the one who sent him off to do whatever it is Roderick does."

"I don't want to ask him. He's disappointed enough in me already. There's no purpose in making him even lower by telling him his son isn't where he was ordered to be." He frowned and sat forward, bracing his forearms on his knees. "Finding new markets for our glass, indeed. No one in the whole of Liverpool had heard of him."

"Why should that disappoint Uncle Harry?" she inquired snidely. "He's used to Roderick's ways. Besides, he has you to order about—*the son of his heart.*" She made it sound a curse. "Even if Roderick does spend the greater portion of his time chasing one female after another, at least he has a life, which is more than can be said of you."

Annoyed flashes stirred behind Max's eyes. "I have never been able to understand you, Felicity. When you were orphaned, my uncle took you in just as he did my mother and me, even though you are not related to him by blood."

"He is my godfather."

"Yes, but he could have put you in a boarding school. Instead, he treated you like a daughter." He waved a hand, indicating her bedchamber. "You know there has never been any meanness or restraint to Uncle Harry's generosity. No drafty quarters in the attic, no measured allowance to remind us of our place. Instead, he welcomed all of us into his home as if we were always meant to be a part of it. Have you no sense of gratitude? Harold Vaughan is kindness in the flesh."

"Kind?" She glanced around the sitting room, as if taking account of the walls lined in silk covering, the elegant Queen Anne furnishings and rich carpeting. "I suppose he has provided well for us, as you are always reminding me, Sir Conscience. You should have been a knight instead of a baronet; your sense of honor is overdeveloped, I declare it is! Oh, don't huff; I suppose I am grateful to Uncle Harry. But I don't feel the warmth of his *kindness,* as you call it, for I don't strain myself to please him as you do."

"I don't strain myself," he protested, but a flash of long-forgotten resentment startled him into silence.

He had been fifteen when his father died, and all formal education had stopped at that point. His uncle saw no need for anything further; Max would be taken into the business just as his eighteen-year-old cousin Roderick had been.

Max's gaze lowered to the carpet as he recalled those early days. He hadn't minded leaving school. It was only his study of painting he'd missed. His tutor had claimed Max possessed a rare talent and declared it a crime that he not be allowed to continue. Remembering the scene between his uncle and the

overwrought artist, a rush of scorn ran through him. As Uncle
Harry had told Mr. Evans, one could hardly make a living
painting portraits. It had been a small sacrifice to his vanity to
give it up, that was all. A man hoping to support his family
made many such sacrifices.

But how strange the casting hall had seemed to his eyes the
first time he'd entered it; the large interior echoing with men's
voices and noises of work; the mixing vats combining sand,
sodium carbonate, quicklime, and other materials that melted—
miraculously to him—into glass. There had been so much to
learn about the formulas, about setting crucibles into hellish
furnaces, and flattening the molten material onto large copper
tables. So much to learn, and he'd had not a grain of natural
facility for any of it; unlike Roderick, whose knowledge must
have passed from his father's blood to his intact, for he'd never
exerted more than a leaf's effort to take it in.

How disappointed Uncle Harry had been in Max's early
attempts at learning the trade. Finally, the older man had given
up. The displaced nephew's talents seemed to lie only in designing patterns for stained glass and etching diamond designs into
crystal, a task he did until this day.

"An artist's work," his uncle often told him, meaning to
compliment; but Max knew Harold Vaughan's heart, that he
thought a man's worth lay in his ability to produce real things,
useful objects for the world of life. Not the airy sort of nonsenses
his own father had sought, to their ruin.

He lifted his eyes and saw Felicity watching him closely,
her lips pressed into a knowing smile. "I am happy with my
work," he said firmly.

"All right, Max," she said, lifting an elegant hand and dropping it. "I know when I'm defeated. But my curiosity remains.
It's not that I doubt Roderick has your formula, because that
would be like him. But how do you suppose he found out about
it, since you kept it so secret?"

"Because he has easy access to my rooms, of course, and
had time enough to take it before he left; I've had the thing
for a few days now, saving it for *a special occasion.*" The

words were filled with loathing. "No wonder Roderick left the day before my birthday. He knew I'd kill him! I wish I'd given it to Uncle Harry the instant it crossed my palms!"

"But he wasn't here to enjoy your public shaming. It's unusual for him to miss the results of his labor."

Max stood and walked to the round table in the corner. A porcelain kitten reclined on its surface, and he fingered it idly. "I know, but it had to be Roderick. There's the forgery to consider. It wasn't enough to simply take the true receipt. No, he must twist the knife by substituting a similar one, proving me the fool twice over."

"And naturally," she said, her eyes crinkling, "you don't recall the formula."

The hand poised over the cat knotted briefly into a fist. "I didn't think it would be necessary."

"Poor Max," she said with a throaty laugh. "You have never had a head for such things. One would think a man who enjoys his work as much as you say you do would be capable of remembering it."

"I would have memorized it, had I the least notion it would be stolen," he told her with a quelling glare. How she loved torturing people, especially him. He had often suspected she was a frivolous woman, and now he knew it.

"Then go to the Frenchman again, for heaven's sake! Surely he will make you a second copy."

A deep silence fell over him as he called to mind the tiny old man, his straggly grey hair falling to his shoulders, and the way his hands trembled as he took the pouch of money. He flashed a look at Felicity. There was nothing to be gained here except condemnation, and he had enough of that for himself already. He moved toward the door.

"Oh, no, Max. You don't know where he is, do you?" She wiped mirthful tears from her eyes.

"Of course I know where he is," he said with admirable calmness. "He has gone to America to make a new life." A trip paid for by himself, he was careful not to add.

She gave an unladylike whoop. "You are an infant, I declare

you are! You expect everyone to exhibit the same trustworthiness as you. Take a wife who is wise in the ways of the world, Max; otherwise, you will be sheared like a lamb at every turn.''

"I won't ask who you are recommending for that position,'' he said, barely keeping sarcasm from his tone. Words were seldom minced among Roderick, Felicity, and himself; they were like brothers and sister in their squabbles, and yet not. "This may come as a surprise to you, but I was not born for your amusement. I hope sometime I can help you as much as you've helped me today.''

"Oh, Max, Max. So dangerous, and so wounded.'' She walked very close to him, her dancing eyes slanted upward. He viewed her with suspicion, but very determinedly kept his ground. In lightning-like progression, he saw a flare of emotion kindle in her face; then she stood on tiptoe and pressed her lips to his. Although he could not help being stirred, he gently, but firmly, pushed her away.

"I have always preferred you to Roderick,'' she whispered. "But you don't care.'' She shrugged away from his grip. "Still tending the flame for Lucy, aren't you?''

His stomach lurched at the name. "I've forgotten she exists.''

Felicity flicked him a look of skepticism and something darker, but she lowered her lashes so quickly he could not read her expression. "Very well, then. I'll tell you where I think your cousin is, since I am certain you're correct; he *must* be the one who stole your formula, and you cannot let him be victorious. I have but one requirement: take me with you.''

"Surely you jest.''

She raised her hands overhead in a luxurious stretch. He averted his eyes from the tantalizing manner in which her gown pressed against her flesh. "Oh, why not? I am expiring of boredom! We won't make a scandal; I shall take my maid.''

"Absolutely out of the question.''

"But I want to help, truly I do. I know I can get your receipt back from Roderick. I'm better at that sort of thing than you are!''

That was true, but he had no desire for the complications

she would bring. He started to speak, but hesitated. Her eyes were playful in their pleading; still; he sensed a deeper longing, a desperation almost, in them. Perhaps he could . . . No.

"I'm sorry, Felicity, but I can't take you. Now tell me where he is before I lose patience."

"Oh, very well," she pouted. "Roderick met a girl named Maryanne Davis on his last trip, and afterward bored me to tears with stories of how beautiful she is. I believe he's followed her and her parents on holiday. Perhaps you'd better sit down before I tell you. Unless I'm mistaken, Roderick has gone to Bath."

He glowered as she launched into fresh gales of laughter.

"Do give my regards to Lucy!" she gasped.

A couple of days following his conversation with Felicity, Max entered the city of Bath on his new bay, Monitor. The animal had covered the miles at a stalwart clip in spite of an annoying drizzle, but the trip had taken longer than Max hoped. Because his journey led almost to the gates of his estate outside Hereford, he had not been able to resist a detour. Since his last visit, the roof of his childhood home had developed holes over the older section, confirming his guess that if restoration was not done immediately, it would be useless. Having spent his savings on the formula, he could do nothing. Perhaps that was as it should be; maybe it was best to let Hastings Hall rot beneath the endless rain like his memories.

He did not believe it for an instant. What an idiot he'd been! He might as well have wagered his fifteen thousand at cards. Or thrown it into the sea.

But there was still hope, he thought, shivering miserably in his greatcoat, the chill sinking deeper into his bones as his horse clopped along the pavement. Should Vaughan Glassworks become the only glassmakers in England with the secret of a true red, they would capture the lion's share of business. Max knew his uncle would be appropriately generous. Before long, he could restore his mother to her rightful home and have a comfortable income as well.

The drizzle, which had plagued him the entire way, had dried to a fine mist. Max was struck anew with the beauty of Bath, even when viewed through a veil of moisture as today. Layer upon layer of golden-stoned buildings marched toward the surrounding hills. No dark pall of firing ovens clouded the sky; merely this gentle fog shrouding all like a half-remembered dream of paradise.

He hated it.

Only the most desperate circumstances could induce him to revisit Bath, for all its pleasantness to the eye. Here had been the scene of his greatest humiliation and his worst disappointment. No one could wish to relive that.

Max sneezed, startling Monitor into a little dance that alarmed a couple crossing the road in front of him. He tipped his hat in apology. There were a number of pedestrians about in spite of the inclement weather, but that was not unusual. The city's one purpose was idleness, and there was aught to do save trail from shop to shop or gossip over the mineral waters.

Eventually he came to the Colonnade and Pump Room. Across from it was the White Hart Inn, the lodging Roderick most preferred. Max entrusted his horse to an attendant and entered, wishing for an instant he'd brought Carleton along. There had seemed little purpose in dragging his man with him; this was no social excursion requiring a valet's administrations. He meant to pay no calls. Regardless of what Felicity imagined, Lucy Munroe exerted no hold over him any longer.

Still, Carleton would have done something with his clothes to make him more presentable. He detested walking into a well-appointed lobby looking like a drowned rat.

The manager was all politeness in spite of Max's appearance, though his small brown eyes flicked over him briefly. He perused the guest book and said that, while a Mr. Roderick Vaughan had resided a brief span with them, he had departed three days before. And no, the gentleman had not left a forwarding address.

Max thanked him and turned slowly toward the entrance, his thoughts desperate. First Liverpool, now this. Surely Roderick hadn't left Bath! He hadn't the time to chase him to the ends of the earth. He was too tired. Worse, Uncle Harry couldn't do without both of them. Though his relative had expressed surprise at Max's request for a holiday, he had been gracious enough to spare him for a while, but not for too long.

He had to think. Instead of leaving the inn, he sank into a chair and leaned his head back, closing his eyes against the look of unease the manager sent his way. It was warm in here. Too warm. Where was Roderick? Always, always near his latest paramour. With sudden illumination—were he not so spent he would have thought of it a moment ago—he pushed to his feet and approached the desk

"Does a Maryanne Davis reside here?" he asked eagerly.

"She does," answered the man without looking at his register. "She stays with her parents, Mr. and Mrs. Douglas Davis."

Frantic as Max was to speak with her, the manager would not give him the Davis's room number, though he was willing to send a message. An uncomfortable half-hour passed while Max waited. At long last, an attractive matron wearing a bombazine dress approached the desk and was directed toward him.

Max rose and introduced himself. When she identified herself as Pamela Davis, Maryanne's mother, he quickly made his request.

"I'm afraid I don't know Mr. Vaughan's direction," she said, her expression chilly. "Nor do I care."

There could be no doubt what had happened here; such had occurred too often in the past. "I believe I can guess the reason for that lack of caring, madam. He danced attendance on your daughter for a significant length of time, becoming important in her eyes, and perhaps your own. And then he dropped from your life with a hurried note. Or a gift of roses."

Her expression grew amazed. "How . . . how did you know that?"

"Because it's what he does, I'm sorry to say, and he's no friend of mine either." That was not always true, but at this moment it was. "If you could give me the least hint of where he might have gone, I would be most grateful."

"Well," she said, mollified, "I know he's still in Bath, for we saw him yesterday in the Park. That's why my poor daughter is in her room at this moment; she so dreads running across him again." She drew closer to him, her tone lowering. "Evidently he's found another foolish girl to pursue; someone with yellow hair, probably from artifice, unlike my angel's beautiful golden red, which God gave her. I don't know the chit's name, but when we saw them at Sydney Gardens yesterday, she was in the company of another woman who looks much like her."

"Thank you, madam," Max said, relief ballooning inside him. "You've helped more than you know."

She appeared intent on detaining him, for she started to touch his sleeve, saw it was wet, and ruffled her fingers in the air with unconscious distaste. "You say he has done this to others besides my Maryanne? Are you pursuing him to defend another lady's honor?"

Hating to disappoint her, he said, "In a manner of speaking, yes."

"Then I hope you at least break his nose. We are leaving before our holiday is finished, and all because my daughter is so heartsick!"

He expressed his sadness at their fate and promised to do his best to damage Mr. Vaughan in some way. Hurriedly taking his leave, he reclaimed his horse and began to search from one inn to the next. Building after building he entered, all of them beginning to look the same. Perhaps he visited some of them more than once.

Roderick could not be found.

The moist air no longer seemed cool; the warmth he gathered in the lodgings had fired heat into his blood—an alarming heat that rippled through his body. He was growing feverish, and he hadn't the time or patience to become sick.

Pray God his cousin hadn't rented a house or cottage. If he

had sold Max's receipt to a rival manufacturer, he'd certainly have the funds to do so.

The thought almost made him cold again.

After what seemed hours of searching, he acknowledged there was only one last place to look; then he would return to the closest hotel and take a room. He reluctantly drew Monitor to the east, crossed Pulteney Bridge, its Adam-designed arches failing to move him in his discomfort, rode down Great Pulteney Street past the gardens and almost to the edge of town, a short distance down a side road, then to the grounds of The Allemande. He dismounted, staring at the yellow-bricked edifice, its columned portico a diminuitive echo of the Colonnade, thinking he'd never meant to stand here again, not on his life.

A fit of coughing seized him, and Monitor shied away, his eyes rolling in alarm. The beast was gaining a false impression of his new master. "I am not always so noisy," he assured his horse, while handing the reins to the lackey who ran through the fog to take them.

"Oh, that's awright, sir, you wouldn't guess at the noises some fellows make," said the pale young man, his green-and-white livery looking less than crisp in the damp. "Don't I know you?"

"No," Max said immediately, his smile dissolving. "You've never seen me before. I'm a stranger. If I seem familiar, it's because a lot of people look like me."

"Huh," said the lad doubtfully, but the baronet was already entering the building.

The reception hall looked the same: Persian rugs patterned in green, navy, and black scattered over a highly polished oak floor; paneled walls painted in light celery with seascapes artfully arranged upon them; tasteful but comfortable sofas and armchairs clustered in small groupings, potted plants dotted around. Every corner bespoke charm, yet maintained a polite distance. How unfortunate the same could not be said for the innkeeper's daughter.

The desk, a massive chunk of mahogany that appeared seamless, faced the doors. He did not recognize the clerk behind it, and there was only an old man sleeping in the lobby. No one could say how long it would remain that way, though, and Max approached the desk rapidly.

"Roderick Vaughan . . ." said the clerk, tapping his quill against the guest book, his gaze wandering toward the ceiling as if to find the name there. Max watched him a moment with seething impatience, then grabbed the book, swirled it around, and ran his finger down the list. There he was. Thank God! Room three-fifteen.

"Is he in?" Max demanded. "I know you're trained to observe the activities of your guests, so you had better tell me."

The attendant's eyes were bulging with indignation. "No. Mr. Vaughan is not in."

"Thank you," Max told him calmly, and retraced his steps through the lobby and outdoors. It took him no more than a couple of minutes to inform the lackey to stable his horse with a good brushing and feed for he might be awhile, then walk to the rear of the building to the servant's entrance. He saw no one in the back hall, where deliveries were received, and paid scant attention to the glances of the cook and his helpers as he strode purposefully through the kitchens. Only when he entered the butler's pantry and found a maid stacking crystal on the shelves did he pause briefly. She was a pretty little mite, and her cheeks flushed at the sight of him.

"I beg your pardon, sir, but you shouldn't—" she began, then hesitated. "Why, if it's not Sir Hastings!"

"You must have me confused with someone else," he mumbled, and reached for the key numbered three-fifteen on the pegboard. "Lost mine," he offered in explanation as he stepped out of the closet.

The servants' stairs were narrow, steep, and dark against the back wall of the inn. He paused briefly at the second landing, his pulse beating far too rapidly for comfort. He needed a long nap and something hot to burn off this fever. But such luxury would have to wait.

Reaching the third floor, he passed through the corridor with growing urgency. Opening Roderick's door without mishap, he relocked it and pocketed the key.

His cousin had engaged a single chamber rather than one of The Allemande's suites. A second's notice revealed that nothing had changed in the inn's decorating scheme during the past eleven months; the bedroom was spacious and arranged around a theme. This one had a forest motif; the carpet was emerald, the walls a lighter green; and the single painting over the bed was pastoral in nature. None of it matched his mood in the slightest.

Immediately he began to search, moving from one drawer to the next, fingering waistcoat pockets and the linings of shelves and trying not to displace things.

Roderick mustn't suspect he had been here. The longer Max could remain incognito, the better. He knew from long experience that confronting his cousin would yield nothing except scornful delight on Roderick's part. The man thrived on dangling people's hopes and letting them fall. Particularly Max's.

How he wished the theft of his formula was a prank. It would be the most cruel one in his cousin's history, but less serious than outright missappropriation. Unfortunately, he didn't trust Roderick's character enough to be able to say one way or the other.

Max flung open the last drawer of the chiffonier, turned his head to the side, and sneezed three times in succession. He thought fleetingly of his horse and would have smiled if he did not feel so sick.

Almost a quarter-hour later, he had searched the obvious places and now began to contemplate the room itself. If he could think like Roderick, where would he hide something?

When his gaze lit on the painting, he dashed to it hopefully; but nothing was hidden on the other side. His glance lowered to the bed. He'd already searched between the mattresses. Now he dropped to his knees and peered beneath. It was then he heard the unmistakable sound of his cousin's laughter in the hall, mixed with feminine voices, moving this way.

For one frantic instant he considered sliding beneath the bed, but there was hardly room enough. With dread, he recalled the narrow balconies that lined the back of the inn and glanced at the French doors that led to them, though Roderick's drapes were pulled over his set. Max scurried there, the sound of his cousin's key in the lock giving wings to his boots.

Scrambling through the doors, he closed them carefully and hoped the drapes would not still be moving when Roderick entered, then stepped to the side of the glass pressing his back against the bricks. There was very little wall between the door and the waist-high barrier, which was solid wood except for little hearts cut at cloying intervals, then a dizzying expanse between it and the balcony to the next room.

He stared past that to the others, frail little rectangles flaunting infinity. None of them were deeper than a yard or wider than a foot to each side of the French doors; just enough room to sneeze oneself over the rail to an untidy demise.

A perverse need for punishment led him to peer over the edge to the others below it, then to those above. A shallow ledge ran from one balcony to the next, an unnecessary ornamentation in his opinion. Perhaps the Munroes had meant them for pigeon roosts.

He hadn't liked these paltry extensions when he'd resided here, and he liked them less now. Not only were they dangerous, but they had been the scene of the most foolish thing he had ever done in his life. Now, to his fevered eyes, they appeared to undulate, taunting him with threats of a speedy death.

How he wished Roderick would leave! But his cousin was walking back and forth inside, slamming drawers and muttering to himself. Over the racket he made, Max faintly heard a single knock, then the voice of Roderick's valet, Henderson. Oh, very fine; Roderick was probably preparing for a dinner engagement or a ball; perhaps he meant to escort the yellow-haired lady Mrs. Davis had mentioned. Naturally he would demand a long soak in a tub, requiring endless pails of hot water to be boiled in the kitchen and carried upstairs at a slug's pace.

A cough tickled at the back of his throat, and Max nearly strangled himself in subduing it. He had hardly recovered when he heard a scratching at the French doors leading to the room next door. Instantly he slid to a sitting position, trying to make himself small.

All was not yet lost, he told his hammering pulse. If Roderick's neighbors exited onto their balcony and spied him behind a heart, he would pretend he belonged here. But he'd have to feign muteness, or his voice would give him away to Roderick.

The mist chose that moment to thicken into rain. He turned up his collar, then pulled his hands inside his sleeves.

Two thumps could be heard as the neighbors' French doors opened wide against the walls of the balcony. "Good; his drapes are pulled," said a melodious voice, a woman's. "I think we're safe awhile. Oh, it has begun to rain. Isn't that a beautiful sound?"

A feminine reply to this, muffled by distance. Then, closer, the voice light and breathy: ". . . imagine how he could manuever himself next door. Do you think he paid . . ." It faded again.

The conversation continued, coming tantalizingly close, then drifting away as the room's occupants moved. Eavesdropping was a thing he despised, but now he listened unabashedly, his need for distraction from his circumstances being so great. Besides, they were undoubtedly speaking of Roderick, and he might learn something useful.

From their conversation, he guessed they were Mrs. Davis's pair of ladies. It appeared Roderick had traded a besotted female for a wiser one. How unfortunate for him. He could almost weep.

" . . . worry, he will soon tire of his game." The more mature speaker again; she owned a beautiful, expressive voice. Wonder if she sings, he thought, and fought a sudden notion to peer over the fence and see if he could glance into her room, find out what she looked like. "But only if we ignore him, though not too pointedly."

"Otherwise, he will think we are trying to attract him by our *lack* of interest," added the other, obviously younger lady.

He grinned and tasted raindrops. He could not believe he

was overhearing instructions in managing gentlemen. No man he knew had ever had such an opportunity. Eavesdropping was undervalued.

"Absolutely," agreed the other. "Now, we have just enough time before dinner to go over this little problem I'm having. Are you willing, or did our walk tire you?"

"No, I'm fine, Mama."

Max's brows lifted. Mother and daughter; that explained the lessons. He heard a scraping noise; chairs being drawn near the French doors? He hoped so; he would be able to hear them better. And now the mother was speaking again, this time with hushed passion.

"He is a scoundrel, a rake, I tell you! Instead of making wagers or racing, he derives his pleasure playing one woman against another! How weak he is, that he can only feel strong when he makes us small!"

Max's smile faded. This was an unexpected change of mood. It did not seem necessary to exhibit such vehemence when the child had been agreeable only a moment before.

"No, I do not believe it. He is too good, too attentive, and very charming! He is not the kind of gentleman who pretends to love one lady while courting another."

"*All* gentlemen are that kind," said the more mature voice. "*Especially* when they are attentive and charming."

He nodded grimly. He didn't appreciate her assault on all mankind, but she certainly understood Roderick.

"No, it's you who is at fault. I've seen how you look at him. What man could resist such lures? To do so would be a mark of discourtesy, Why, he probably pities you!"

"Pities me! If anyone is to be pitied, it is you! Has he begged *you* to marry him?"

Max's ears perked. Had Roderick been caught at last?

"Are you claiming he has asked for your hand?" came the trembling reply.

"We have only to set the date."

Max shivered, though not because of the rain. Lord, but the mother was heartless!

"No!" the girl cried. "You shall not have him!"

A brief, taut pause. "Put that pistol away! Do you imagine murdering me will accomplish anything?"

Max's eyes grew very wide. He cast a wild look over the fence but saw only the open doors.

"Yes, I do. You can't have him if you're dead."

Max had had enough. He crouched to a stand, thinking furiously. He could not sit here while a mother and daughter slew one another over his cousin. He had only two alternatives open to him: burst through Roderick's room and endure the ignominy of being discovered or risk his life by stepping along the ledge to the next balcony.

"Please do not shoot me," the mother entreated. "I have not said I intend marry him!"

"As if anyone could say *no* to such an opportunity!"

There was no time to be lost. Without looking down, he flung his leg over the rail.

Chapter Two

Gwendolyn held up a hand to indicate the need for time to reflect. Camille scooted back in her chair and arched her neck backward, slowly and pleasurably rotating her head.

"I was afraid of that," Gwendolyn mumbled, scanning her writing with distaste. "Too histrionic by far, even for a comedy."

Camille set the pages of the script on the table and covered her yawn with delicate fingers. "But the women are going to join forces against him, you said. *That* will be amusing. I rather liked the interplay of the characters."

Gwendolyn gave her daughter a gentle smile. "That's because you enjoy melodrama. You would take to the stage in an instant did I allow it."

"No, Mama. The performing would be nice, but I shouldn't like to travel always."

"What an intelligent girl you . . ." Alarm filled Gwendolyn's eyes. "Did you hear something?"

"Hear what?"

"Help," called a masculine voice softly. Gwendolyn exchanged an astonished look with her daughter, then rushed to the balcony.

A man was clinging to the outside wall midway between her room and Mr. Vaughan's, his arms splayed against the bricks, the heels of his boots hanging over the ledge. One side of his face was pressed against the wall, the other turned toward her. A single green eye implored her from beneath dripping dark hair. His mouth worked soundlessly.

"Oh, dear heavens!" she cried, and heard Camille gasp behind her.

"Stuck," said the man. "Help."

"Don't move! There is a gentleman next door. I'll fetch him!"

"No," he begged. "Don't tell Roderick. And keep your voice down."

A few heartbeats passed. So he was acquainted with Mr. Vaughan, was he? Well, this was not the time to ask searching questions. She could not stand idly by while a fellow creature plunged to his death. Yet he was out of her reach by at least a hand's span; she could determine that without trying.

Her frantic gaze swept the balcony, but there was nothing there to help. Perhaps if she had a rope, she could tie it to the bed and swing the other end to him. If there was time, she could knot bedsheets together. Oh, there was no time for anything! He was so pale he looked ready to fall any instant!

She peered over the edge of the balcony and saw a slim extension at its bottom: room enough for a small foot. Without thinking further, she hiked up her skirt and climbed over, and then, with one arm gripping the rail, extended the other toward him.

"No, Mama!" Camille cried. "Come back; you will fall!"

"Hush, child. Anchor me." Tears in her eyes, her daughter immediately clutched her arm with both hands, then crouched to add further weight. Swallowing hard at her thoughtless daring, Gwendolyn told the stranger, "Come, sir. You have only a few inches before you can touch my hand."

The single eye she could see had rounded to an almost perfect circle during this operation, and now he said in quiet, urgent tones, "What . . . are . . . you . . . doing?"

"I should think it would be obvious. I'm trying to save your life." She patted the bricks with her hand and extended her fingers again as if to say, *Hurry up!* Her boldness was bleeding away with each raindrop; much longer in this position and courage would desert her entirely.

"Go . . . back . . . this . . . instant!" he demanded. "There's no point in both of us falling."

"Listen to him, Mama," Camille entreated. "Please don't do this."

Gwendolyn, summoning every ounce of strength to her eyes, kept her gaze firmly pinned to the stranger's. "Don't argue with me. Just come."

There passed a small length of time wherein his green eye searched hers. She felt the oddest tension pass through her during those long seconds, as though a kind of connection was growing between them. Doubtless it was because of their life-and-death situation, for it was not possible for her to feel a bond with any man. Thus, when she sensed his terror leaving him, she experienced a surge of relief, a relief that was to be woefully short-lived.

"You won't be able to support my weight," he said calmly. "If I touch that beautiful hand, I'm afraid I'll clutch it all the way down." He made a brave attempt at a smile. "I do thank you for the offer."

"You won't make me fall. Come, sir. You can make it."

The green eye closed briefly as he took a shuddering breath. "Climb back, madam. You have shamed my courage into returning, but I won't move until you're safe."

He meant it; she could see his look of stubborn resolve. After an instant's indecision, she raised one leg and was about to lift the other when her foot slipped. The sudden loss of balance teetered her weight in the wrong direction. Both slippers flailed in the air. Camille cried soundlessly, her grip tightening to steel. Gwendolyn clung desperately to the rail, the wood biting the underside of her arms as her toes sought the ledge. She had time to think only, *I am going to die!* before a strong arm circled her waist and boosted her into her daughter's embrace.

When her senses returned, she found herself sitting on the balcony, her back braced against the rail and Camille snuggled against her. On her other side, the stranger had collapsed into the corner with head tilted back and eyes closed to the rain, his chest moving up and down rapidly.

He must have sensed her gaze upon him, for his lashes lifted. Although she was inured against the hundred-and-one ways a man could use his eyes to charm the opposite sex, she could not resist responding to the tired smile in his.

"Thank you," he said.

"I believe it is I who should be thanking you," she returned.

"No. Had it not been for me, you would never have gotten into such a predicament." He shook his head in embarrassment. "I was fine until I became dizzy for a moment. Then I panicked. I apologize for my cowardice."

"You didn't look cowardly when you came to Mama's rescue," Camille said. "I wouldn't dream anyone could move so fast on such a little surface. Thank goodness you did!" She dashed tears from her eyes and gave her mother another hug. "This was much worse than last week's disaster!"

Patting her daughter's back consolingly, Gwendolyn explained to the baronet, "A wheel broke on the carriage we'd hired. No one was hurt, but it served to make my daughter's nerves more fragile."

As the stranger's gaze shifted to Camille, Gwendolyn studied his face for warning signs. He appeared politely attentive, nothing more. That was to the good, for this one was quite attractive with his startling eyes, dark hair, and tall, muscular build. Camille was at a vulnerable age, and she might find it hard to resist his lures, did he send forth any.

And now his glance returned to her, a warm emotion flashing in his eyes. Again she felt that odd pull. Well! Was it herself she would have to guard after all these years? Ridiculous.

"I have no recollection of it," he said. "Only that your mother saved my life." He pushed a soggy lock of hair from his eyes. "I'm just happy to see my foolish journey accomplished its purpose."

When both ladies stared at him inquiringly, he explained, "Your affection for one another has been restored."

They continued to regard him in bewildered silence. He indicated Camille with a gesture of his hand and began to speak slower, as if explaining to the slow of understanding. "You immediately put down your pistol to help your mother when you realized she was in danger. That alone should show you where your loyalties lie. I'm sure you won't ever again become so angry or jealous that you feel . . . murderous . . ."

Gwendolyn's world seemed to be tilting. The man had obviously overheard them reciting lines. She sent a mute appeal to her daughter, who was giggling uncontrollably. Camille had not thought how devastating was this discovery, and now her merriment faded as she caught her mother's disturbed air. Gwendolyn struggled to her feet, the man's gaze following her with utter confusion.

"Did I say something amusing?" he asked.

"I think we had best go inside," she answered grimly. "Then you can explain how you came to overhear us—and who you are."

The suites in The Allemande were arranged with a bedchamber on either side of a sitting room, which connected to a balcony. It was into this middle room the ladies led him, to a dainty chair he at first refused because of his sodden state, then accepted when he realized that he was actually feeling quite feverish. Hasty introductions were exchanged; after which, in spite of Mrs. Devane's grave look, a look he could not understand, she took pity on him and rang the bell for the maid, stating her intention to order tea.

"We must talk," she said, "but we'll understand one another better if we are comfortable." After rifling through a chest in the corner, she handed him a thick towel and excused herself, saying she meant to exchange her wet gown for dry clothes, her daughter having already disappeared into her bedroom to do the same. Max thanked her, but she was already gone, the door closing firmly, the snapping of the lock as loud as a pistol's firing. He was so edgy he jumped.

While he waited, Max ruffled the towel through his hair, removed his greatcoat and spread it across a chair to dry. He spied a mirror over a low bookcase and went to it. Using his fingers as a comb, he tried to restore some order to his closely cropped hair. He gave this up as a lost cause and peered downward into the glass at his grey jacket and waistcoat; they were reprehensibly wrinkled, but dry enough; the pantaloons were too snug to be crushed. His cravat was shocking. He did his best to retie it.

Suddenly, his fingers stilled. The flushed face in the mirror stared back at him with a surprised expression. He was preening like a debutante before her first ball. But it was only politeness, he assured his image, which now took on a doubtful look. The ladies were beautiful, yes, but he wanted to appear his best for more esoteric reasons. Mrs. Devane had saved his life; therefore, he should present himself decently at least. He owed her that much.

Even if she had been so cold as to nearly unhinge her daughter's mind a few moments ago. He found it difficult to reconcile the two impressions he had of this woman. And of her daughter, for that matter, who seemed sweet as an angel now that he had met her. He could more easily imagine a babe in leading strings wielding a gun than she.

Thinking now of the ladies' conversation, he glanced at the room's furnishings, searching for the pistol. Possibly it would be best if he took the weapon and hid it, just in case. He wandered past the two settees set at right angles from the fireplace, looked at the table separating them, then the smaller tables at each end. No pistol lay there promising death, nor was it on any of the scattered chairs. Only two piles of paper covered in a flowing script. As neither appeared to be a letter, he could not prevent his eyes from reading the first few words, and then he was caught. He grasped one stack, read a few lines, looked to the other pile. He began to laugh.

Mrs. Devane entered the room looking extremely elegant in

a high-necked lavender gown striped with white. Her beauty stopped his breath for a moment. She did not seem at all moved by *his* appearance; she only viewed the script in his hands with a coolness that iced his bones.

Recovering from his laughter, he replaced the papers. "I'm an imbecile," he said, still unable to contain his smile. "I should have known you are both actresses."

Hope flared in her eyes for a moment, and he could not account for it. But the light as quickly died. "No," she began, and was interrupted by a knocking at the door.

Fearing it might be Roderick, he motioned toward her bedroom, a question in his eyes. She nodded and waited for him to disappear from sight. The visitor was only the maid, and as soon as Mrs. Devane ordered tea he joined her in the sitting room, taking a seat opposite her on the settee.

"Why are you so afraid Mr. Vaughan will find you?" she asked immediately. "And what were you doing on his balcony? I assume that's the point from which you began your journey to mine."

He told her, the words pouring from him like oil from a cruse. He did not stop even when Camille joined them, looking fresh and pretty as a butterfly in her cream muslin. It occurred to him the fever was making him babble, but the intensity with which they listened encouraged him further.

"I don't understand why you think Mr. Vaughan stole your formula," Camille said when he finally ground to the finish.

"His life is a game," Max told her. "He delights in manipulating people. His moving next door to you, for instance, is typical. Shadows you at every step, does he?" Camille's wide-eyed nod urged him on. "Which one of you is he pursuing, or is it both? Although I suppose your husband . . ."

He looked inquiringly at the older of the two ladies. He could see no sign of a masculine presence here, although Roderick did not always confine himself to unmarried females. When Mrs. Devane apprised him of her widowhood, he felt a tide of relief, then expressed his sympathy guiltily. "He has begun his siege, I warn you," he concluded.

"You don't have to warn me, Mr. Hastings," Mrs. Devane said. "I am fully aware of such behavior in *gentlemen*." Cynical lights sparked in her eyes.

"Only certain gentlemen," he ventured, a little put off by the all-inclusiveness of her statement. It reminded him of the words in the script she had recited moments before.

A second knock came at the door. Max made as if to retreat again, but when the maid called, "Tea, mum," he relaxed. As Mrs. Devane opened the door for the servant, however, he had cause to wish he'd made that exit. It was the same young woman he'd found in the butler's pantry. Her eyes widened as she spotted him.

"Sir Hastings," she murmured, her amazed glance consuming him and the ladies as she rolled her cart into the room. "Oh, I mean . . . you're not him, you said."

"Yes, I am," he said resignedly. There was no use in confusing the poor girl. "Though I hope you won't tell anyone. I'd like to keep my presence here a secret for a while."

"Even from Miss Munroe?" she asked as she placed the tea service on the table.

So Lucy was still unwed, was she? That was a surprise. *"Especially* from Miss Munroe." He locked eyes with the maid, willing severity into his expression. When merriment flickered in hers, he felt his heart drop.

"Yes, sir, I promise," the girl said, a giggle in her voice. She backed from the room, and he was certain he heard laughter coming from the hall as the door closed.

Returning his vexed attention to the two ladies opposite him, he saw they watched him with nearly identical looks of curiosity.

Mrs. Devane began to pour tea into a cup painted with blue roses. "I take it you are acquainted with the owners of The Allemande," she said smoothly.

"Yes. I've stayed here before. Last summer." He made his words deliberately curt. Hopefully she wouldn't inquire further.

For a moment he thought he was successful in his wish. After determining he took neither sugar nor cream in his tea, she passed him a cup and saucer. He drank deeply, the dark liquid soothing his throat. Mother and daughter sipped delicately, and then he felt Mrs. Devane's eyes center on him like a flame seeking truth.

"Did your wife accompany you on your visit?"

"I am as unfettered as you see me," he answered, pleased that she had asked. Perhaps it meant she was interested. Not that he wanted her to be.

"Miss Munroe is quite lovely," she said.

A fleeting image of a cloud of raven hair, ebony eyes, and crimson lips floated past his mind's eye. "She is indeed." He set his empty cup on the table. Mrs. Devane would surely take the hint if he changed the subject. "But no more lovely than my present company. Have I thanked you sufficiently for your hospitality?"

"More than sufficiently, Sir Hastings," Mrs. Devane said. "Even though you were not totally honest with us."

"Not honest? I'm sorry; I don't understand."

The lady smiled charmingly, but something in her eyes made him doubt the smile's sincerity. "You did not tell us you possessed a title."

"Oh, that. I didn't think it necessary to speak of it."

"But you are so modest. Are you a knight?"

"Baronet," he said uncomfortably.

Camille reached for a scone and balanced it on the edge of her saucer. "Most of the titled people I've known are very quick to say if they're peers. I believe they want to impress."

Max had often found it so, which was why he assiduously avoided mentioning his own appellation. He could hardly say as much, so he mumbled, "A baronet is not really a peer, I must remind."

"Now, Camille," Mrs. Devane enjoined, "Sir Hastings is not of that sort or he would not be here. The entire city of Bath has fallen out of favor with the peerage in recent years, now that the middle classes—that would be you and I, dear—have made it their resort of choice." She nibbled a petit four, then dabbed her mouth with a linen napkin. "Oh, but I had forgotten. Sir Hastings is not here for pleasure."

His fever was not too high for him to sort out her meaning. "Madam," he said tightly, "I have not chosen to make an issue of something I cannot help being born with. I beg you to do the same."

Her shoulders stiffened, and the self-composed light in her eye flared angrily for a fraction of an instant. Just as quickly, her mask of politeness slipped back into place.

He watched the transformation avidly. There were more levels to this woman than one would suspect at first glance. Interesting levels. Just what did she hide behind her polished veneer? He discovered a sudden need to know and fought it. There was no time for this sort of nonsense. Last year's experience had cured him of dalliance forever.

"You are correct, of course," she was saying, her perfect lips displaying beautiful teeth. "None of us can change the circumstances of our birth."

"It is what we do with our lives afterward that matters," chimed Camille in the manner of one reciting a familiar refrain.

He looked from one lady to the other, his senses filling with delight. There was something afoot here, and he was determined to discover what it was.

"Why were you practicing that play if you're not actresses?" he blurted out.

Silence dropped over his fair companions like an invisible blanket. Neither one moved, though the girl cut a worried look at her mother before venturing shakily, "Because we enjoy reading aloud?"

Since she had made it a question, he also looked to Mrs. Devane, who appeared to consider, then discard her daughter's reply as if she found it wanting. She took breath as if about to speak, then hesitated, her gaze drifting to the side, mayhap searching for a response in the fabric of the chair. She's trying to compose a lie! he thought with certainty. Now why would she think that necessary? The hunter's instinct within him sharpened.

"I saw a name on the topmost page," he said. "The author's name. A Madame Rose." Mrs. Devane's breathing quickened, and alarm flew into her daughter's eyes. "Who is she?" he continued relentlessly. When they remained as quietly desperate as two netted birds, his suspicions were confirmed. "This is delightful! One of you wrote that play."

"I did," Mrs. Devane said immediately. "My daughter had nothing to do with it."

He laughed. "You sound as if you're guilty of a crime." He recalled the subject matter that had caused him to scale the walls. "Although I suppose you could have been, indirectly, had I fallen." He chuckled encouragingly. When they persisted in remaining silent, the mother discreetly gnawing at her lower lip, he abandoned his attempt to engage their mirth. "I don't understand why you're so despondent. There's nothing shameful in such a hobby. I myself once enjoyed painting . . ." He looked from one to the other searchingly.

"Do you not know about Lady Scandal, sir?" Camille asked. At her mother's quickly indrawn breath, the girl wilted. "Oh, dear. I'm always speaking out of turn."

"It's all right, child," Mrs. Devane said, patting her arm. "If Sir Hastings stays more than a day in Bath, he will learn the truth anyway."

"What truth?" he demanded, and was overcome with a round of coughing. Mrs. Devane quickly poured him a fresh cup of tea, and he downed it even though the pot had cooled to lukewarm.

"You're ill," she said. "You should rest."

"What truth?" he repeated.

Mrs. Devane stood, smoothed her skirt, and crossed to the passageway at the end of the settees. She slowly began to pace, as if she did not want to see his face as she spoke.

"You have come to Bath seeking your formula, Sir Hastings," she began. "In doing so, I've heard you ask the maid for secrecy. When you were hanging from our building a few moments ago, you begged us not to tell Mr. Vaughan of your presence. Am I correct in thinking you don't want him to know you are here?''

Although he could not see what her question had to do with the subject at hand, he nodded. ''I hope to search his room more thoroughly. If I confront him directly, he'll never tell me whether he has the formula or not.''

''Then you understand the need for secrecy. We will keep your secret, but you must be willing to honor ours.''

Spreading his hands outward, he said, ''Of course.'' The woman totally baffled him, but she was fascinating. He followed her movements back and forth with fixed attention.

''When my husband died two years ago, he left nothing behind for Camille and me,'' she said. ''There was only a small pittance I'd managed to save during our years together. I realized I'd have to earn our bread in some fashion, and the only skill I had was a small talent in spinning stories. I tried to sell children's stories at first, but no publisher was interested in them. In desperation, I showed one publisher a play I had written for a Christmas pageant at chapel. He told me it showed promise, but I must think of something unique that would distinguish it from the multitudes of others he received daily.

''By this time, a year had gone by. My savings were gone. My husband's estate was entailed and passed to his brother. Camille and I had leased a cottage near the manor house, for we could not afford to travel far. Finally, we could no longer pay the rent.'' She stopped and gave him a direct look. ''I was half-mad with worry, Sir Hastings.''

''Was there no family to whom you could turn?'' he asked angrily. Why did no one help them? He would have. The brother-in-law was unspeakable for not doing so.

''No.'' Her answer vibrated with unspoken nuances, and he wondered at it. But then her expression lightened. ''At that time, there was an *affaire de coeur* that became the subject of every drawing room within gossiping distance of Bath. If you were here last summer, perhaps you heard of it. Lionel Pocken-ridge?''

He shrugged his shoulders. "The name means nothing to me."

Camille gave him a delicious smile. "How could you have missed knowing about him?"

"Perhaps Sir Hastings was too involved with his own concerns," Mrs. Devane said.

This was too close to the mark to ignore. "Perhaps I was here at the wrong time."

"Nevertheless," Mrs. Devane continued, giving him a knowing look he did not appreciate, "Lionel Pockenridge was ... How shall I put it politely? An opportunist. He prowled every assembly and haunted the pump room looking for a wealthy wife. And finally, he found one in Madeleine Finney."

"She was plain as ditchwater," Camille giggled.

"My goodness, Camille," said her mother, stifling a smile, "the poor woman couldn't help how she looked. At any rate, they were married. What Mr. Pockenridge didn't realize was that Madeleine's father had gambled away his fortune the night before the wedding. Mr. Finney told no one and let the marriage proceed."

Camille selected another scone and waved it merrily as she spoke. "Everyone said Mr. Pockenridge got exactly what he deserved. It was so amusing that Mama wrote a play about it; only she changed their names and a few of the events. She added another character, a pretty lady that the Pockenridge character fell in love with but rejected in favor of the wealthy spinster. It made the story even better!"

"The play debuted last fall," Mrs. Devane said. "It did well enough that, instead of starving, we are now as you find us."

Camille chewed a morsel of her scone and swallowed quickly. "She has written four others since then, all based on true events. That's why Madame Rose is sometimes called Lady Scandal."

Max had been listening with growing disappointment. "Your writing is not a hobby at all, then," he said in a musing voice, speaking the obvious while his mind raced. He could not believe this elegant, refined woman would scribble such trash.

Camille's expression grew serious. "No, it is our livelihood. And you mustn't tell anyone that Mama writes those plays. Society doesn't like intelligent women."

"I fear you are wasting your breath, dear," Mrs. Devane said, regarding Max haughtily. He had not known brown eyes could look so cold. "Can you not see he disapproves?"

Pain, sharp as a rapier, sliced through his head. "I'll keep your little secret," he said irritably. "Whether I disapprove or not is beside the point. I gave my word."

"I am greatly comforted by that," Mrs. Devane said. "Isn't it a fortunate thing, Camille, that the person we found jumping from balcony to balcony is a man of honor and not otherwise?"

Max felt pressure building. She could tell him he was ugly, that his manners were reprehensible, and his mind thick as mud, and it would be all right. But he would not tolerate having his integrity questioned.

"And you are the authority on honor, I gather," he said, immediately regretting it when Camille gasped. If he were not so unwell, he would never have spoken so disrespectfully to a lady.

Mrs. Devane gave him a quelling look. "Am I to take it you believe a woman who earns her living is without honor?"

"I beg your pardon," he said through gritted teeth. "I should not have spoken as I did."

She waved a hand negligently and returned to her seat. "No, please elaborate. I am interested in your opinion. It's important for my daughter to understand how the masculine mind works."

He glanced back and forth between them. "Very well, I'll tell you how I feel. There's nothing wrong with earning one's living. I do it almost every day. But one's choice of occupation is another matter."

"Ah," she said. "Then you don't believe a lady should write. Perhaps my daughter and I would have been more *honorable* in your eyes if we milked cows."

"Don't be ridiculous. It's not that you write, it's *what* you write. You are making commerce off the misfortunes of others, and I don't know how you can."

Camille leaned forward, eager to defend her mother. "But these are not nice people Mama parodies. They *deserve* it. Foolish, selfish, *mean* people."

He snorted. "I have never known anyone who wasn't foolish, selfish, or mean upon occasion."

"How unfortunate for you," Mrs. Devane said in that fluid manner of hers, her composure returning in full. "And I can see we will never change your mind on this issue, Sir Hastings, so let us agree to disagree, shall we? I am certain we've occupied enough of your time today and that you will want to be about your business . . . your honorable business of searching Mr. Vaughan's room when he is not there."

Max could not help laughing. *"Touché,* Mrs. Devane. Remind me not to cross swords with you again." He was relieved to see an answering spark in her eyes, faint though it was. "If you're not totally out of sorts with me, I'd like to ask for your mercy in one other matter. Could you tolerate my presence until Roderick leaves again? I know he won't stay in his room this evening; he never does. Once I'm sure he's gone, I'll go next door and search, then be out of your lives forever." And that will be a shame, he thought suddenly, for in spite of her reprehensible occupation, Mrs. Devane intrigued him.

She looked as if the idea of his staying pained her. Was she so angry with him, then? Perhaps it was because he was a stranger. The Devane ladies had been gracious to put up with him this long, and unusually trusting. "Don't trouble yourself," he heard himself say, and began to rise. "I can wait elsewhere. It was unforgivable of me to ask."

"Not at all," Mrs. Devane said, and motioned for him to return to his seat. "You shouldn't go back into the rain; your chill will get worse. It will only be for an hour or so anyway; the inn serves supper at seven, and Mr. Vaughan plans to dine here. He told us as much when we saw him at the park this afternoon."

"He always dines here," Camille added, wrinkling her nose and grinning. "Everyday he asks if he may take us to the opera or a play or for supper, and each time Mama refuses. And every evening, there he is in the dining room, and somehow he never fails to sit near us!''

"Roderick never gives up easily,'' he said. "Usually he doesn't find it necessary. I'm relieved your mother is wise enough to avoid him.''

Mrs. Devane met his gaze squarely. He saw pleasure in her eyes, but wariness as well. *You have nothing to fear from me,* he told her silently. She might be captivating, but he had more important issues at stake than a light flirtation.

Chapter Three

One of the best things about growing older is having the freedom to wear vibrant colors, Gwendolyn thought as she regarded her image in the mirror one final time before leaving her bedroom. She had attired herself in an evening gown of rich coral, and the cameo-and-pearl necklace resting in the cleft between her breasts added a touch of dramatic contrast.

The brilliant hues would make an excellent foil for her daughter's fairness, could she wear such at her age. It seemed a pity fashion limited young girls to virginal whites and pastels, but mayhap it was for the best. No advantage could be gained in making Camille more attractive than she already was. It grew hard enough to keep the suitors at bay.

As Gwendolyn entered the drawing room, she found Camille dressed in a pale blue gown and waiting in the chair by the French doors, watching the rain. The girl turned and smiled, then glanced pointedly at the gentleman on the settee, a question in her eyes.

Sir Hastings lay sleeping beneath the blanket Gwendolyn had given him earlier. He looked helpless as a child and totally appealing in his slumber, unlike her second husband, whose mouth would open wide as a barn door to emit snores that could rattle windows in the next village.

For a moment she contemplated letting him sleep, but that was foolish. The maid would not be able to hold onto *that* secret, should she discover him here tomorrow morning. Gwendolyn leaned down and, subduing a ludicrous, tender urge to brush the hair from his eyes, vigorously shook him awake. He came to instant consciousness, his jade eyes meeting hers in total bewilderment.

"We are going down to dinner, Sir Hastings," she told him. "I doubt we will see you upon our return, so my daughter and I will take our leave of you now."

He swung his legs to the floor, the blanket falling to his ankles. She bit back a smile at his hair, which had ruffled to a peak. "Yes, of course," he said gruffly, then cleared his throat. "Thank you both for your kindness."

Pushing away a prickling of her conscience at abandoning him, she offered her hand, then moved aside for Camille to do the same. His eyes burned bright with fever, and he should be in bed instead of contemplating the activities of a thief. But he was a grown man and not her responsibility.

Pausing at the door, she said, "I think if you wait about a quarter-hour, you will be safe in entering Mr. Vaughan's room."

"All right, thank you."

He looked subdued and rather pathetic. Her heart twisted sympathetically. "I wish you success in finding your formula."

"I'll find it," he mumbled automatically.

"Don't fall back asleep," Camille warned.

"I won't," he promised. He seemed to come to a sudden alertness. "Wait."

Gwendolyn and her daughter paused inquiringly.

"I . . ." He appeared to be thinking furiously, but after a few seconds, his shoulders slumped. "It was a pleasure meeting you."

"And you as well," she said graciously. "Even if the circumstances were a trifle . . . unusual."

She closed the door reluctantly. It was odd how sad she felt. She knew she'd carry that image of her last sight of him—tousled head, rapscallion grin, and all—for a long time. Feeling Camille's curious glance, she threw off her moodiness, exchanged a smile with her daughter and led the way downstairs.

The Allemande's dining room occupied an entire wing on the east side of the building. As no rooms were above it, the ceiling was unusually high and decorated with oak beams and rafters, giving it the feel of a rustic cathedral. With stone floors and undraped, mullioned windows, the room also possessed the feature of noisiness. Gwendolyn rather liked the echoing structure, which made conversations blend into a cacophonous broth of privacy.

Tonight the room bustled with even more activity than usual. Gwendolyn remarked upon it as they were led to their table by their waiter, Andrew Hibbs, a middle-aged man whose mustache made him look more severe than he was. He and his brother Richard served the dining room alone at most meals, and Gwendolyn believed it was overwork that made him perpetually irritable.

"The Munroes are dining downstairs tonight, madame," Andrew responded.

"That doesn't happen often," Camille said.

"No, miss, but their oldest son is down from Oxford, and they like to put him on display. That wasn't me as said that, mind."

Gwendolyn smiled as he drew her chair. "I didn't realize they had another son."

"Well, let us thank God they do," he said feelingly. "If all they'd raised was that brat-boy and the siren, they couldn't appear in public with their heads up."

Camille gave him an innocent look as he handed her a bill of fare. "Is that how you speak of me, Andrew? Am I a brat or a siren?"

"You and your mother are angels," he said fiercely, "except when you fish for compliments like that. Now read your menu and tell me you want the roasted pork, because that's the only thing fit to eat tonight. Unless you want a bout of sickness over the fresh sole, which is about as fresh as my brother's stockings.''

"We'll take the pork," Gwendolyn said immediately, having learned by experience to trust his judgment in these matters.

"As you wish, madam," he said with a formality that caused Camille to chortle, then took the menus and wove his way among the tables to the kitchen.

As soon as he left, the girl leaned toward her mother and said with soft eagerness, "What did you think of Sir Hastings?"

Gwendolyn, who had been arranging the napkin across her lap, paused for the briefest instant. "I'm more interested in what *you* think of him."

"I like him, even if he does have strange ideas. He made me angry when he talked about your plays as he did, though. You have more honor than ten ladies—or ten gentlemen, for that matter!"

Although she gave her daughter an appreciative glance, Gwendolyn could not quell an uneasy feeling. Sir Hastings had touched upon a sore spot with his accusation. He could not know how she disliked writing the plays!

The first one had been amusing; in it she had poured out a lifetime of frustration and disappointment about the cages that Society placed around not only herself, not only women, but everyone.

But each play following had been harder to write; she fought increasing pangs of guilt, pettiness, and spite as she did them. She shared these feelings with no one, especially not her daughter, who would be devastated to know and would beg her to stop. The simple truth was, Gwendolyn could not afford to cease composing gossip-ridden farces. She was feathering their nest, and until she knew herself and Camille to be solvent, she would continue.

Mischief danced across Camille's face. "At the least, our afternoon was not dull. Did you ever dream we would have a visitor enter through our balcony? And a handsome one, too. He is so daring!''

"You may call his actions daring; others would consider them foolhardy,'' Gwendolyn said primly, and leaned back when Andrew returned with rolls, butter, and bowls of chicken consommé. Surely the child had not been attracted to him. She was exhibiting a dangerous interest in the appearance and manners of gentlemen of late. The next years were going to be difficult.

Camille eyed the waiter impatiently until he rambled away, then whispered, "But, Mama, he thought he was saving our lives!'' Her quicksilver expression grew apprehensive as she glanced toward the door. "Oh, dear. Mr. Vaughan is here and coming this way. I hope Sir Hastings has good fortune finding his ... whatever it was. Why do we not invite his cousin to sit with us tonight? We could detain him longer, so that ... Oh, good evening, Mr. Vaughan,'' she said musically.

Gwendolyn, who was seated with her back to the entrance and so had been unable to see the gentleman until this moment, greeted him politely. Tonight he had dressed conservatively in shades of brown, except for a waistcoat striped in red and gold that drew one's eyes like a flag.

"You should both be banned from the dining room,'' Mr. Vaughan said, a gleam sparkling in his pale brown eyes. Before they could take offense, he added smoothly, "No one could be interested in food when such a feast for the eyes is present.''

While Camille made no effort to stifle her giggle at this extravagance, Gwendolyn could scarcely force a polite smile. "You flatter us, Mr. Vaughan.'' Seeing her daughter's pleading look, she added reluctantly, "Would you care to join us this evening?''

"You honor me.'' He sat so quickly she blinked. Seconds later, a frowning Andrew huffed over with a bill of fare. "What do you recommend, my good man?''

"There's fresh sole tonight,'' he growled. "Cook's specialty.''

"That sounds good. Bring me a double portion; I'm unac-

countably hungry.'' Mr. Vaughan handed over the card and
waved him off. He whisked a napkin to his lap with a flourish,
then glanced quizzically from one lady to the other. ''What?
Did I miss something?''

''N-Nothing,'' sputtered Camille. Avoiding her mother's
eyes, she lengthened her face in an effort to appear serious.
''Tell me, Mr. Vaughan, do you like to play games? I have
always wondered.''

Gwendolyn gave her a daughter a significant look, which
was ignored. The gentleman appeared puzzled.

''Games? Do you mean cards or parlor games?''

''No.'' Camille took a sip of her soup, her lips trembling to
contain a grin. ''I am talking about playing pranks on friends.
Or relatives.''

He cocked his head, contemplating her with interest. ''I've
done my share. What about you, Miss Devane? Do *you* like to
play games?''

Not liking the turn the conversation was taking nor the wicked
light in their companion's eye, Gwendolyn sat straighter in her
chair, drawing his attention to herself. ''You have mentioned
your family's business before, Mr. Vaughan, but nothing at all
about the manner in which it is done. Exactly how *does* one
make glass?'' Smiling archly at Camille's dismay, she added,
''And pray don't spare any detail. I want to know everything.''

Max sat at the foot of his cousin's bed in total discouragement. He had searched every possible hiding place. The formula
was not here. Perhaps Roderick kept it on his person. Truth
was, he could have hidden it anywhere between Bath and Blackpool. The only thing left to do was confront his cousin with
the theft. But that would not work, either; to have him in a
position of weakness was exactly what Roderick fed upon, and
he would delight in prolonging Max's agony forever. If he
could just devise some way to trick it from him . . .

He could not plot anything now, however. Weariness and
the ague had sapped all sharpness from his brain. The best

thing to do was to seek a room at an inn and rest. Tomorrow he would think of another plan.

Feeling the weight of the world on his shoulders, he moved to the door, opened it, and stepped into the corridor. He was not lucky enough to be alone this time, though; a young woman stood some yards away, rapping persistently at the Devanes' suite. It took only a fraction of an instant to recognize the owner of that halo of crisp dark curls and goddesslike figure. Instantly he moved backward and tried to close the door, but it was too late; Lucy had seen him. She gave a gladsome cry and scurried toward him, arms extended.

"Max, Max!" she squealed, and pressed him into an embrace he could hardly refuse to return, though he did so stiffly while trying to ignore the allure of her soft, warm body. She wore a pink muslin gown cut to display her plump breasts to advantage, and he had all he could do to keep his eyes above her dimpled chin. "I told Betty she could not be right when she said you were in the Devanes' room, for of course you would be in Roderick's! She is so stupid, even for a maid. Oh, it is good to see you again! What brings you back to The Allemande? But perhaps I should not ask that, it is too shameless of me!"

Her tiny, dark eyes sparkled like chips of polished glass. Of course she would think he had come to see her; Lucy's thoughts did not often venture outside her own shadow.

Gingerly, he searched his heart for signs that old wounds might be reopening, but so far she had triggered none of his former responses. Perhaps time did heal all. Or, as he had suspected more than once over the past year, he had been under some kind of witchery spell last summer and had come to his senses at last.

That much was good. But now all hope of secrecy was lost. Lucy could no more rein in her mouth than she could her bosom. Even if he turned and ran into the misty night, Roderick would know he had been here. He would have to fabricate a reason, and fast.

"I've come to see Roderick. On business."

She gave him a playful, knowing look. "Of *course* you

have. You don't speak with one another often enough in . . . Liverpool, was it?''

''Blackpool.'' She was still clinging to him, and he paced back a step as inoffensively as he could.

''You won't admit it, will you?'' Her lips curled teasingly.

''Admit what?''

''That you came to see me. As if you didn't know, as if Roderick didn't write you that I am still unwed.'' She laughed gaily. ''Go on, tell me he did not.''

''He did not.''

''Oh, you are such a one for teasing! But it's true.''

''Is it?'' She spoke as if she were bestowing a great gift. Something nasty uncurled inside him. ''Why? I thought you had the old duke boxed and tied with a ribbon.''

''Max, Max, the things you say!'' She tittered, then became solemn. He suspected theatrics were at work until she said, ''He died.''

''Oh. I am sorry.''

''He had just asked me to marry him.'' She spoke in dreamy, hushed tones, bringing her folded hands to her lips as though lost in memory. ''And when I said yes, he gave me a kiss. It was the first time I had allowed him to touch me, and it was horrible, Max! Not at all like your pleasant kisses! He smelled of onions and garlic and snuff and dead old meat!'' She shuddered. ''And so, when he grabbed his heart''—Lucy dramatically clutched at hers—''I thought he was pretending, and I—I laughed at him.'' She turned woeful eyes to Max. ''He fell to the ground, twitching horribly.'' Her voice dropped to a whisper. ''I fear the last words he heard in this world were mine as I shouted, 'Stop it, you ridiculous old fool!' ''

Max could think of nothing to say. One of the doors near the end of the hall opened, and a family of four headed their way. Lucy put a restraining hand on his arm as they passed, as if she feared he would walk off with them. ''Come, Max. Do join my family for dinner. Bryce has returned from school, and you must meet him. I vow you will love him.''

He subdued a shudder of distaste. "Is he anything like your younger brother?"

"No one is like Albin," she said, with admirable understatement in his opinion. Her glance swept over him. "Hurry and change, won't you? And tell Roderick he may join us as well."

"Roderick's already gone down."

"Very well, then. Hurry! I'll be waiting in my parents' apartment." She stood on tiptoe and kissed his cheek. "We have much to talk about, you and I!"

He watched her trip away with harried eyes. Why had he not refused? It was still not too late; he could leave a brief note for her, another for Roderick, both full of lies, and run like the devil. Or he could return to his cousin's room, select some of Roderick's best wearing apparel since they were of a size, and bluster into the dining room as if he owned it. He was quite hungry, after all, in spite of his throbbing head.

He would go to dinner. He had little to lose now.

His decision had nothing to do with Mrs. Devane's presence in the dining room, he assured himself, although it would be pleasant to see her again. He retraced his steps to Roderick's room.

Andrew had been correct; the roast pork tasted juicy and delicious, and Camille was consuming her portion with enthusiasm. Gwendolyn suspected boredom over Mr. Vaughan's recitation of the workings of a glass factory to be responsible for that, however. Even she had not expected such a litany.

"Is everything to your liking?" Andrew asked beside her elbow, his manner disdainful when he glanced at Mr. Vaughan.

"I can't taste the fish for the sauce," their guest complained. "What kind of spice is this?"

"Strong," replied the waiter.

"I could not have described it better. Bring me a slice of that pork the ladies are eating. I'd rather digest pond scum than this."

"I'll see what can be arranged," Andrew said beneath his breath as he carried off the offending plate.

Mr. Vaughan frowned. And then his glance moved to the door behind her, as did Camille's; both of them appeared so astounded that Gwendolyn could not refrain from twisting her neck to look.

The Munroe family was entering the dining room. Mr. and Mrs. Munroe were a tall, slender couple, their stiffly correct posture making them seem even more willowy. Both lifted their chins as they walked, though one and then the other nodded regally to customers as they passed. Behind them came their children: first the boy, Albin; next, a tall, fine-looking young man, obviously the guest of honor; then beautiful Lucy and her escort, whose green eyes swept the room nervously until spotting Mrs. Devane.

The morsel of bread Gwendolyn was eating slipped down her throat before she was ready. She reached for her glass of water and gulped.

"Mama, are you all right?" But Camille's attention became distracted, as her gaze was pinned to Sir Hastings, who was leading Miss Munroe their way. "Do you see who— *Ouch!*" Casting a resentful look at her mother, she bent to rub her ankle.

"I don't believe my eyes," Mr. Vaughan said, rising. "What in blazes are you doing here, Max? And in my clothes?"

Sir Hastings was wearing a black jacket and trousers with an ivory waistcoat, Gwendolyn observed, and looked devastatingly elegant, though the coat appeared a trifle tight across the shoulders. Only the hastily tied cravat gave away his tense state of mind—that and his wary eyes darting between Camille and herself, begging silence.

Lucy laughed merrily. "I knew it! I knew you did not come on business, Max! Why did you not confess the true reason? I won't be offended, I assure you!"

"I am here on business," Max said, with a meaningful look for Gwendolyn and her daughter. "What an amazing thing, Roderick. When I found you weren't in your room, I found a key so that I could enter and pen a note about my arrival. When I exited, there was Miss Munroe, who was kind enough to insist I take dinner with her family. You and I can discuss our business later, but who are these lovely ladies with you? Do introduce us.''

With only a tightness around his lips revealing his irritation, Mr. Vaughan reluctantly did the honors. Gwendolyn fell in line with the charade, and Camille made an admirable performance of meeting him for the first time, though she looked ready to burst with laughter.

Finished with the pleasantries, Roderick repeated, ''But why are you wearing my clothes?''

At that moment, the oldest Munroe sibling reached their table. ''Our parents are waiting and sent me to fetch you,'' he said to his sister, his friendly glance scanning the faces at table, then returning with such a directness to Camille's that a shiver of warning went down Gwendolyn's spine. ''Hullo, everyone. Will you not introduce me, Lucy?''

His sister impatiently performed introductions, Bryce locking his eyes with Camille's the whole of the time. ''Well, come then,'' Lucy said irritably. ''If Mother and Papa are waiting, we had better go.''

She tugged both gentlemen away. Camille's gaze followed Bryce longingly, Gwendolyn saw with deep distress. She did not know who disturbed her more, the dangerous young man with an eye for her daughter or the dashing older one, whose unanticipated presence stirred a part of her she hoped was dead.

Life was taking on unwanted complications. It was what she had come to expect where gentlemen were concerned.

She watched Sir Hastings take his seat at a large table near the center of the dining room. Although he spoke pleasantly to Mr. and Mrs. Munroe as he settled himself, his restless eyes sought hers with a look of desperation that both amused and concerned her.

Distantly, she came to realize Mr. Vaughan was speaking. ''You seem quite fascinated with the Munroes' table. Both of you.'' He did not appear pleased by his observation.

"They are a handsome family," Gwendolyn said smoothly.

"Indeed." Once again he glanced toward the center table, his piqued gaze following the line of hers. Suddenly, his interest quickened, and his eyes returned to Gwendolyn, a watchful smile forming. "My cousin would affirm that, especially if you were speaking of Miss Munroe. He believes the sun rises in her."

"*Does* he?" Gwendolyn had suspected a story when Sir Hastings had spoken of his previous stay at The Allemande, but he'd successfully dodged explanations. She glanced across the room, surveying the baronet and Lucy with what she hoped was a detached interest.

Mr. Vaughan's grin widened annoyingly; he appeared pleased at capturing her so easily. But he could not speak further, since Andrew was gliding toward them with a dish of pork, which he set before the gentleman. Gwendolyn masked her impatience until he departed, then bit back rising irritation as Mr. Vaughan methodically sliced a large morsel of meat, plopped it into his mouth, closed his eyes, and chewed with satisfaction. Slowly, his lashes lifted, his amused eyes staring directly into hers.

"Now that," he said, after swallowing, "is good." Maddeningly, he began to cut another slice.

She was beginning to understand Sir Hastings' description of his cousin's liking for games. "Mr. Vaughan," she said rapidly, not caring if she played into his hands or not, "you have hinted of something between Miss Munroe and your cousin. Pray do not tease us."

"Did you want to hear that old tale?" he asked innocently, wiping his mouth with his napkin. "I'm sorry; I didn't realize. It's not a pretty story, I warn you. I'm rather ashamed to speak of it. Max has often made me glad our surnames are different when he gets into his scrapes, but last summer was the worst."

Even Camille was caught by this. "Oh, do tell us!"

"Very well," he said tiredly, "since you asked." He set down his knife and fork and leaned toward them. "My father doesn't often take holidays from work." He grimaced. "Let me rephrase that. Until last summer, he had *never* taken a holiday. But my mother had endured enough of that. She took to her sickbed in protest. There was nothing truly wrong with her except boredom, but she vowed never to rise again unless Father took her to Bath as Mr. Wilkey had taken *his* family. No man can tolerate a crying, complaining woman; therefore, my father booked rooms for the entire family here at The Allemande, and we stayed for three weeks.'' He lifted his fork again and stabbed at his bowl of peas. ''Most of us did, rather. Father could only bear idleness for two days before he felt he must return to the business.''

''During our visit, Max began to pay court to Lucy.'' His glance drifted toward the Munroes' table. ''It doesn't take a scholar to see why. She's a delectable lass. But she is . . . How shall I put it? It's not in me to speak poorly of a lady's character. Let us just say she enjoys gentlemanly attention more than is usual and loves to play one against the other. And she's most assuredly looking for an advantageous match.''

''Many young ladies feel it necessary to find the best match,'' said Gwendolyn, her censuring tones trembling with remembered pain. ''Often their parents push them into marriages they don't want in order to fill the family coffers. Or for reasons of pride.'' She glanced aside, lest Mr. Vaughan read her history in her eyes.

''Yes, of course,'' he said, curiosity evident in his voice. ''The Munroes certainly want the best for their daughter, but they don't have to push. She is as eager as they are. Last summer's actions proved it.'' He straightened his cravat without needing to; it was styled flawlessly in the *primo tempo*. ''I myself enjoyed her attentions before discovering the direction of her thoughts, and then, naturally, removed myself from the field. Max was not so fortunate. He followed her like a lovesick puppy. And Lucy pretended an interest in him.''

As he paused to consume another morsel of meat, Gwendolyn regarded him cynically. She suspected more lay behind his words than he was telling. Something in his cavalier manner hinted at wounded pride, the rejected suitor. It seemed the

rivalry she had sensed in Sir Hastings that afternoon was recip-
rocated in full. What could cause grown men to act so?

Mr. Vaughan drank a few sips of his wine and set down his
glass. "If you ask me, I'd have to say she was most attracted
to his title. The Munroes have fortune enough in this place and
don't need to marry money. But to have a title grafted into the
family tree . . . they wouldn't be the first to aspire to such. So
Max was her favored escort until the Duke of Charlington came
along."

He snorted. "That's when her true colors began to show.
No woman could have preferred the duke to my cousin; even
I will say as much. God knows Max is no prize, but Charlington
was an old toad."

When Camille laughed, he grinned and raised his glass.
"Lucy launched herself at him like an invading general. To do
her justice, old Charlie didn't put up much resistance. When
it became apparent he favored her, she tried to cut Max loose."

He shook his head and rolled his eyes. "He was having none
of it. He is"—he turned his empty glass to the side, as though
examining the lines of the crystal critically —"a stubborn man.
Once he gets an idea in his head . . . Well, Max thought he
could win her back by acting the perfect suitor."

His gaze drifted toward Sir Hastings, one side of his mouth
lifting ironically. Gwendolyn imagined she saw affection in
that glance as well as disgust. "I cannot tell you all the foolish
things he did for fear of boring you headfirst into your plates,
but does a white horse and gig, all decked with ribbons and
bells give you an idea?"

This hardly seemed worthy of Mr. Vaughan's scorn, Gwendolyn thought. Her lashes lowered as she watched him butter
a roll. He appeared to be the worst kind of gentleman; one who
would belittle another's efforts in love because his own were
mundane in comparison.

Mr. Vaughan's eyes met hers and flickered for an instant,
as if he sensed her disapproval and was surprised by it. "But
the worst, the very worst thing, the action that caused the most
snickers and gossip and finally led to our having to leave Bath

several days early, was the night he hired a group of minstrels to serenade Lucy outside her window. When she came to the balcony, Max shouted up some ridiculous poem he'd composed. I suppose he had to speak loudly so she could hear. Trouble was, so could everyone else. Heads began to pop out of rooms like badgers from their dens.''

Camille burst into giggles. "Oh, poor Sir Hastings! He must have been terribly embarrassed."

Her daughter's amusement wormed its way into Gwendolyn's heart. Despite her pity for the baronet, she pressed her fingers to her mouth to hide a smile.

Mr. Vaughan sighed deeply, as if in great regret. "Such is the madness of love, but that's not the worst of it. Any guests who didn't observe the performance directly were told about it in great detail by Lucy's little brother. He was proud of himself for cutting it short. Max had only got through a few of his lines when Albin threw a bucket of water over his head.''

"Oh, dear." Gwendolyn could not prevent casting a strained look at the baronet. Camille, too, looked at him, as did his cousin. The object of all this mirthful attention had turned his head aside to attend a remark of Lucy's; slowly, as he pivoted back, his eyes fell upon them. He straightened, the color draining from his face. Gwendolyn swiftly looked away and pretended an interest in her food she no longer felt.

"Why is Miss Munroe not wed, then?" Camille asked, when she recovered her breath. "Did she change her mind about the duke?"

"Oh, he died," Mr. Vaughan said carelessly. "About a month after we left." He snapped his fingers in Andrew's direction and pointed to his plate, mouthing for more. "Asked her to marry him and dropped dead at her feet."

Max observed his cousin's table with growing hostility. They were laughing at him. Even Mrs. Devane, whom he'd thought to be more genteel than that. But he had no logical reason to think so. She was capable of deceit; her occupation proved it.

One day he would stop being surprised when women disappointed him.

He had little doubt of their subject. Roderick had repeated the story of his idiotic behavior countless times in the year following his disgrace. How his cousin relished doing so, too. If there was one person in his acquaintance who had not heard of his ill-fated declaration of love to Lucy Munroe, he would like to know him or her. Possibly he would have to move to Australia to find such a one.

Returning his attention to the occupants of his own table, he gazed from face to face. He was so tired. Tired of wondering if he would ever find the formula. Tired of Mr. and Mrs. Munroe's probing into why he had come; tired of Lucy's arch declarations that *she* knew why he was here, and just in time, too; for didn't she have four beaus dangling after her? And Albin . . . He didn't like to think he could harbor thoughts of murdering a twelve-year-old, but he did. Only Bryce seemed inoffensive, but perhaps that, too, would change when he knew him better.

"You have not begged my forgiveness yet," Lucy sang, biting a strawberry while staring intently at him.

"Why do I need to ask your forgiveness?" Max asked sharply, sick to death of her flirtations. Last summer's attraction filled him with perplexity. She was beautiful, yes, and possessed a body designed to heat a man's blood to the boiling point; but what madness had caused him to overlook the paucity of her brain?

"For not writing me even once." She pouted playfully.

"Do pardon me. I had no inclination a newlywed duchess would be longing for my letters."

"His Grace passed," Mrs. Munroe said shrilly, her nasal voice sending shards of pain through Max's head. She was all but deaf, and he suspected she compensated by trying to make everyone else the same. "Our Lucy never did wed him, though he wished for it with his dying breath."

"Yes, madam, I know that now." He gulped a few swallows

of wine. Putting down his glass, seeing all eyes fastened to him as if expecting further comment, he added, "Unfortunate."

Mr. Munroe, his mouth full of meat, gave a few huffs, juice spattering across his chin. "You could say so. Broke my poor girl's heart. Don't get all that many lords around here, my lord."

"Sir," Bryce corrected.

"Yes, son?" Mr. Munroe said affably.

The young man chuckled. "Sir Hastings is not a lord, Papa; he is addressed as 'sir.' "

" 'Tis too confusing," Mrs. Munroe shouted. "Royalty should all be spoken of as lords and ladies to keep it simpler, I'm thinking."

"I hope you don't entertain the notion that I have royal blood, madam," Max said hastily. "Baronets are considered commoners."

"Anybody can see that by looking at you," Albin smirked.

Max directed a look of loathing at the boy while Mrs. Munroe rapped her glass to draw the waiter's attention. At the same time, she viewed Max with a deflated expression. "Only the best is good enough for our Lucy. We shan't rest until she becomes a lady."

A sneeze saved Max from the necessity of making an answer. But Albin, whom Max feared possessed a sixth sense about one's true feelings, was not deterred.

"The wives of baronets are called ladies," he said, his lips pulling back from his teeth as he watched Max.

"Oh, that's right," Mr. Munroe's voice reflected renewed interest. "For a minute I was thinking that was only for the wives of viscounts and on up." He paused a moment as their waiter, Richard Hibbs, reached them. As soon as Mrs. Munroe ordered him to bring lemon pudding for everyone, the innkeeper continued, "How long are you staying with us this time, Sir Hastings?"

"To be truthful, I haven't yet booked a room."

"What nonsense is this?" the innkeeper was saying. "You'll stay in one of our best, I insist on it! Remain at least long enough to get over that case of sniffles. I'll even give you a commoner's rate, what?" He laughed uproariously.

Max looked across the room. Roderick was certainly smitten with Mrs. Devane; he knew him well enough to recognize the signs. Camille received only the crumbs of his attention; even his appetite was less vociferous than usual.

In spite of Max's present predicament, perhaps it was just as well Lucy had discovered him leaving his cousin's room and spoiled his initial plans. Now that Roderick knew he was here, there was no reason to run. Why should he not stay awhile, not only to recover the receipt for red, but to rescue Mrs. Devane from his relative's wiles?

Not that she needed rescuing, he counseled himself. *Recall her duplicitous nature.* And she had laughed at him. He lifted his fork and stabbed the congealing plate of meat, making designs in the pork since he could not stomach eating it.

"You really should take up my father's offer," Bryce said. Startled, Max glanced up to see the young man was not looking at him, but Camille. "No doubt your cousin would appreciate the company. He seems well acquainted with Mrs. Devane and her daughter, by the way."

And you would like to be, too. Especially with the daughter.

This was a fortunate development. Mrs. Devane would probably be relieved to know such a suitable young gentleman was interested in Camille. She had expressed concern at Roderick's attention, though Max knew she had little to fear there except for herself. Yet she might be grateful did he play matchmaker and ensure the girl's removal from harm's way.

"He does know them quite well," Max said to Bryce. "I believe Miss Devane has been hoping to find more young people her own age, too. I wonder if I put in a word if you would be willing to accompany us on an outing soon."

"Why, yes," Bryce replied immediately, making an admirable attempt at coolness in his tone. "I would be pleased to oblige. If the young lady wishes it, that is." Max felt a nostalgic sympathy for his eagerness. He had been much like him, once.

"You ought to go see that traveling circus on the outskirts

of town,'' Mr. Munroe said. ''They've got all sorts of beasts there, and magicians and acrobats.''

Lucy frowned in distaste. ''Oh, Papa. We'd best do anything else. When the wind blows this way, the smell is awful!'' She reached for the baronet's hand and squeezed. ''I'm so glad you are staying.''

''For a few days perhaps.'' As subtly as possible, he removed his fingers from hers.

''I did not doubt you would for a second,'' Lucy said with a brilliant flash of teeth. ''You do so enjoy teasing, Max, but you have made me very happy!''

''Oh, yes, Max,'' cooed Albin in his grating soprano, his eyes full of dark promises. ''You have made us *all* very happy!''

Chapter Four

"You came all the way to Bath to tell me *that?*" Roderick's gaze raked over his cousin as he crossed one leg over the other. "Did you think I didn't know it? My sire *always* wants me to return."

Max moved uncomfortably in his chair as he scoured his mind for inspiration. The two gentlemen were seated in the room Mr. Munroe had hand-selected for the baronet. Although it was not a suite, the chamber was more spacious than Roderick's and boasted a large bed with an intricately carved oak headboard. Done in deep crimson and green, the room's theme was the hunt; an enormous painting of gentlemen and ladies riding to hounds hung above the bed, and a bearskin rug lay on the carpet beside it. Unfortunately, the chamber was on the same floor as the Munroes' apartment—"First level's best! Too high for passersby to bother us, but low enough to jump if there's a fire!" Mr. Munroe had told him with a braying laugh—but Max shuddered to think how accessible he would seem to Lucy. She had certainly looked content when they bid their good nights.

Roderick lingered with the Devane ladies only a little while

before following him upstairs. Max scarcely had time to order
his bag delivered from his horse before Vaughan charged into
the room. And now his cousin was watching him with lively
attention. Which was not surprising. If he was as guilty as Max
thought, he had to know why he was here.

Games and more games. How he longed for uncomplicated
people in his life.

Unfortunately, living beneath Roderick's roof had taught him
to plot strategies as well, for self-defense.

"You've caught me," Max said. "That's not the only reason
I came." He waited, hoping for a guilty response from his
companion, but Roderick remained unmoved. "I decided I was
overdo for a holiday."

Roderick snorted. "You? I never thought to hear that. Has
the sea burst into flames? Did Napoleon escape again?"

"You're not the only one who enjoys leisure."

"Max, you don't know *how* to enjoy leisure. You're never
happier than when you're bent double after twelve hours of
grinding circles into blown glass."

The baronet's eyes glittered dangerously. "Is that what you
think?"

"What other conclusion can I draw? You've lost all sense
of fun, old man. Didn't used to be such a stick when you were
a lad."

"You sound like Felicity," he said resentfully.

"Ah, Felicity. How is the child? Still plotting to leg-shackle
one of us?"

"She is as you left her, Roderick."

"The chit never gives up. But Felicity's got the right of it
if she's been advising you to enjoy yourself more."

Now it was Max's turn to give Roderick a scornful look.
"Perhaps it's as well one of us takes an interest in the business."

"Yes, and you glory in it, too, don't you? Making your
Uncle Harry proud?"

Regarding him steadily, Max leaned his head back. Across
from him sat the man who held the key to his future, and he
would do well not to fall asleep.

"You could do the same," he said hoarsely. "He would burst with fatherly pride if you treated your work with more seriousness."

Vaughan ran his hands along the velvet arms of his chair. "No, Max. I leave that to you. For me, life is to be savored."

"That's fine so long as your pockets remain deep. How are your funds holding out these days, if I may ask?"

"You may not," Roderick said, his tone injured. "How would you like me to inquire about yours?"

"I'll tell you gladly. My purse is exceedingly light. I'm embarrassed to admit I may have to throw myself on your mercy."

"Amazing! You spend next to nothing. Well, don't look to me for a loan. Write your favorite uncle. I'll be doing well to cover my own shot when I leave." His glance moved over his cousin. "Suppose I shouldn't be surprised you're on Poor Street, since you've been reduced to stealing my clothes."

Max couldn't help smiling, though he felt a ridiculous disappointment that his cousin had not taken that opportunity to confess. Hoping Roderick would be moved by his poverty was a feeble dream at best, he supposed.

For an instant, the scalding thought that Roderick might not be responsible for the theft singed his brain. But if not his cousin, then who? There was no one else who could do it; especially not in the way it was done.

No, Roderick was making it difficult, that was all. What would be the amusement in his trick if Max was not made to sweat a little?

Very well, then; he would participate in the contest for a day or so. Perhaps a week, he amended, recalling a pair of soft brown eyes and golden hair. After that, a more direct approach would be in order. And if it involved his fists, he wouldn't object in the least.

"I apologize for that," Max said. "At the start I only intended to remain overnight, but I've decided to lengthen my stay. I'm sending a messenger to fetch Carleton with my clothes." Along with a letter of explanation to Uncle Harry, he reminded himself.

"And until then you'll be mucking up mine, I suppose. If there was any danger you'd look better in my rags than I do, I might be offended. As it is, welcome to them. Except for my new wine-colored jacket; I'll shoot you for touching it." He tilted his head thoughtfully. "You're staying longer than you planned? Might a renewed interest in the innkeeper's daughter be responsible?"

Max swallowed the denial that instantly rose to his lips. He could not wish for a better cover to explain his continued stay. "Old feelings die hard," he said, nearly choking on the words.

"Then you're more of an idiot than I thought. Wasn't last year's punishment enough?"

The baronet raised his head irritably. "A pretty face can make a fool of any man, as you well know. And what about you? Your dinner companions tonight were uncommonly fair."

Roderick smiled faintly. "Yes, both of them, though I prefer the older for her experience. She's proving deuced hard to win, though."

"Has Roderick Vaughan met his match?" Max asked mockingly.

"I'm a long way from despair. Mrs. Devane projects a cool air, but I suspect has a warm center." A challenging gleam lit his eyes. "It promises to take longer than usual, but I will melt that icy exterior, I promise you."

Max's lashes lowered to mask a deadly look. His cousin's arrogance enraged him. He was speaking of a fine lady willing to risk her life to save a stranger's. Although he could not approve of her scandalous occupation, he understood the necessity which led her to it. She deserved better than Roderick's schemes of seduction.

And yet . . .

An insidious idea began to take shape in his mind. He dismissed it as unworthy. It returned.

Roderick was dazzled by Mrs. Devane. Should she exert her charm in his direction, he would be willing to do anything, say anything to please her. Even to the divulging of the whereabouts of Max's formula.

The baronet blinked. What was wrong with him? That refined lady could not be used in such a fashion. He could not risk her virtue, no matter how badly he wanted answers. She would never agree to such a thing, anyway. Fever must be confusing him.

But nothing would happen so long as he was around to guard her. And guard her he would, whether she wanted to assist him or not.

"I might be able to help," he said, damping his ire to speak in civil tones. "A group outing should seem less threatening. Perhaps a picnic. I could invite Lucy and her brother as well."

"You may try, and my best wishes to you," said Roderick. "I've attempted to interest her in such an activity for days; but as you say, a greater number might appeal." He clapped his hands on his knees. "Well, I'm away. The night is young, and I've some living to do."

As Roderick rose to approach the door, a desperation Max could no longer suppress made him follow.

"Roderick. Is there anything you want to tell me?"

Vaughan regarded him with bright eyes. "Such as what? Don't ask me to say I love you, because I don't. Though your ears are nice. I've always admired them."

Max sighed, pushed him into the corridor, and closed the door. Then he walked to the wash basin and splashed water across his face. His head might be splitting, but he could not rest yet. His hands shook ever so slightly as he ran his fingers through his hair.

What a tense evening it had been, Gwendolyn thought as she sat at her dressing table, brushing her long hair. Most disturbing. After dinner had finally drawn to a close, she'd returned Camille to their rooms as quickly as possible. Her daughter had been disappointed in not being allowed to attend an assembly, but Gwendolyn could not take the chance young Mr. Munroe would follow them. Or Mr. Vaughan. And certainly not Sir Hastings, who looked to be staying at The Allemande after all, since he had walked off with the owner's arm across his shoulders.

It was impossible to avoid mixed feelings about his remaining longer. He seemed an odd combination of heady masculinity and comedy. She suspected the woman who eventually married him would spend her time either laughing or weeping. If he did not remain a bachelor, that was, for he was approaching the age where most men made up their minds one way or the other.

How old was he? she wondered. From his appearance he could be anywhere from twenty-five to thirty-five. Probably the younger age, which would explain the tender feelings he prompted within her. Maternal feelings, that was what they were. He was certain to be significantly younger than her thirty-two years. Everyone seemed to be, except for very old people.

Setting aside her brush, she looked at her rosewood desk and sighed. She still had at least an hour's work to do. Mr. Alferton, the stage manager at the theatre, a man she had never met directly but who communicated with her through an anonymous mailing address, had requested two more skits for the spaces between acts of *Lydia's Secret.* Repeat visitors were growing tired of the current ones. The skits were merely humorous sketches meant to appease the audience as scenery was changed backstage. Neither should take long to write, except it was difficult to be amusing when tired. Gwendolyn moved to her desk and stared at the wall, flicking her quill against her cheek as she thought.

Concentration proved impossible. The startling events of the day continually played through her mind. The astouding entrance of Sir Hastings into her life . . . the shattering moments when she slipped and his arms buoyed her to safety . . . his unexpected arrival in the dining room . . . and the threat his continued stay offered.

It was ridiculous to be old enough to realize what was happening to her but too young to put death to the emotions. Maternal feelings, indeed. She had been caught by a pair of green eyes and a charming, direct manner as easily as any schoolgirl would be. Even Camille had better sense.

The only thing to be done was to bury those feelings, and there was one sure way to do that: *write*. The quill began to move rapidly as she recounted Sir Hastings' wooing of Lucy. Laughing at someone and then feeling passion for him did not pair easily, she hoped. And laugh she did as the words fell onto paper, her wont for exaggeration magnifying the situation which Mr. Vaughan had recounted.

When she finished, she read the whole with sad pleasure. It was one of the most amusing pieces she had ever written; Mr. Alferton would have been pleased. But selling Sir Hastings' story had never been her intention; catharsis was. She read it through once more, then slid it into her refuse pot. There. Now that she saw the baronet as a ridiculous figure of fun, he could be nothing more to her.

Unfortunately, she still had two skits to write. After rising from her chair and stretching for a few moments, she began to work again. She had almost done with the first one, a sentimental frippery about a young girl's first waltz, when she heard a faint thump outside her bedroom wall. It came again; three short, quiet raps, as though someone meant to signal her. And then a light knocking at the sitting room door. Quickly she donned her robe, knotted its belt, and padded to the entrance.

Her heart lurched when she saw Sir Hastings, though some part of her had known it all the time. He looked weary, but no more sick than he had appeared earlier. Mayhap dining with an old love had been good for his health.

Unfortunately, he did not strike her as ridiculous in the least. So much for writing one's madnesses away.

"I'm sorry to disturb you," he whispered. "May I come in? I have news I think you'll be relieved to hear. I could come back in the morning, but I hoped to arrange this tonight since my time here is limited."

Anyone might open their door and see them. She could not allow scandal to touch her daughter. With some disquiet, she stood aside for him to enter. "Very well. For a moment only."

As she went to sit opposite him on the settee, she said, "I must say you've stirred my curiosity."

"Then I won't delay in quenching it. Camille is asleep?" When she nodded, he continued, "It appears Bryce Munroe is quite besotted with your daughter."

"I'm not blind, Sir Hastings. I was aware of that."

He looked taken aback at her lack of enthusiasm. "Then perhaps you'll be glad to know I've suggested we might all take an outing together, along with Roderick and Bryce's sister."

"You *what?*" Her posture stiffened. Had she imagined herself attracted to him? He had crossed an unforgivable line with his interference. "I cannot believe you would do such a thing without my consent!"

He stared. "Naturally nothing will be done without your consent, but I don't understand why you aren't willing. You said you were concerned about Roderick's attentions to her."

"True, but that doesn't mean I'm eager to replace the notice of one gentleman with an even more attractive one—at least in my daughter's eyes."

"Then she is interested as well." His expression grew more baffled. "Miss Devane is a vivacious, charming young lady. Don't you want her to mix with others her own age?"

"Sir Hastings, my daughter is hardly sixteen years old."

He hesitated for a fraction of time. "I had not realized she was so young; she appears older. But I wasn't suggesting a private assignation, only a group activity to provide harmless entertainment."

"Harmless!" She pushed to her feet and walked to the mantel, knitting her hands together. "What do you know of harmless?"

"Mrs. Devane, surely you're overreacting." He watched her warily, as one might observe a madwoman. It made her even more furious.

"Overreacting, is it?" She forced her voice to remain low, though she could not hide the quiver of emotion in it. "Do you know how old I was when I wed for the first time?"

ness. "I, and I alone, will decide when
ertainly won't be when she's sixteen."
er, if she had her wish, but she would
sfaction of knowing that. She glanced
Now if you don't mind, I'm very tired."
oth hands to his temples. "I have been
Forgive me. The search for the formula
ing. I suppose I hoped that if Roderick
ould be in your company, he might le
a slim hope at best and selfish of me to
beg you will forget the past few moments

a few instants, then stood, anger spurting
of the man, to steal into her room a
anted opinions about her childrearing i
old him about herself, and now this!
n unaccountably low opinion of me, Si

not," he said rapidly.
guise my identity doesn't mean I'm will
f a—a deceiver."
ght that—"
would draw that conclusion." She raise
d as she spoke, pacing a few steps awa
a kind of logic in it, I suppose. If one h
mind. A *narrow* one."
e said commandingly, the words burstin
d his control. "Shall I tell you the truth
anted to spend time with you myself."
tly. Long seconds passed as they regard
s very tall; her eyes were on a level wi
vas flushed, his eyes bright, but that mig
knowing all she did of men and their li
ression reflected sincerity. Aware that I
vay, she set her chin to fight losing it.
I would have guessed, since you plann
nroe on your picnic."

"No, but I have a feeling you're going to tell me." His forehead creased. "The *first* time, did you say?"

"I was sixteen! Do you think I want my daughter to repeat my mistakes?"

"I'm sorry," he said awkwardly. "I didn't know." He cleared his throat. "How many times have you been married?"

She breathed a prayer for patience. "You are missing the point entirely; but if you must know, I've been to the altar twice."

His face was alive with questions, but he didn't ask them. That was well; it meant he possessed at least some breeding and good manners. Her irate heart began to slow to a more normal rate. She reseated herself and regarded him as calmly as she could. He already knew her most dangerous secret; perhaps if she told him a little of her past, he would understand her fears for Camille. And then he would go, please God, and leave her alone.

"I fell in love for the first time with the vicar's son, Harrison Allworth. At least, I thought it was love, but I was too young to know the meaning of the term. It was my mother's fondest wish was for me to marry a peer."

"Not an uncommon ambition."

"I know. Therefore, when a viscount's horse went lame a mile or two from our house and Lord Devane hobbled to our door, he seemed a godsend to Mother. Especially when he collapsed from the walk and needed to recuperate for a few days. He was not a healthy man, nor a young one." *And his favorite form of exercise was raising the port decanter to his lips.*

"By the time he'd recovered, I was betrothed. Against my will."

"Doubtless you can guess the result. Harrison and I eloped. I cannot tell you of the hue and cry that resulted. Both sets of parents cut us off. And then, almost immediately, I became with child. Harrison was little more than a babe himself; he was not trained for anything and could not support us."

Not that he was willing to try, she failed to add.

"He did have some luck with cards, and we existed by gambling and outrunning our creditors. Sometimes I did laundry and washed pots for our dinner." She lowered her gaze. "During Camille's first year, she did not lay her head on the same pillow for longer than a week at a time."

Sir Hastings looked appalled. "I'm sorry."

"We had some happy times," she said simply. *But not nearly enough to compensate for the suffering.* Except for the gift of her daughter. Anything would have been worth that.

His eyes searched hers, a thousand thoughts in them.

"After we had been married two years, Harrison died." She kept her tone even, for she liked to think of herself as an emotionally controlled woman, at least outwardly. But the words still possessed the power to shake her. "We were staying at an inn on the Dorset coast, just outside Weymouth. Camille was sick, and Harrison rode out during a thunderstorm to find a physician the innkeeper had recommended. Lightning struck an oak tree and split it. He was found pinned beneath the tree the next morning."

Sir Hastings said nothing, but the sympathy in his eyes almost undid her. She continued rapidly, "There was nothing I could do except return home to beg my parents' support. They were willing to give it."

Her teeth set in remembrance. No need to tell him of her mother's recriminations, her constant complaints. Gwendolyn's life was ruined beyond repair in her parents' eyes. And then the miracle happened.

"Eventually, Lord Devane received word of my widowhood. He forgave my lapse, and we were married." She was unwilling to say more, but slammed shut the gates of memory which taunted her with images of the viscount's drunken face and his brother's brutal one.

"Your mother had her way at last," he said.

"Yes."

"But it was not your wish," he said gently.

Something within him reached toward her; she felt it as surely as if he had risen from his seat and glided his fingers

along her cheel
was imagination

"Arthur Deva
ure of kindness,
For that, I will

Sir Hastings
eyes. She wonde
when he said, "
all this time."

"No, I will no
deeply, she finish
so you would un
will not be force
necessity, or by
exposed to perso
dreams of roman

"You continue
His eyes were so
to him. After a
protect her from t
to let her try her

The warmth in
to be telling me v

He stirred forv
"No one, only an
for disaster. Reins

"Camille is no

He leveled a pr

Her stomach tig
one's soul to a str

"The circumsta
I are closer than m
values my opinion

"I doubt that wi
thought appeared t
long do you plan to
to begin mixing wi

She prayed for
she is ready; and
Or seventeen or
not give him the
pointedly at the d

He briefly pres
speaking out of t
has clouded my
were relaxed as
something slip. It
push it." He rose.
ever happened."

She stared at hi
through her. The
night, impose his
spite of all she ha

"You must ho
Hastings."

"I assure you,

"Just because I
ing to play the pa

"No, I never th

"But naturally
her hands heaven
and back. "There
a particular slant

"Mrs. Devane,'
from him as if be
I asked because I

She stopped ins
one another. He
his cravat. His fac
be from fever. Ye
she thought his e
wrath was ebbing

"That's not wl
to include Miss M

He briefly closed his eyes. "You've been listening to my cousin. My relationship with Lucy ended long ago, but I could hardly ask Bryce without including her."

"Well. You needn't ask either of them. Mr. Vaughan has invited me repeatedly to walk with him, or go for a carriage ride. If I should accept and see if I can discover something, would you then leave us in peace?"

He made no effort to hide his amazement. "Are you speaking of seeing him *alone?*"

"Yes. my daughter has promised to visit an elderly friend of ours tomorrow, so it will be the perfect time."

He started to say something, then began again. "Thank you, Mrs. Devane, but I can't allow you to risk yourself on my behalf." He smiled briefly, giving her a tender look that made her heart skip a beat. "Not again. You'll be in more danger with Roderick than you were on the balcony."

How exasperating he was. Now that she had expressed her willingness, he was reluctant. "I'm not a child, nor am I subject to the flatteries of a rake. Believe it or not, I have dealt with his like before."

They were standing very close to one another. His eyes swept her face, a sweet tension growing between them. Suddenly he moved toward the doorway, and she could not say whether she was happy or dismayed.

"I do appreciate the offer," he said, turning the knob and holding the door slightly ajar, his fingers clinging to it as if to an anchor. "But now that I've had time to consider, I realize it's useless. Roderick's very cunning."

"It seems worth the effort to me, Sir Hastings. Do you imagine I never had occasion to use my wits when I was married to Harrison? Sometimes it made the difference between bread on the table and hungry dreams."

He paused, his restless eyes seeming to search the room for words. "Why are you willing to do this?" With a disarming smile, he added, "It can't be only that you want me out of your life. If that's all you wish, I will go. You don't have to earn my absence."

She glanced aside. "It's *your* formula, is it not? I cannot bear injustice. What is more, I love a mystery." *Would that those were the only reasons,* she thought miserably, and not this overriding need to help him that had sprung unbidden inside her breast.

Slight disappointment edged his expression. "Very well. I can't stop you, I suppose."

"No, you cannot."

"Then my best wishes go with you." He stared at her a moment longer before bending swiftly to kiss her cheek.

The door closed softly behind him. She put her fingers to her face; then, spurred by an impulse, she clenched the knob and pulled. But he was already gone.

As she glanced up and down the corridor, she was certain the door to Mr. Vaughan's room clicked shut.

For several seconds she regarded it in doubt. She tried to recall the last words she and the baronet had spoken. Like all conversations, it was already fading, leaving behind only impressions. Well, there was nothing she could do about it. Perhaps a visit from Sir Hastings to his cousin explained the slowly closing latch.

She entered her sitting room, then walked quietly into her daughter's chamber. Camille was curled on her right side, her favorite sleeping position. A shaft of moonlight lit the curve of her cheek and her soft skin. Pale lashes flickered over a dream. Gwendolyn stroked back a moon-silvered curl that had fallen across the girl's nose, a blaze of love filling her heart.

You shall never feel want, she vowed. You will have the life you deserve.

It was something she did every evening, this ritual, this prayer. Saying it with conviction and frequency, she believed, would make it come true.

But tonight, for the first time in a long while, she had misgivings.

"Oh, my dear," she whispered, "how shall I protect you when I cannot protect myself?"

Chapter Five

Max woke shortly after eight the next morning after a restless night interrupted by feverish dreams and coughs. He felt hollow and spent, and the image in his mirror looked haggard. After eating a breakfast of eggs and toast in his room, he returned to bed and slept soundly until half-past one.

When he awoke the second time, he felt much better. His fever had broken, and the scratchiness in his throat was almost gone. Brimming with renewed energy, he ordered hot water, had a bath and shave, and attired himself in the spare set of clothes he'd brought, a green jacket with beige waistcoat and pantaloons.

He slipped cautiously into the hall, on the alert for signs of Lucy Munroe. He counted himself fortunate she had not already pounded on his door, but then she never was an early riser. His pulse didn't steady until he reached the stairs.

It was time to see what, if anything, was transpiring between Mrs. Devane and Roderick. In the light of day and the perspective of a clearer head, he felt his fears for her multiplying. If anything happened to that brave lady, *anything,* be it insult or injury, he would strangle his cousin with his bare hands.

He nodded to a couple of ladies descending past him on the stairs, then turned to enter the corridor when he reached Mrs. Devane's floor. He had gone only a few steps before he saw a man carrying a valise exiting from her room. The stranger was short and thin as a reed, his shabby clothes hanging loosely on him. The lower half of his face was pale, giving hint of a recently shorn beard. He possessed a furtive air, and Max's hackles rose.

The man's eyes widened as he spied the baronet. Stiffly, he began to walk in the opposite direction, toward the servant's stair. When he realized Max followed him, he darted a panicked look over his shoulder, then broke into a run. The baronet sprinted after him, demanding that he stop. The stranger's boots clattered down the stairs with so much force that Max thought he'd fallen or at least dropped the bag. But when Sir Hastings arrived at the stairwell, he saw the man continued to clomp downward, the valise clutched to his chest, the bald spot on the top of his head flushing with exertion.

Max used the handrail to leap several treads at a time. He was gaining on him, but he had to move faster. Once the man reached the ground floor, he would be hard to catch. Corridors ran in all directions, and there were the outside exits to worry about.

He was nearing the first floor when a maid turned from the hall to the stairs. She carried a large pot of water in her arms, and Max ran into her headlong. Water sloshed over them as she tried to hold onto the bowl, but to no avail; the pot slipped from her hands, the remaining liquid spewing upward in a deluge. She cursed under her breath, her plump cheeks darkening with rage.

At least, Max thought, feeling moisture seep through his clothes to his skin, crowding his way past her at the same time, the water was warm.

By the time he arrived at street level, the man was nowhere to be seen. There was no use huffing back and forth in wet clothes while trying to find him. Sir Hastings trotted upward past the maid, who was kneeling to sop the puddles with a towel, muttered an apology which she ignored, and climbed on to the Devanes' room. As he feared, the door was locked, and no one answered his knock.

He reversed direction and hurried down the stairs again to where the maid worked. She sat back on her haunches and eyed him indignantly. After repeating his apology, he asked her if she had seen the man he'd been following.

She wiped her nose with her sleeve. "I saw naught but you and a flood," she said resentfully.

"He was leaving Mrs. Devane's room, and I'm afraid he may have stolen something."

Suspicion bulged her eyes. "Thieves at The Allemande? No, that's not likely. It ain't never happened before."

"There's always a first time," he said, impatience making him curt. "Do you have a passkey to the rooms?"

"I do," she said with reluctance.

"Then come open Mrs. Devane's chamber for me. She could need our help."

"Don't know nothing about a man," the maid said stubbornly. "I can't leave this mess for someone to fall over."

"Give me a towel, and I'll assist you." To her astonishment, he snatched the cloth from her hands, swiped rapidly as she squawked a token protest, then pulled her to her feet. "Now hurry."

She allowed herself to be pulled along, a hazy smile lifting her cheeks. Less than a moment later, he stood within the Devanes' sitting room, the maid hovering near the doorway. Just in case *he* should turn out to be the thief, Max thought wryly.

Nothing seemed to be wrong. He had expected the furniture to be in disarray, or the contents of drawers to be spilled over the floor. Pacing through the rooms, he felt like an intruder. Perhaps he'd misread the situation. The man could have been a relative or a messenger. Maybe he had run because he thought Max meant to do him harm.

He saved Mrs. Devane's bedroom for last. With a feeling bordering on reverence, he glanced at her dresser, her desk,

her bed. She had lain here last night, after he left. The scent
of her, the stamp of her strong personality, was upon the room.
But his mooning accomplished little, and the maid was beginning to watch him with suspicion again. He moved toward the
threshold, his hand brushing the edge of the writer's desk.

It was then he heard it. A soft, slithering sound. Nothing
about the noise suggested it belonged in a lady's bedroom. It
was full of wrongness. Inappropriateness. Evil.

Softly, he paced closer to the desk, his breaths quickening.
The drawer lay slightly ajar, the way an owner might have
closed it were she in a hurry. Yet every other surface of the
room bespoke an elegant neatness, an eye to detail that a writer
would understand.

He stared at the desk. And heard a faint rattle, sensed the
anger rising behind the wood. Turning his head, he looked at
the maid, who still stood in the doorway. She, too, had heard
it, her eyes growing large and afraid.

"What is it, sir?" she whispered, almost soundlessly.

The movements within the drawer became frenzied. The
drawer bumped; the opening widened. Something dark writhed
within, something graceful in its fluid, whipping motions; something elegant but sinister.

Max edged backward, his arm extended to guide the servant
away. She needed no urging. As a narrow, leathery head probed
its way from the drawer, she exclaimed, "Mercy sakes, Lord
preserve us, 'tis a serpent like in the Garden of Eden!"

"Quiet, woman," he said in a hushed voice, his glance
searching the small parlor for a weapon. The quilt he had rested
beneath yesterday lay across the back of the settee. He seized
it, grabbed the shovel from the fireplace, and returned to the
bedroom. At each movement the maid shadowed him, though
she kept carefully behind, wringing her hands and begging him
to stop, crying he would be bitten, he would, and why didn't
they close the door and run for help?

"What's your name, miss?" Max asked, his eyes following
the snake as its head wormed higher, its body gliding sinuously
from the prison of the desk.

her to think of Camille instead of herself, he
...er than his own mother, he had never known a
...an. He tried to imagine Lucy or Felicity showing
...1. His imagination failed him.

...did you and Roderick go today?'' he asked in a
...trying again to stir her from the despondency that
...pon her the moment she'd discovered what had

...ked at the Royal Crescent,'' she answered tone-
...vas unable to learn anything about your formula.

...know you are in a hurry to return home. I hope
...ave to leave without finding it.''

...ula? He had forgotten it entirely.

...ght stunned him. How could he could forget the
...tant thing in his life? His future, his fortune, was
...As was his mother's. But now it had receded into
...s of his mind, replaced by something much more

...of little consequence at the moment. Besides, I don't
...eave until we have an answer to what happened

...ulder curved inward as she moved slightly away.
...kind, Sir—Max. Had it not been for you, Camille
...h of us, might be dead. For the second day in a row
...cued me, and I believe that is enough. I've already
...ow grateful I am. I'll never forget what you've done.
...ly no one could be expected to do more.''

...to do more. I need to make sure you're safe.''

...ked at him, and he was shocked to see the coldness
...s. ''Our well-being is not your responsibility.''

...mpossible not to be hurt. Then he remembered wha...
...ld him about her marriages. No doubt she'd suffered
...ds of both husbands. Perhaps she distrusted all me...
...ntentions. If she did, that was unfair, and it irritate...

...'t know what's going through your mind,'' he sai...
..., staring at the horse's ears as he spoke, ''but let m...

''H-Hettie, sir,'' she sniffed.

''All right, Hettie,'' he whispered, ''When I move forward, you move back. Don't wait to see what happens. Get help, but slam the door behind you, all right?''

''Oh, sir. Please don't do this!''

He darted a firm look in her direction and waited until she met his eyes. ''We can't take the chance it will escape and hide somewhere else. Now prepare yourself.''

Hettie moaned, and inwardly he echoed the sound. He had little confidence in his ability to subdue the reptile. Like many Englishmen, he had never seen one other than in books; they were that rare, and certainly had no business in a lady's bedroom—especially *this* lady's.

The snake had nearly unwound itself from the drawer. Rage spurred him to action. He launched the coverlet over it, and both reptile and cloth fell to the floor. At the same moment, Hettie screamed and flew out the door, banging it shut with enough force to dislodge a painting from the sitting-room wall.

The serpent was undulating rapidly toward the edge of the quilt. Before it could emerge, Max clutched the handle of the shovel in both fists and slammed it, blade downward, again and again, as the snake thrashed back and forth, its rattle chilling his blood.

At last, when he felt the blade cut through, he forced himself to stop.

Max waited, his heartbeat gradually steadying. The snake's movements continued, but he was sure the head had been severed. Cautiously, using the shovel, he lifted the coverlet, then flung it aside and studied the striped body of the reptile for a brief time. Only the most civilized part of his mind dissuaded him from chopping it to pieces.

Had Mrs. Devane opened her desk drawer, she would have fallen victim to a horrible death.

The fault was not the serpent's but that of the man who had left it here. Why had he done such a thing? It was incomprehensible.

There came a noise from the corridor, and he swerved in

relief. It would be best to have the carnage cleared away when Mrs. Devane, *Gwendolyn*, returned. But it was not Hettie's voice he heard as the door nudged open.

"That's strange; it's unlocked," Gwendolyn said, her curiosity evident. "I wonder—"

Seeing him, she stopped, her pleasant expression fading to perplexity. In the corridor behind her stood Roderick, who entered the room the instant he spotted his cousin.

"Well, Max. One never knows where you'll turn up next. Dare I ask what you're doing here? And why are your clothes wet?"

Before the baronet could answer, Hettie and two footmen burst through the door. Without pausing to acknowledge the others, she headed for Max, saying loudly, "Oh, thank heaven you're all right! Did you kill that horrible devil?"

"Kill?" Gwendolyn's fingers moved to her throat.

Max took her hand. "I'll explain in a moment," he told her softly. "For now, I want you to wait outside. I need to remove something. And we must check your suite more thoroughly."

"Check . . . my suite?" repeated Gwendolyn.

"In case there's more snakes," Hettie supplied helpfully.

A little more than an hour later, Max, dressed in dry clothes courtesy of his cousin, hurried toward the inn's stable carrying a medium-sized box. Several grooms looked up as he drew near, gazing past him. Hearing rapid footsteps approaching, he turned swiftly, then relaxed when he saw Mrs. Devane. Her pace was so brisk that she held her jaunty blue bonnet in place with one gloved hand. In the other, she clutched a matching reticule.

"That magistrate is not going to do anything!" she exclaimed.

"I know." He began to move forward again. She hurried along beside him.

"Do you know what he said to me? *These things happen,*

Mrs. Devane.' I'd like to hear him say in *his* bedroom."

"I suppose finding the source of a beyond the ordinary duties of a mag

"But you're going to look, aren't you're intention in coming to the sta

"I hope to try."

"Then I'm going with you," she argue all you like, but it was *my* room the safety of my child."

He gazed into her determined eye crumble. "Very well. I'll hire a gig."

Soon they were cropping along in pulled by a well-groomed black, headin that Mr. Munroe had mentioned at dinn he could think to do. At their feet la contents.

As they traveled, Gwendolyn eyed but maintained a taut silence. To divert did you manage to break away from R

"I pled a headache."

"That should have been believabl ripped apart drawer-by-drawer would

"The room doesn't matter." She flas "Shall I ever feel safe again?"

He wanted to slide an arm around h her hand. All he could do was touch course you will. I'll speak with Munro put a new lock on your door. If he do

"Who could have done this, Sir Ha

"That's what I hope to find out." H a cart filled with flowers. "I know another long, but don't you think w experiences for you to call me by my

Ignoring the question, she looked at "That thing could have crawled from ter's."

How li thought. selfless w such conc

"Wher light voic had falle happened

"We lessly. I'm sorry you won

The fo

The th most imp tied to i the shad urgent.

"That intend t today."

Her s

"You a or I, or b you've r told you But certa

"I wa

She lo in her ey

It was she had at the ha and their him.

"I do forcefull

assure you I have no designs on you when I say I want to help. I'm not trying to intrude, any more than you did when you decided to spend time with Roderick this afternoon. I'm motivated only by a fondness for a very kind and courageous lady and her daughter. And if you think I'm going to abandon you while there's any chance of your being in danger, you are sadly mistaken."

There was a long silence. Unable to bear it any longer, he slid a look at her. She had half-turned toward him, and her eyes were moving rapidly, her face solemn. Their covert glances met and held. And warmed. Her lips trembled, fighting a smile.

Satisfied, he grinned and returned his attention to the busy roadway.

Reaching the outskirts of the city a short while later, Max drove toward a meadow containing a number of cheerfully colored tents. The afternoon was a fair one; there was a good crowd milling about on the grass and, from the sound of intermittent applause and laughter, an equal number enjoying a show within the largest tent. He parked the gig, tucked the box beneath his arm, then led Mrs. Devane to the first attendant they saw, a ticket-taker. Max fired a few questions, and they were pointed to the owner's wagon. Mr. Eddison was a stout gentleman with a thick beard that trembled when Max displayed the contents of the box.

"Lud, lud," he said miserably. "Did you have to kill him? Feidler reported a missing snake from the reptile exhibit last night. Don't know how it got out. That's a rattler from the American West, that is. Or was." When he lifted the tail and eyed it with sad fondness, Gwendolyn averted her eyes. "As deadly as they come. Do you know how hard it is to get these over here? Where did you find him?"

"In my desk at The Allemande," Gwendolyn said.

"What?" He looked back and forth between them. "Now see here, you can't lay it on us. We've never lost an animal before. And I can't believe he would crawl across town and into somebody's desk!"

"No one's accusing your circus of anything," Max said.

"Tell me about your serpent handler, this Feidler. Is he a smallish man, thin, with a bald spot?" As the manager regarded him blankly, he added, "He might recently have had a beard."

"Feidler is taller than you and has a bushy red head." Mr. Eddison looked thoughtful. "Though we do take on locals when we need an extra pair of hands, and that sounds like a fellow we hired a couple of days ago. Had to give him the sack last night." He leaned closer to Max, his onion-scented breath nearly driving the baronet backward. "Little problem with the bottle. Didn't stay at his work. What was his name, now? Drinker, Dinkums . . . no . . . Deevers! That was it!"

"Do you know where he lives by any chance?"

"No, but Birchwood might. He's my clerk." Mr. Eddison told him which wagon was his, then peered up at Max, wrinkles rippling outward from his eyes. "Why're you looking for Deevers? You think he did this?"

"Let's just say we have a few questions for him," the baronet answered cryptically, placing a guiding hand at Gwendolyn's elbow. He could not be sure the circus owner was trustworthy, and he didn't want Deevers to be warned. "We may have some work for him."

"Well, luck go with you. I'll keep the snake, if you don't mind. Might be able to use the skin for something."

Max looked at Gwendolyn. She widened her eyes in distaste and nodded. The baronet handed the box to the manager, thanked him, and led her down the steps and toward the clerk's wagon.

Mr. Birchwood was a very short man who would not have appeared plump except for his pillow-like stomach. His small hands were resting on that rounded middle, and he was snoring when Max peered into the open door of the wagon. The noise of their arrival brought the man to immediate wakefulness. He sat up, jerking his feet from the ottoman to the floor and giving them both a wide smile.

"Hello, hello," he said gladly, reaching for Max's hand, then Gwendolyn's as they climbed into the caravan. Sweeping

"Be prepared for anything," Max said softly as they drew into the yard. "I wish you had stayed in the village."

The muscles in Gwendolyn's legs spasmed at his words, but she set her mouth firmly. "We can't be sure this is his house. Even if it is, he might have had nothing to do with what happened."

He cocked an eyebrow. "Have you ever hunted?" When she shook her head, he said, "There comes a time when you are certain your prey is just over the next rise. You feel it in the small hairs at the back of your neck; you scent it in the air. Perhaps it's the smell of fear."

Her breathing quickened. "And . . . you feel this way now?" It was shattering, how the man possessed the power to absorb her in his words. He could cast spells, she believed.

"I do." His shoulders straightened. "But," he said brightly, "I could be wrong. Such has been known to happen."

At that moment, a woman walked from the house, a naked baby perched on her hip. Max hailed her and asked the necessary question.

The woman, who identified herself as Lila, was dressed in a colorless skirt and blouse. She ran her gaze across the horse and gig, then Max and Gwendolyn. The dark bags beneath her eyes, the downward droop of her mouth, gave her a defeated air. Her envious thoughts were so transparent to Gwendolyn that she felt a stab of pity.

"Deevers is gone," Lila said finally, shifting the baby's position.

"Do you know where?" Max asked.

"No. He don't tell me anything, and I don't want to know."

Moved by sudden impulse, Gwendolyn opened her reticule and removed a pound note, then stepped down from the gig. Hearing Max's surprised movements behind her, she gestured to prevent his joining her on the ground.

"We must find him," she told Lila gently, her eyes entreating as she pressed the note into the hand of the woman, who slid it into her pocket without comment. "If he is the man we're looking for, he may have information that could save someone's life.''

"Teddy?'' Lila asked scornfully. "He can't help nobody's life. He's in trouble, ain't he?''

Gwendolyn's pulse began to speed. "Why do you say that?''

"Cause he's always in trouble. Can't keep a position. Won't take care of his young 'uns. Leaves me alone to do it myself.''

Swallowing disappointment, she asked, "How long does he usually stay away? Are you sure you don't know where he is?''

The woman's gaze traveled from Gwendolyn's bonnet to her tiny boots, but she said nothing. Desperately, Gwendolyn nodded toward her baby.

"Your child is beautiful. I have a daughter myself, and I want to protect her. The man we're looking for put her life in jeopardy. Can you understand why this is so important to me?''

"I don't know where he is,'' Lila said dully. The baby began to fuss. "He ain't coming back. Told him not to. I ain't seen him since last night.'' She jiggled the infant, making its low wail vibrate. "Going to find me somebody better.'' Her eyes lifted longingly to Max.

With tears of frustration gathering, Gwendolyn turned and moved toward the gig.

"Told him to stay away from that man,'' the woman called after her. "I knew he meant trouble.''

Gwendolyn veered. "What man?''

"Don't know his name. The man that took him home last night. I saw 'em talking yesterday, down near the shed. Asked Teddy what it was about. He said it was something to do with his work at the circus, but I knew better, 'cause they got rid of him. He says, 'Why did he pay me then?' and I says, 'Probably 'cause you'll do anything for a drink,' and he says, 'You're right about that,' and I says, 'Give me some of it then for the babies,' and he says, 'Work and make your own,' which is why I told him to get out for good.''

Gwendolyn, whose spirit had lightened at Lila's sudden loquaciousness, felt dejection consume her again.

"What did the man look like?" Max asked from the gig.

The woman appeared to search her memory. "Medium sort of fellow. Not too stout nor too skinny. Tall as you, I'm thinking. Toffy clothes. Not old, not young. Not good-looking as you."

That certainly narrowed it down, Gwendolyn thought with gloom. Nevertheless, she thanked the woman, left her name and address should Mr. Deevers return and promised a reward if she contacted her, then returned to the carriage. Max jumped down to assist.

"How discouraging," she said as he turned the gig toward Bath. "We're no closer to the truth than before."

"We've learned a few things. Deevers was undoubtedly the man I saw, but now we know he was only an instrument."

"Then some other stranger is behind the murder attempt. A man your height who is not too thin or fat or especially good-looking. Is that supposed to comfort me?"

Instantly, he dropped the reins and cupped her face in his hands, his eyes searching hers tenderly. She could not breathe. Her mind screamed, Flee! while her heart pled, Stay. Her heart won; she felt her lips tremble for his kiss.

But a glint of caution and sensibility came into his expression, and he did not touch her lips but pulled her into a warm embrace, carefully avoiding her bonnet so as not to crush it, almost as a brother would. Almost. She could have wept with disappointment and relief.

"I hope to comfort you," he said quietly. "Don't be afraid, dear lady; tomorrow is another day. We will find him."

Chapter Six

Visitors to Bath were more likely to attend the Pump Room than residents, but, sometime during the night, Sir Hastings had slid a note beneath Gwendolyn's door suggesting they meet there shortly past noon. Thus, on the afternoon following what she believed she would hereafter think of as The Day of the Serpent, Mrs. Devane found herself beginning yet another circuit of the large room.

Were it not for the presence of her daughter, she would find it boring in the extreme. The place teemed with people, many of them very finely dressed indeed, which she knew was the point of the exercise. The ladies paraded; the gentlemen watched, though some escorted their female companions. Very few actually drank the medicinal waters.

Fortunately, all the others seemed too involved in their own concerns to listen to her conversation with Camille, which naturally centered upon the events of yesterday. The girl was very distressed, the mystery occupying her every thought. Gwendolyn wished she could have kept this knowledge from her, but it was impossible since so many people knew about it. By breakfast time, thanks to Hettie's loose tongue—or perhaps the footmen's or even Mr. Vaughan's—the residents were buzzing over the shocking news that a reptile had been found in one of the rooms.

"Where is Sir Hastings?" Camille said despairingly. "He will know what to do, won't he? What can be keeping him?"

Gwendolyn had been wondering the same thing and frowned, turning yet again toward the entrance. On this occasion she was rewarded by the sight of the baronet, who was nudging his way through the mob and looking searchingly around. She exclaimed and began waving her reticule and fan, as did Camille, until he, along with a good many others, could not help seeing them.

They greeted one another warmly, too warmly on her part, Gwendolyn immediately thought. It was alarming how glad she was to find his concerned eyes resting upon her, to hear his anxious questions, "Are you both all right? Did anyone disturb you on the way over?"

Gwendolyn assured him of their good health and safety. "One of the footmen accompanied us here, as you suggested in your note." Noticing curious glances from a trio of ladies passing by, she lowered her voice. "Perhaps we had best walk."

Max immediately offered both ladies an arm, and they began to stroll. "I didn't like leaving you alone this morning, but I thought a public place like this would be safe."

"I'm sure it is," Gwendolyn responded. "We would have done something anyway; gone shopping or for a drive. Camille and I aren't going to let this incident destroy us. We refuse to become prisoners of fear, don't we, darling?"

Camille agreed, though her tone carried less conviction than her mother's. "What shall we do, Sir Hastings?" she entreated. "How can we find this terrible man and stop him?"

"Don't worry, child. The wheels are in motion. I've just returned from the traveling circus, where I spent a longer time interviewing people than yesterday. It occurred to me last night that perhaps the man who hired Deevers might have gone there to hire him. Eddison knew nothing, or he would have said so yesterday: but he put me in touch with one of his men, Feidler, who confirmed that a stranger had been around looking to hire someone familiar with snakes in order to play a prank—''

"A prank!" Gwendolyn declared indignantly.

Max chuckled. "My words precisely. Apparently Feidler thought so, too. He told the man he wouldn't do it, though he noticed him speaking to Deevers afterward."

Gwendolyn stopped, her excited eyes boring into his. "Was he able to tell you anything about this person?"

The baronet looked pleased. "Several things. First of all, he is much as Mrs. Deevers described; a rather ordinary-looking man. Brown hair, tallish, medium weight, nice clothing. But the worker told me he possessed an accent. He wasn't able to place it, however. Not surprising, because the fellow was hard of hearing."

"A foreigner, then," Gwendolyn murmured. "I know few foreigners."

"And," Sir Hastings said, a lilt in his voice, "he was able to give me a name. Paul."

"Paul . . ." whispered Mrs. Devane.

"Mean anything to you?"

"Nothing at all." she said, dismayed. "I have no acquaintance with anyone of that name. Have you heard of such a person, Camille?"

"No," she said miserably. "Oh, but if only I had, we could find him and everything would be over!"

Max patted her arm consolingly; then, with a deflated look in his eyes, he led them back into the stream of people. "The name could have been false, I suppose. The accent faked."

He was quiet a moment, but she sensed an inner turmoil. It struck her that she could easily read his moods, though his face was no more expressive than any man's. This curious insight harbingered no good, she feared. She was becoming too attuned, too dependent on his leadership. How easy to lean on him, how comforting to hand the reins of her life and her daughter's to this charming, capable man. This weakness in herself she could not allow, for with such abdication went one's autonomy. She had vowed never to fall into that position again.

Of course, her worryings might be for naught. Sir Hastings had been careful to say nothing out of the way, nothing which might be misconstrued as an indication of a man falling into the kind of affection which led to bridal raillery.

But she was no longer a green girl. She knew the signs. A special light came into his eyes when he looked at her. The frequency with which his arm brushed against hers, the way his fingers lingered upon her waist when assisting her from the gig yesterday, that gentle note in his voice; these could not be explained as only the attentions of a solicitous gentleman.

Now should *Mr. Vaughan* treat her the same—and he tried to do even more in his exaggerated, practiced way—*his* performance meant nothing. But there was much more depth to Max. Therefore, accordingly, she would have to be more careful.

"Gwendolyn," he said, pulling them to an empty spot near the wall and lowering his voice, "I hesitate to ask you this, but feel I must. Does anyone besides myself and Camille know about your writing?"

"I've told no one else." Her puzzled air gave way to a rising anger, and, given her recent thoughts, she was almost grateful for it. "Oh, no. Surely you don't think someone means revenge! I recall how you disapprove of me. Naturally you'd think of that first."

"I don't disapprove of you in the least. But it's worth considering. Remember how easily I discovered your secret."

"Yes, but you happened upon us in a way we could never dream to expect."

He smiled. "That's true. But there must be other times when you leave your suite unguarded."

"When we're away, I'm careful to secure my manuscripts."

"I think we know how effective locks are," he said, with feeling. "My formula was under lock and key as well."

A dismal look flickered in his eyes, but she was unwilling to sympathize at the moment.

"There must have been opportunities," he continued. "Discarded papers, for an example. Anyone might find them. I've seen the maids putting refuse from the rooms into a big container which they leave unattended in the halls for long moments of time."

Camille touched Gwendolyn's arm. "We must think of everything, Mama," she pled. "What if someone *has* found out? Though *I* haven't told anybody, I promise!"

"Naturally you haven't, dear, and please don't be so worried; you'll make yourself ill." She returned her gaze to Max. "Even if someone has made such a discovery, I cannot believe he would become incensed enough to attempt murder."

"Perhaps if someone felt his life had been ruined by a parody, he might," he said slowly.

"I've ruined no one's life!"

"Can you be certain?"

Gwendolyn's temper was so inflamed by this, she pushed past him and marched toward the exit, leaving Camille to rush after her. But it was Max who reached her first. She shivered as his hand closed upon her forearm, and, with a nervous glance at the crowd, she fell in step with him again rather than create a scene. Camille scurried to her other side and linked an arm in hers.

"I am not your enemy," he said, his mouth set in a grim line. "I believe what you say, Gwendolyn, and I know your intentions. But an unbalanced person might not. Think about your past plays and the characters you've represented. Can you recall anyone who seems more unstable than the others?"

"I have never in my life had an enemy," she said stubbornly. At that instant, hard, colorless eyes flashed into her memory. A downturned mouth between quivering jowls. A long, narrow nose with two bumps in it from a long-ago fight. "Except . . ."

He lifted his brows inquiringly.

"Max, there you are!" cried a feminine voice gaily. Lucy Munroe, devastatingly lovely in a spotted muslin trimmed with pink lace, glided toward them on her older brother's arm. Gwendolyn's disappointment was mirrored in the baronet's face, but not her daughter's. For the first time this morning, she smiled, and the smile was for Bryce alone.

Politeness deemed they must greet one another, though

Gwendolyn felt the tension in Sir Hastings' arm and wondered if he had truly recovered as he'd declared. There was nothing reticent about Miss Munroe, nothing to show anything amiss had ever passed between them. She clasped his hands and moved so near that he was forced to step backward.

"Max, I could almost believe you were avoiding me if I didn't know better," she said with an energetic laugh. "Bryce and I searched for you yesterday and then again this morning. I was worried about your illness, but I can see you have made an astonishing recovery. You look very well indeed, does he not, Bryce? I cannot believe you found a serpent in Mrs. Devane's room and then hacked it to pieces! Papa is so upset! He's afraid everyone will think the rooms are infested! Is it true that the beast spit at you and you caught the poison with the edge of the shovel, and was there really a nest of snake eggs under the bed?"

There was nothing to be done but submit to Miss Munroe's strong leading, and in the next seconds, Gwendolyn found herself sharing the baronet's escort with Lucy, while young Mr. Munroe quickly offered his arm to Camille. It was a thing that worried her even more than her unfinished conversation with Max, and she watched the pair with a mother's eye as they continued their amble.

She could not be displeased however, to see Camille's spirits lighten enough for her to laugh and to speak with her normal animation. Accordingly, Gwendolyn set her teeth to endure Lucy's chatter. And reserved her thoughts for potential murderers.

Since it proved impossible to free himself from Lucy, Max accepted with a grudging grace that he would not be able to speak privately with Mrs. Devane until they returned to The Allemande. By then it was time to dress for dinner, and Lucy, whose family partook of most of their meals within the Munroes' private apartment, pressed the three to join them—especially "dear, sweet Camille," for whom she claimed to have developed a particular fondness. It would have seemed remarkable to Max, since she had spoken no more than five words to the girl, if he didn't recognize the lovesick gleam in Bryce's eyes. What really surprised him was that Lucy had noticed, but perhaps her brother had instructed her in advance.

The invitation was fortuitous for Camille. He only wished the dinner could take place without him. Lucy's determined pursuit, so well appreciated last year until she threw him over for the duke, made him feel like a fox at the hunt.

He was tempted to claim he intended to take all his meals in town, but he could scarcely protect the Devanes if he did that. Therefore, he endured another uncomfortable dinner with the Munroe clan, and even the presence of Gwendolyn hardly lessened its agony.

Family and guests crowded around the table in the small dining parlor. As green-and-white garbed maids served them, Mrs. Munroe yelled question after question about the serpent, while her husband decried any responsibility for its presence. Albin kicked him repeatedly beneath the table, apologizing snidely each time, claiming he thought it was the table leg. And Lucy babbled on as usual, directing every comment his way. Bryce was the only Munroe to exhibit good sense. He had a mild temperament and a gentle way about him that brought a bloom to Camille's cheeks every time he spoke. Max hoped her mother approved.

For a woman of strong feelings, Gwendolyn was unusually adept at hiding emotion. He had never known anyone so poised. During the interminable dinner, she spoke graciously when given the chance, and her lovely face registered interest and good humor to even the most stupid comments. He caught himself watching her lips when she talked. If he kissed that beautiful mouth, would she respond with a civilized smile and a few calming words?

Reluctantly, he acknowledged to himself that he would like to find out.

Only once during the evening did her smooth exterior waver, and that was when Bryce suggested a picnic.

"Sir Hastings suggested the possibility of an outing the other night," he said, his eyes on Camille, "and I was wondering if we might proceed with that tomorrow. Perhaps the ladies would be interested in a carriage ride to a spot I know in the country. Or a walk to Beechen Cliff."

"Oh, yes!" Camille responded immediately, with Lucy eagerly joining in. "There is nothing I should like more than a carriage ride. Or a walk!"

Gwendolyn's fork hung suspended over her dish of peas. "I hope you haven't forgotten our plans, dear."

Camille's face fell. "Plans?"

"You remember," her mother prodded, with a significant look.

"What is so important that it can't be postponed?" Lucy cried. "Oh, I suppose that's rude. But won't you consider doing whatever it is some other time? Nothing is more fun than a picnic, and Bryce doesn't have long to stay before he returns to Oxford."

Camille's expression became a portrait of pleading. Max watched the silent battle between mother and daughter with interest. He wanted to urge Gwendolyn to soften, but knew better. A respite could do no harm. The investigation—*both* investigations—appeared stalled, and all three of them were filled with tension. Especially the girl.

"It would be relaxing," he said, in spite of his earlier intentions. He looked deliberately from Gwendolyn to her daughter.

The skirmish within continued for a few seconds, and then, with an air of strained grace, she capitulated. "I cannot hold out against so many high hopes."

Lucy squealed happily, and joyous looks passed between Camille and Bryce. The drive in the country was decided upon, and the time of departure was set for eleven o'clock.

"I hope you don't expect me to go," Mrs. Munroe declared. "I'm hostessing a whist party." She considered Gwendolyn, blinking her small eyes. "You're welcome to join us if you'd rather let the young folk traipse about by themselves. They don't understand how we mothers must rest to conserve our vitalities!''

''Careful now, Mrs. Devane,'' the innkeeper said with a guffaw. ''My wife will pluck you like a chicken; she's that good with the cards, she is!''

''I believe I possess enough energy for a picnic,'' Gwendolyn said, so dryly that Max laughed out loud.

''How wonderful,'' Lucy said, her voice lacking enthusiasm. Brightening, she added, ''I know! We must invite Roderick Vaughan, and then everyone will have an escort! When we are done, I'll write him a note!''

''I don't want to escort anybody,'' Albin stated. ''But I'm going.''

A chorus of negatives rang out from all the gentlemen at the table. Max's was the loudest of all.

''I'm glad you changed your mind about tomorrow,'' the baronet said as he walked the Devanes back to their suite a short while later.

''Are you?'' Gwendolyn's voice was cool as she inserted her key in the new lock.

''So am I,'' Camille said feelingly. ''Thank you, Mama.''

It was hard to remain irked when her daughter looked so happy. Tomorrow's engagement would lighten Camille's mind; therefore it was worth it. She would keep her eyes on Bryce Munroe, that was all.

Toward Max, she felt less forgiving. ''I thought our time might be better spent on more essential matters.''

''That's what I want to talk with you about, if you will allow me to come inside for a moment,'' he said.

Gwendolyn permitted him to enter, and, pausing only to place her reticule on the credenza, she joined her daughter in sitting opposite the baronet on the settee. Max crossed one leg over the other, looking very much at home in her sitting room, she thought uneasily.

''We were talking of enemies when the Munroes found us

at the Pump Room,'' he said. ''You were about to mention someone.''

''Oh, yes. Although it doesn't pertain to the matter at hand, my husband's brother was never fond of me.''

''Uncle Bernard,'' Camille said, her tones hushed.

Gwendolyn sighed and lifted a hand expressively. ''We needn't worry about him, though. Arthur's been gone for two years, and we've heard nothing from Bernard since the funeral. Why should he take it upon himself to kill me now that I'm out of his life?''

''Could there be the question of an inheritance? Maybe one you didn't know about?'' Max asked.

''That would be delightful, but there was nothing left to inherit that wasn't entailed.''

The baronet appeared to mull this over. ''Nevertheless, it would be worth inquiring.''

She was not so certain. The thought of seeing Bernard again was an unhappy one. ''I'm sure there can be no connection. He does not meet the description at all.''

''We must explore every possibility if we hope to be successful,'' he said. ''The foreigner, if he is foreign, could be another go-between.''

She exchanged a troubled glance with Camille. ''The estate is little more than twenty miles west of here, on the outskirts of Halleydale.''

''That's well. We could return in a single day if we leave early enough.''

''If we hadn't laid plans for tomorrow, we could go in the morning.'' She could not resist saying it, though it would be hard to choose which outing she dreaded more. ''Unless we tell the Munroes we can't make their picnic.''

''No, Mama, we cannot do that,'' said Camille with an imploring look. ''How impolite it would be to ruin everyone's plans!''

''We can visit Devane on the following day just as easily,'' Max said.

Gwendolyn gave him a cutting glance. "Yes, so long as he does not decide to murder us in the meantime."

The corners of Max's lips lifted ever so slightly. "I thought he was above suspicion."

"Not any longer," she said irritably. "Now that you've made me aware the assailant could be anyone, I see suspects everywhere."

When Camille uttered a sound of distress, Gwendolyn's heart fluttered. She swept to her feet and walked to the end of the settee, her fingers caressing the top of her daughter's head as she passed.

"I'm sorry, darling. I really don't suspect everyone; our situation is not so bad as that." She began to pace, feeling like a caged animal. "And I apologize to you, too, Max. It's only that I need to do something. Waiting is so difficult for me. Mr. Alferton has requested a new play, and I haven't even finished the one I'm currently working on. I'm too unsettled to write."

Max rose and took her hands in his. The understanding she saw in his expression soothed the loud riot in her mind to an anxious murmur.

"No one wants this to end more than I," he said. "Tomorrow will be only a day's interruption, dear lady. And there is safety in numbers."

After gazing searchingly into his eyes, she nodded. The awareness of his physical presence, his tall strength, the dry crispness of his skin against her soft palms, almost broke her control. She glanced at their linked hands, then at her daughter, who was observing with bright interest. Stepping back immediately, she gently slid her fingers from his.

Hoping she had not offended him by her actions, she determined to sound more agreeable at least. "I have just thought; the day need not be wasted. Since my escort has been decided for me"—here she could not help inflecting with humorous resentment—"I can make another attempt to find the whereabouts of the missing receipt."

A curious blend of emotions pooled in Max's eyes. "Don't trouble yourself. I'll confront Roderick at the first opportunity.

The time for playing is done. If I admit defeat, he'll give over.''
His face took on a remote look. ''Eventually.''

''I hope you are right,'' Gwendolyn said. ''You know him
best.'' Her tone was agreeable, almost meek, but she intended
to help him whether he wanted her to or not. And she thought she
knew a way. ''Does he—is he a man of independent means?''

''Roderick?'' He looked surprised. ''He earns his living from
the business as I do. When he accumulates enough, he spends
until it's gone. Then he goes home to work for more. Uncle
Harry doesn't grant my cousin an allowance or he'd never
return.''

''I see.'' This was exactly what Gwendolyn wanted to hear.
''I was merely curious,'' she said to Max. Sensing he needed
more, she fabricated further, ''He'll be running out of funds
soon and will probably have to return to Blackpool.''

''Doubtless.'' His puzzled look gradually faded. ''And as
for escorts,'' he added, a note of threat sounding in his voice,
''Miss Munroe is going to be put straight on that.''

Camille's lips curved impishly, her gaze moving back and
forth. ''She will be very disappointed.''

Max smiled. ''We'll all be disappointed if we oversleep
tomorrow.'' After exchanging polite good nights with them,
he took his leave.

When Gwendolyn closed and locked the door behind him,
she turned to find her daughter's eyes dancing with speculation
and delight. ''Sir Hastings is very fond of you,'' she said.

Hurriedly, Gwendolyn walked to the mirror and began
unpinning her headress. ''Naturally, he is. He likes everyone.''

''But he doesn't call everybody 'dear lady,' nor have I seen
him hold Lucy Munroe's hands as he did yours just now.''

''He was giving comfort, Camille. Don't make so much of
simple human kindness.'' The pins would not loosen. She was
going to have to sleep all night with this horrible thing hanging
halfway off her head.

''And you have grown attached to him as well!'' Camille
said, in the triumphant manner of one who has uncovered a
secret.

Gwendolyn could not fail to see her daughter's tilted head and lively expression in the mirror. She took both hands to the headdress and pulled fiercely. There came a gentle sound of lace tearing, but it finally surrendered, loosening several long strands of hair to fall onto her shoulder as it did. Sighing, she set the ruined headgear on the credenza and faced Camille.

"There are no men in my life, child, nor shall there be. I am content with the two of us. More than content."

Camille's face grew long. "But why?"

The child's emotions were so easily read that a stranger could know her every thought, Gwendolyn told herself with dismay. All her coaxing on guarding one's feelings had been useless. But it was an honest face, and a beloved one.

"You know why. Marriage means death to a woman's spirit, her *self.* I have told you so many times, and you've seen the truth of it in action. Do you not recollect how difficult it was for us, all those years I was married to your stepfather? We could not so much as take a walk without asking his permission. Every item of clothing that needed replacing must be begged for individually; he refused to give even the smallest allowance. How much better our lives are now! Our thoughts and desires are bounded only by the limits of our industry and application."

"But all gentlemen cannot be as Papa Arthur was!"

Gwendolyn sat beside her daughter and rested a light hand on her shoulder. "You are young, my darling, and full of a girl's dreams of love. I was once the same about your father. He was everything one could wish for: handsome, charming, brimming with ideas."

Unfortunately, those ideas had not included the labor that would bring them to pass, but she would not disparage him before Camille.

"Still, my existence centered around *his* life, not my own. Oh, don't misunderstand; I wanted to be with Harrison. But had I wished otherwise, what could I have done, a young woman with a baby? An unspeakably precious baby, by the by."

Camille smiled feebly. "I think it would be wonderful to

center my life around my husband's,'' she said slowly. ''If I loved him enough.''

It would be easier to explain a sunset to a person blinded from birth, Gwendolyn thought, and kissed her daughter's forehead resignedly. ''Time for bed, child. I must be up early tomorrow to write before we depart.'' She marveled that she so easily kept devastation from her voice.

Chapter Seven

The next morning dawned fair and promised to be cooler than normal. A perfect day for a picnic, as the members of the party kept repeating to one another. They set off in three curricles provided by The Allemande. Bryce and Camille took the lead; Mrs. Devane and Roderick were next, and Sir Hastings and Lucy followed, the boy who would mind the horses perched on the back. A fourth carriage would come later with servants and food, there being no confusion as to young Mr. Munroe's destination. He had been to the ridge many times before, he said.

From the flicker in her daughter's eyes at this comment, Gwendolyn knew she was wondering how many young ladies he'd taken to the same spot. She seemed ready enough to forgive him for it; as the curricles sprang into motion, her smiling profile attended his every word. She would get a crick in her neck if she didn't stop.

After a few moments of furious observing, Gwendolyn became aware that Mr. Vaughan was speaking to her. "You needn't worry about your daughter," he said. "Bryce has good hands and a light touch."

"What?"

"With the horses," he said, with a slow smile.

"Oh." She flashed him an uncomfortable look, then returned her gaze to the conveyance in front of her. They were traveling on Great Pultney Street now, heading eastward from town, and traffic was lessening, the distance between buildings and houses increasing. Before many minutes passed, Bryce turned onto a smaller road that threaded among the hills. She was aware of the beauty of the countryside they passed, but only vaguely.

"You are crushing my feelings," Roderick said.

"I beg your pardon?"

"Not once have you commented on my elegant handling of the reins nor my masterful way with the horses."

She gave a perfunctory smile and switched her glance back to Camille, who was giggling helplessly at something Bryce had said. Mr. Munroe faced her, his head tilting upward as he laughed. He was not watching the road.

"Shall I hail them?" Vaughan said abruptly. "I believe three could be crowded into that seat if none of you breathed."

Her gaze swung to his and held. She saw a curious blankness in his eyes and something darker. She could ignore him no longer; the boundaries of politeness forbade it. The thought brought to mind an earlier promise to herself, and she unconsciously darted a glance at the carriage behind. Lucy spoke with animation; Max stared stonily ahead, though he brightened when their gazes met.

"You must forgive me," she said, swiveling back to Roderick. "This is the first time my daughter has been in the company of a gentleman alone."

"I would hardly call her alone. But worry is one of the required duties of motherhood, I suppose."

"Yes, I believe it is." After a moment's hesitation, she added hesitantly, "There are so many duties of motherhood, Mr. Vaughan."

"And you are an excellent example of its virtues, as you are in numerous other areas. Truth, I don't know when I've met a lady who embodied such a litany of sterling qualities: beauty, taste, conversation . . . character . . .''

This seemed a little much for even Roderick, and she could not like how his eyes dipped across her as if she were a sweet in a confectioner's shop. Yet there was a strange lack of conviction in his words, almost as if he did not trouble to convince her his flatteries were real. It seemed odd. Had he given up? She hoped not, for then her idea had no chance.

She forced spirit into her eyes. ''Thank you, sir. You are very kind, more kind than I deserve.''

''Surely no one could be more deserving than you of every suitable reward.''

Again, his words held the ring of falsehood. Stirring uneasily, she put on her most companionable smile. ''Would that it were so. But no one deserving could possibly fall into the situation that I . . .''

After the pause lengthened, he raised one eyebrow. ''Please continue, Mrs. Devane. You have whetted my curiosity.''

''I shouldn't speak of it,'' she said reluctantly.

''Well, if you think you shouldn't, I won't press.''

Odder and odder. After an interval, she said in a woeful voice, ''My departed husband often said I was improvident. I fear he was correct.''

His eyes flicked her way. ''Oh, have you run up a milliner's bill, lovely lady?''

''How I wish it were so simple as that. No, I fear Camille and I have . . . many debts.''

''You amaze me. Although you're both always beautifully garbed, you've never seemed like spendthrifts to me. Of course,'' he added lightly, ''I haven't known you long.''

''There are more ways to lose funds than overshopping, Mr. Vaughan,'' she said sadly.

''Ah,'' he said with a knowing look. ''Cards, I presume?''

''You are very perceptive.'' They were passing a meadow speckled with little clouds of sheep, and she averted her eyes to watch them. She had not known how distasteful playing this scene would prove. ''My greatest fear is that we might be thrown from The Allemande.'' She swallowed, finding the lie hard to digest.

"Surely the Munroes would not be so unkind. Bryce will fight for you; I'd be willing to swear he would.''

An annoyed frown creased her brow. "If only we knew someone wealthy enough to lend us money temporarily, just until our trust's next payment, then all our problems would be solved.''

"All of them? How wonderful that must be. Would that *my* problems could be dealt with so easily.''

Her mouth tightened. She would say nothing further; he could not have failed to understand.

After a long pause, he glanced at her, his eyes holding regret. "You are in need of a loan, then?''

Her heartbeat accelerated. "I fear so," she said, turning her lashes downward.

"How much?" he asked softly.

She contemplated for a few seconds. "Ten thousand.''

"Ten! Good lord! How came a woman to lose so much?''

"It is horrible, I know it. You ... this is so embarrassing, but our needs make it necessary ... you don't know anyone who might ...''

She waited breathlessly. This was the point at which she hoped he would volunteer. If he admitted to having so much, it must mean he possessed the formula, since the baronet had told her he was not independently wealthy. He would be forced to try to sell the receipt or use it in the factory to obtain the funds necessary. But before he did either, she would tell Max, and he would have enough proof to force Roderick to admit his theft.

"And if I did know of someone?" he asked slowly, "What are you willing to give in exchange?''

She took his meaning at once. "How dare you speak so to me?" Her voice shook in outrage.

His eyes were centered on the road ahead, but a grim smile appeared at his mouth. "Why so surprised? You're a woman of experience, both in love and wagers, not an innocent young virgin. How can you ask someone to sacrifice so much, when you are not willing to do the same?'' His smoldering glance caressed her face. "Although with me, it would not be a sacrifice, I promise you."

Clenching her teeth, she said, "Then . . . then are you saying you have the available amount?"

"If I did, are you saying you would be accordingly grateful?" he returned.

He was teasing her in the most shameful manner possible and enjoying it. It was a pity he wasted himself so. He was a presentable-looking man. To be desired by him would appeal to a few misguided women, she could not doubt it.

Yet there were some lines of honor which could not be crossed, no matter what the reward.

"No," she said. "I would not."

By noon, the party reached its destination, a lovely spot at the base of a nest of hills. After Bryce declared the walk to the top would be invigorating and well worth their time, the group left the curricles and horses to the care of the tiger and began to climb.

The path was merely a trail of beaten-down grass carved into the hillside and did not offer a convenient passage for more than two to walk abreast. Therefore, the couples fell into line as they had on the drive over, with Bryce and Camille leading the way. The upward slope was gentle, Max thought; certainly too gentle to cause the great gasps of breath Lucy was inhaling. If she would talk less, possibly she could avoid the appearance of a consumptive.

Directly ahead, Gwendolyn walked a little apart from Roderick. She had not accepted the offer of his arm, he noticed, and her bearing was stiff. When his cousin made an occasional comment, Mrs. Devane's responses were brief. Only with the greatest difficulty could Max restrain himself from bounding ahead to see what was the matter.

"My goodness, Max, walk slower, will you?" Lucy fussed. "I'm delicate, not a lumbering Amazon like some." Her eyes bored resentfully at the back of Mrs. Devane's head. "It's very hot, isn't it? How do you gentlemen bear the heat with your coats?" She began to twirl her parasol erratically. Max flinched, then dodged as it caught the brim of his hat. "Pardon, but I am weary to death of carrying this thing." When he made the obvious suggestion, she cried, "No, I can't throw it in the grass! Do you want me to become brown?"

As this did not appear to require an answer, he made none.

"Oh, why did we not go to the Pump Room?" she cried after a brief pause. "Or we could have taken tea in a shop where it would be dark and cool inside. That would have been wonderful!"

"You were happy enough about a picnic last night," he said with irritation.

"Yes, but I didn't know then that you would be such a glowering old thing today."

He looked startled. "Is that what I am?"

"You didn't used to be. But you haven't listened to a word I've said all morning. I cannot fathom it, Max, truly I cannot! I know how much you care for me. I was remarking about it to Betty after breakfast. She remembers how you sent bouquets of my favorite roses to my room every day last summer. It was so romantic! No one has loved me so well as you, though I have had many admirers who have tried." Her exquisite features clouded further. "Still, your attentions have not been what they should be today. Every time I looked up, you were staring at the carriages ahead, and now you are still not noticing me! Is it that you find Camille attractive? She *is* a comely thing, but young. Very, very young. Bryce has caught her eye, anyway; have you not seen it? And I know you could not be thinking of her mother, for she is too old—far older than you; she must be!"

Max sliced a look of disbelief at the lady at his side. She was the most self-absorbed creature he'd ever met, yet she remained strangely innocent in her vanity. Only her own wishes mattered to her, but he believed she held no malice in her disregard for the feelings and motivations of others. She was like a very young child, without empathy and without conscience.

He recalled how he'd been ensnared last year. There was a fascination to such single-minded purpose when it was combined with deadly beauty. Thank God he could see clearer now.

"Has it not occurred to you that my feelings have changed?" he asked.

She blinked. "Changed? How could that be? Nothing is different. I am the same. You are the same."

"Lucy." His glance wandered restlessly over the surrounding hills as he gathered patience. "Do you recall cutting me dead when you had the duke in your sights?"

"Oh, that. Surely you aren't still jealous. I told you Charlington died. He means less than nothing to me now."

He absorbed this for a moment.

"His shade must smile to know you remember him so tenderly."

Her trilling laugh rang over the hills.

"Max, you could always make me happy! Oh, this is much better. Now you are more like your old self." Impulsively, she drew nearer to him, her parasol returning to a dangerous closeness. "I knew Bryce was wrong when he said you had no partiality for me. How can he judge, when he's seen us together only once or twice?"

Max closed his eyes briefly, opening them upon Gwendolyn. Roderick had caught her arm and was pointing out a distant cottage in a cove. Children played in the field beside it, and a cow moaned behind a fence attached to the house. Gwendolyn did not appear unduly moved by the picturesque scene. The baronet increased his stride.

"Oh!" Lucy whimpered. Her hand, which was crooked in his arm, pulled downward as she sank slightly. "My foot! Look and see, won't you, Max? I think there's a rock in my shoe! Oh, the pain!"

Stifling a sigh, Max knelt on one knee as Lucy braced her weight on his shoulder, raised her gown a few inches and lifted the injured appendage toward him. Hesitantly, he slid the slipper from her foot and tipped it. A tiny pebble rolled out.

The couples ahead had heard her cries. "Are you all right, Lucy?" Bryce shouted.

"Yes, I believe so, though it hurts mightily!" she cried back. "A large rock was in my shoe!"

"It's no wonder you've been complaining about the walk," the baronet grumbled as he restored the slipper to her foot and rose, slapping dust from his cousin's pantaloons. "Why didn't you wear walking boots?"

"Because I have none that go with my blue. Do you see how exactly the shade of my slippers matches my gown?" She began to hobble forward, leaning heavily on him. "Ouch. Oooh." Abruptly, she yelled, "How much further, Bryce?"

"We are almost there!" he reassured her.

"You have been saying that for hours!" In softer tones, she added as an aside, "He's not a bad brother, but he doesn't understand that ladies are to be pampered, not sent on long rambling hikes across mountains like goats."

Max regarded her for a significant interval, his face solemn. Misinterpreting his interest, she cast a fetching look upwards, her features conveying satisfaction.

Suddenly, he said, "You're right; I have been beastly to you today. But if I've given the appearance of ignoring you, it's because I'm preoccupied."

"I knew it must be something of the kind," she said forgivingly. "We shall forget it ever happened."

"Would that I could, but the problem remains to plague me."

"What problem is that?" she asked with little concern, her thoughts occupied with the folding of her parasol, which she then began to use as a cane.

"It's a rather delicate matter."

A butterfly floated near her head. Squealing, she used the parasol to bat it away. When she recovered, she said, "You can tell me anything, Max. No one is more wonderful at keeping secrets than I."

"All right," he said, with the appearance of great reluctance. "Here is my dilemma. I'm at an age where the prospects of settling down with a wife have begun to seem attractive." Her lips arced upward. Rapidly, he continued, "I've always hoped to restore my ancestral home—"

"Yes, I remember you told me that last year," she said encouragingly.

"—over which my mother will have as much control as she wishes, since it was robbed from her too soon."

The smile faltered a little. "As I remember her from last year, your mother is a very kind lady. She is not the sort who puts her desires over that of her family's."

"She is beyond estimation, and her taste in refurbishing the estate will be impeccable."

"Oh, but she is probably too elderly to make so many decisions on her own. She would not, say, prefer Hepplewhite over Chippendale to the extent that she would force her personal taste over everyone."

"As to that, I don't know, though I can assure you her choices would be elegant. And practical as well."

Her eyebrows moved expressively. "Practical?"

"Yes, for all the little ones I hope to have. They can be very hard on furniture."

Her laugh sounded brittle. "My goodness, Max. How many children do you expect?"

"I've always hoped for twelve."

"Twelve!" Lucy screeched.

"I could be content with eight, I suppose, but all my dreams must now be modified."

She tossed the parasol to the ground and removed a lacy handkerchief from her sleeve, fanning herself with it. "That's for the best, I'm sure. Yes, modify by all means."

"About the children, never. But my dreams for restoring the estate must be delayed. I've lost my savings through an unfortunate investment, and now I'm afraid my future wife will have to content herself with living at my uncle's house indefinitely, perhaps forever."

"Forever?" she asked weakly.

"Yes, but it won't be so bad. Uncle Harry's abode is not too near the glassworks; you can scarcely see the smoke from

the windows. And before dawn, when the workers pass by, they are not terribly noisy; one grows used to falling back asleep for an hour or two before starting our daily tasks. I have a very nice bedroom. There is even a small sitting area attached, and on Sundays Uncle Harry allows me to use his chaise to drive the family to chapel. So it's not as though my wife and children will never have diversion."

Lucy made no reply to this. After a moment, he shot a sideways glance at her. Her features were uncommonly serious, her dark eyes lost in thought. His brows lifted as he tried to stop a smile.

By this time, the walkers had reached the crest. The view of the surrounding area was everything that could be wished, with hills rolling outward around them like waves. Here and there, cottages interrupted the flow of green, and cows could be seen grazing upon several rises. Trees clothed many of the hillsides, and bird melodies echoed upward from them.

It was very peaceful and quiet. Too quiet. Bryce and Camille, who had chattered the past hour and more without stopping, became shyly mute when their companions joined them at the brow. The remaining couples were equally silent.

The baronet was more determined than ever to find the cause of Gwendolyn's estrangement from his cousin. But there was no easy way to accomplish this. While he felt Lucy would have no objection now if he sought a private interview with Mrs. Devane, he could hardly expect the same cooperation from Roderick, who was ostensibly her escort for the day. He would have to wait for a more opportune time.

Thus the minutes ticked off uncomfortably, with the youngest couple moving from one vantage point to another, and the rest of them making desultory attempts at conversation. When the servants arrived at last with the picnic accoutrements, panting with exertion from the climb, the glad cries of welcome were far beyond what could normally be expected.

The four footmen became the unhappy center of attention as they unloaded their burdens. The put-upon glances they exchanged attested to their feelings; surely they had never been subjected to more direction in the simple matter of setting up an outdoor meal. No, they must not put the two small tables together *there,* for the ground sloped. And *here* was too much sun. The cloth they spread upon the tables was declared to have a spot, though nothing could be done about it now. The benches had no backs, and yes, they might fit easier into a chaise, but the ladies would become tired with no support for their spines.

Every item unpacked from the baskets must be commented upon. The boiled chicken looked good. Were there no peaches among the fruit? Had cook baked the bread that morning or was it last night's? Why had they brought only white wine?

By the time the participants settled themselves at the table, the faces of the footmen looked to be stamped from the same aggrieved mold.

Finally, a measure of contentment came to the party as they prepared to enjoy the repast. Bryce smiled as one of the servants poured wine into his glass, his gaze glowing upon Camille, then moving to his sister.

"You're very quiet, Lucy."

"No one can be expected to talk every minute," she snapped, and popped a healthy morsel of chicken into her mouth. At the next instant, she spat it into the grass with noises of revulsion.

Bryce's eyes widened at her unladylike behavior. There was no time for condemnation, however, for Camille gasped, seized her wine and drank. She took only a sip before crashing the glass to the table, her eyes watering and round with hurt disbelief.

"How *awful* the cheese is!" she opined. "And the wine . . . is it supposed to taste like this?" Gwendolyn, her own face puckered in distaste, began to pat her daughter's back.

"Someone has emptied the entire salt cellar onto this chicken!" Roderick proclaimed.

All of this occurred within a few seconds, seconds in which Max had yet to take the first bite. "Don't touch the food!" he commanded.

"Wonderful advice, but your timing could be better," said Roderick with a pained expression.

Gwendolyn's gaze immediately sought the baronet's, and

the distress in her eyes deepened to shock. Camille's fingers flew to her neck as she looked from Sir Hastings to her mother.

Max surged to his feet and leaned his fists on the table. "Did anyone actually swallow anything? Is everyone feeling all right?"

Immediately, the color drained from Camille's skin. Turning frightened eyes back to her mother, she whispered, "My throat is burning."

"That's because of the briny wine, my dear." Roderick threw his napkin on the plate and stood. "Are you trying to put everyone in a frenzy, Max? The food isn't poisoned, for pity's sake; someone in the kitchen made a mistake, that's all."

Lucy's terror-filled eyes glowed like dark mirrors. "How do you know? There's a horrible taste in my mouth. I could be dying at this very moment, and no one is doing anything! I am so young and have my whole life before me!"

Bryce also rose, blazing fury at the footmen. "What *has* happened here? Why is the food spoiled?"

From the beginning of the furor, the servants had been exchanging troubled glances and looking helpless. Now the tallest of them, a slim young man with brown hair and a trembling chin, paced forward. "I don't know, sir. Cook said he made everything fresh this morning. We only put the chicken and all in the carriage; we didn't have nothing to do with how it was made." He swallowed. "Though we're sorry, sir. Very sorry."

"You should very well be sorry!" Bryce threw an agonized look at Camille. "You've given my guests discomfort, and that's unforgivable!"

Max held up a calming hand in Mr. Munroe's direction as he stepped to the footman, who looked as if he wanted to cry. "Could anyone have had access to the baskets after the cook finished packing them?"

"I don't see how, Sir Hastings," he said with a quivering voice. "Soon as cook rang the bell, we came to put them in the chaise."

"Fred, hold a minute," said one of the footmen, a man who could almost have been the first servant's twin, excepting he looked older. "There was . . ." He darted a look at Bryce, then slumped. "Oh, well. Pardon." He cleared his throat. "Nothing."

Max approached him. "Don't hold anything back, man! This could be very important."

The second footman squeezed his eyes shut, took a deep breath, and said on a single exhale, "I hate to say it, on account of you, Mr. Bryce and Miss Lucy, but I saw Master Albin coming from the pantries right before we went into the dining room, and he had that look on his face we all know well and to our sorrow; and I says to Davey, 'He's been up to somethin', sure as I'm alive,' didn't I, Davey?"

The footman in question nodded solemnly.

Bryce knotted his fists. "Albin! I should have guessed immediately!"

"He wanted to come with us, but we wouldn't let him, and this is his revenge," said Lucy, enraged. "And after I played quoits with him, too, for hours last Saturday. Oh, the ingratitude! If Mama will allow it, I shall slap him, I declare I will! My mouth is so dry, I fear I will never be the same again. Why is there no water? What a horrible, horrible day this has been!"

After Miss Munroe's speech, there seemed no better prospect than to return to The Allemande, since nothing could be adjudged safe from Albin's treachery. The footmen rapidly sprang to work. Max offered escort to his glowering companion, and the picnickers began to tread downhill.

His relief could not be measured. Though his fingers ached to get at the villainous child, the party's discomfort could have been much worse were Mrs. Devane's enemy behind it.

It lightened his heart when Gwendolyn recovered enough to send him a faint smile. By the time they reached the curricles, even Camille had regained a measure of composure as Bryce's unending apologies led her to comfort him repeatedly, saying no harm had been done, they were all fine, and the outing had been the happiest day of her life.

Chapter Eight

Clouds were darkening the sky when the travelers arrived at the inn. As the couples disembarked from the vehicles and gathered on the sidewalk, Bryce again begged their pardon. He offered to send refreshment to their rooms, but all declined since dinner was so near. After exchanging a few private words with Camille, he marched off with his sister on his arm, both promising retribution to their remaining sibling. Lucy hardly glanced at Max as she flounced away.

Roderick expressed his intention to escort the ladies to their rooms, and after an appropriate interval of impatient waiting, the baronet went to the Devanes' suite and knocked softly. Gwendolyn looked tired when she admitted him to the parlor; and he did not accept her offer to sit but stood near the door. Camille could be heard moving in her bedroom.

"You have come to set a time for our journey to Halleydale, I imagine," she said.

"That, and to ask how you got on with Roderick today. You looked . . . uncomfortable."

Turning aside, she laughed lightly. "I believe we were all uncomfortable."

For a moment, he scrutinized her averted face, then touched her chin with his forefinger, gently guiding her to look at him. She stepped back warily, and his arm fell.

"That's not what I meant. I'm talking about before that unfortunate meal. The two of you were hardly speaking. Did he do anything, or say something, to offend you?"

"No, no, of course not." She blinked rapidly. "I've been a little out of sorts today; perhaps that's what you noticed." Again she shifted slightly away, her fingers moving restlessly against the material of her gown.

"Gwendolyn." He grasped her shoulders and peered into her eyes. "You are a terrible liar. What really happened? You didn't try to find out about the formula again, did you, and he became rude? I told you not to do that."

Her expression became resolute. "I know what you said, Max. Nothing happened, I tell you."

After the space of several heartbeats, he released her. "Very well, then. I'll ask Roderick."

"No," She pressed a hand to her heart, then attempted to smile apologetically. "I mean, how ridiculous you will seem, quizzing him about whether he has said something to me or not. There is no reason for you to act in this—this protective manner."

"Isn't there?" He could not restrain himself from moving closer. How he ached to crush her to him, to bury his fingers in her hair, to taste her lips. He wanted this woman more than he had ever wanted anything in his life. He longed to shield her from all danger and harm, to draw her against his chest and never let go. But her anxious brown eyes stayed him, and he must content himself with only a light touch to her arm, a gesture she could interpret any way she wished; as comfort, as encouragement, or passion delayed.

He was moving from admiration to love. He felt the surety of it coursing through every muscle, every vein, to his very bones. But even as the conviction pumped through him with each heartbeat, he acknowledged the futility of it. Gwendolyn did not need him or anyone, and he had nothing to offer her;

not even a home. The thought was as cooling as a blast of winter. This time it was he who stepped backward.

"You won't say anything more, then?" he asked softly.

Her eyes swam with emotions he could not discern. "There's nothing else to speak about," she replied, her lips barely moving. "And I'm certain that if you persist in asking Mr. Vaughan, he will tell you the same."

"Very well." The fragile mood had broken, and he straightened his shoulders. "Are you and Camille taking dinner downstairs?"

"Yes, and she wishes to attend the Upper Rooms afterward. There is a concert tonight."

"May I escort you there?" he asked immediately. "I don't like to think of you alone on the streets at night."

"I'll hardly be alone. You know what crushes these things are, and we'll hire chairs before and after."

"Still, it would ease my mind to accompany you, if my presence is not too distasteful."

"Distaste—? Oh, Max, of course you are welcome. No one could ever hold you in distaste."

With only the hardiest manning of his muscles did he prevent a smile. It was ridiculous how happy her faint praise made him.

"I only want you to think a moment as I've been doing today," she continued. "Perhaps we will never find the man who placed the serpent in my room, or the man behind him. It's possible the entire incident was a mistake, as you suggested. If we don't discover him soon, if he doesn't make another attempt, then we must go on with our lives. You cannot protect me forever."

She was warning him off, he knew. A spark of ire began to burn. "Why are you speaking of forever, Gwendolyn? I'm only talking about tonight."

"Of course you are," she said hastily. "I—we would be happy to have your escort."

"Good," he said in gruff tones. He suggested a time when they could meet for dinner and the entertainment.

She agreed and, standing aside while he crossed the threshold, bid him farewell for the moment.

"I'll see you in a little while, Gwendolyn," he said with a bow, then stepped back and waited.

Seconds ticked by. Her eyes darted to the left, toward Roderick's door, then back to him. He could hear her fingernails tapping against the knob. Still he remained immobile. The taut instants grew into a full minute, then more. Behind Mrs. Devane, Camille appeared in the open doorway and smiled faintly, her curious gaze roaming between them.

"Are you . . . are you not returning to your room?" Gwendolyn asked finally.

"Aren't you?" he countered.

Her fingers fluttered to her throat. "Yes." She darted a nervous look at her daughter. "Of course."

The door closed softly. His teasing smile faded; his eyes narrowed. There could be no greater confirmation than this that something had transpired that afternoon between his cousin and Gwendolyn. Something ugly.

It took only a few seconds to cover the distance between her room and Roderick's. Despite wanting to pound on the door, he tapped softly. In case she still listened.

"I need to speak with you," he told Roderick as the door opened.

"Can't it wait, old fellow? I'm trying to dress for dinner, and Henderson is off having my cravats ironed."

Max scanned his cousin's disheveled appearance, the half-buttoned shirt hanging over his pantaloons, feet clad only in stockings. "No, it can't wait. I don't care what you look like." He moved forward.

Vaughan reluctantly stood aside to accommodate him. "Sounds ominous. What is it? Aren't you pleased with the cut of my jacket? I'll admit it doesn't suit you, though Millicent Deveridge came close to swooning when she saw *me* wearing it."

The baronet forced a tight smile. "I have appreciated your generosity with your wardrobe, but that's not why I'm here."

"Well, strike me; I'd hoped it was." He gestured toward the set of chairs by the French doors, and both gentlemen sat. "Thought you might be coming to say Carleton had arrived with your rags and that I could dress myself without worrying if you'd stolen what I wanted to wear the next day."

"I expect him at any moment." Keeping his expression neutral, he asked bluntly, "Did you enjoy yourself this afternoon?"

"Is *that* what you wanted to know? What a considerate relative you are." Crossing one leg over the other, Roderick gazed thoughtfully at the ceiling. "Enjoy, enjoy . . . Now, let me see. First there was a drive in the poorest-strung curricle I ever hope to bounce in again, then a long, hot walk up a dusty hillside to eat food salted well enough to last 'til Armageddon. What was there not to enjoy?"

"You know what I mean. Your companion. Mrs. Devane—"

"Ah, Mrs. Devane. A lovely lady."

A familiar frustration gnawed at his stomach. Had he ever had a conversation with his cousin when he wasn't led down looping pathways? "She seemed very quiet today, almost as though she were . . . affronted about something. Disturbed, even."

"Max, you amaze me. I've always said you're the most sensitive fellow I know. Imagine your worrying about my companion when you had such a beautiful one of your own." He spied a tiny dark spot at the knee of his pantaloons and, clucking his tongue, moved toward the basin. "Clothes are a symbol of life, don't you think? A great joy when new, but requiring constant upkeep." While he spoke, he lifted a towel from the small stack on the table, moistened it, and bent to scrub the stain. "Then, when an item is old and soiled with the dirt of this world, there is only one thing left to do: throw it out. Sad, isn't it?"

"Spare me the philosophy. What did you say to Gwendolyn to make her so upset?"

"What a firebrand it is," Roderick said beneath his breath, and he continued scrubbing for a few seconds, then delivered a look of mild reproach. "Gwendolyn, is it now? How came you to address her so familiarly?"

Max saw his mistake, then realized it didn't matter. He would never allow her to risk quizzing Roderick again. There was no further need for secrecy anyway, for he intended to demand the formula directly. As soon as the question of Roderick's conduct that afternoon was settled.

"I consider her a friend," he said.

"Do you? And a close one, too, from the fiery look in your eyes. How quickly you've moved from an acquaintance made only a few nights ago to such . . . friendship. Could it be your act of killing the reptile has made you feel as though you were her protector from some anonymous fiend? That would be like you. From the time I've known you, that's how your mind has worked. Nothing is ever simple; things don't happen by accident in your world. It could not be that this man you saw leaving her chamber was simply a window-washer, and the snake a runaway from the woods."

"When was the last time you saw a rattler in the woods?"

"It could have escaped from that circus that's pitched tents outside of town."

Max's suspicions were instantly alerted. "What do you know about the circus?"

"What do I—? Good lord, Max, do you suspect me?"

The small hairs at the back of his neck still bristled, but the baronet coaxed his muscles into relaxing. "No, of course not."

"Because I can assure you I'd never touch one of those things."

"I know you wouldn't."

Roderick might fail to be many things he should, but no one could say he wasn't fastidious. Though if he'd been the one to hire Deevers . . . But why would he?

Cynicism darkened Vaughan's eyes. "But the thought entered your brain—didn't it?—that I might have done such a horrendous act. This is exactly what I was talking about. You believe there's always a reason for things and that you can control the outcome if you work hard enough, even if you must stretch rational thought to its breaking point. But in my view, the miracle is that we don't all awaken with snakes in our beds."

For a millisecond, Max considered telling his cousin about yesterday's search and the things it had revealed. But there was nothing to be gained by it; Roderick would be of no help. Only his own plans were important to him. He could never be disturbed, never be counted on to walk away from his path to aid someone else.

Vaughan floated the towel on the surface of the water and returned to his chair, lengthening one leg toward the window. "Do you think my breeches will dry in time for dinner, or shall I have to change again? How dreary a prospect. Almost everything I own is at the washerwoman's or on your back."

"She wouldn't tell me, either," Max said.

"What's that?"

"Gwendolyn. When I asked her what was wrong between you this afternoon, she claimed nothing."

"Oh, so you asked her, did you?" He breathed in noisily. "Doesn't surprise me that she said nothing was wrong. Doesn't surprise me at all. You'd better be careful, old fellow. She's poison in silk."

"Guard your tongue, Roderick. You're speaking of an exceptionally fine lady."

"Don't get top-lofty with me, Max. I knew you before you could grow a decent beard." He bent his knuckles and examined his fingernails. "I suppose our allegiance goes back far enough that I'm obligated to tell you. For your own sake, before you make yourself the fool as you did last year. Lord, what a baby you are!"

Max waited, his eyes glowing cold death upon his cousin.

Vaughan met his gaze unfalteringly. "Very well. It pains me to say your exceptional lady asked to borrow money from me this afternoon."

This was so unexpected that Max blurted, "She did what?"

Vaughan closed his eyes briefly and nodded. "Ten thousand pounds."

An incredulous silence lengthened while Sir Hastings allowed the words to sift through his mind. He could not resolve them with what he knew about Gwendolyn Devane. If she needed funds, she would have asked him, not Roderick.

Yet, she knew he was searching for the receipt for red, that he had lost his savings and had nothing.

No. Such a thing was unthinkable. She was a successful playwright. His cousin was lying. Again.

"I don't believe you."

Roderick shrugged. "Believe what you like, but she did ask. I told her I didn't possess that much, and how badly I regretted having to refuse, especially when she offered her favors as collateral—"

Light exploded behind Max's eyes.

He launched himself at Vaughan, throwing a blow that landed on his cousin's cheek. The chair toppled backward, carrying them with it. "Tell me you lie!" he demanded, his face inches above Roderick's, his fingers clutching the edges of his shirt.

"I'll tell you nothing except that my cousin is insane!" Roderick grunted angrily, and pushed, dislodging Max to the side.

Both men struggled to their feet, eyeing one another with rage and caution as they circled. "You've always been a liar," Max said between clenched teeth. "But now you've reached the very bottom, Roderick. Spinning tales about a lady who is above reproach. I'm ashamed of you."

"Spare your shame for yourself," Vaughan said, fingering his injured cheek as he paced.

"What do you mean by that?"

The words seemed to ignite him. He pounded a fist into Max's middle. The baronet bent forward and groaned, clutching his stomach with one hand, grasping the arm of the chair with the other.

"You dare to plead ignorance of your own scheming ways?" Roderick queried, panting. "As if you weren't aware that for years you've toadied to my father for everything you could get. Poor, fatherless Max!" His tone became mocking. "Always in

the right, the ever-faithful, ever-dutiful nephew, with your *'Yes.
Uncle Harry, I'll do anything you say, Uncle Harry; I am so
grateful for your generosity, Uncle Harry,'* until it would take
a saint to measure up! And the inevitable result is that no one
can, not even his true son!''

Though he struggled to regain his breath, Max could not
miss the hurt, a long, barricaded history of it, behind his cousin's
words. Still bowed from the nauseating effects of the blow, he
lifted his eyes.

''I never intended—''

''Silence!'' Furiously, Vaughan grabbed him by his shoulders and shoved him against the glass doors, a crack resounding
through the room and shooting fireworks in Max's head. ''Don't
pretend you don't know what you've done.'' Vaughan removed
his grip with a flourish and stepped back. The baronet began
to slide downward, his stunned gaze locked with Roderick's.

''Is ... this why you took the formula?'' He gasped.
''Revenge?''

Something moved in Vaughan's eyes, a faint startlement that
Max interpreted as a direct hit. Though the look was quickly
masked. Triumph coursed through the baronet despite the ache
in his skull.

''I don't have an inkling as to what you mean,'' Vaughan
said edgily.

''And you were accusing me ... of pretending ignorance,''
Max taunted.

''No, truly. Have you lost a formula? What's it for? A new
medicine?''

''Why don't you give it over, Roderick. The game is done.
You've given me one of the most difficult weeks of my life,
I admit, but—''

''*Have* I? Thank you. Nothing you could ever say would
please me more.''

Max slowly worked his way to his feet. ''I know you did
it. I don't know how, nor do I really care. All that matters is
that you restore the receipt for red to me.''

''Receipt for red? Are you talking about glass? Surely you

haven't jumped on that dead horse again. Has some charlatan duped you, and now you hope to lay the blame at my door? Or are you simply raving?''

"The substitution was one of your finest efforts," Max said heatedly, keeping his voice low with only the tightest effort. "Did you laugh as you copied Soufrière's handwriting? Was it difficult finding stationery to match his, so that I wouldn't suspect anything at a glance? I admit you couldn't have been more successful. My embarrassment at my birthday dinner was everything you could have wanted.''

"Your birthday? What, did you present this formula publicly, then?'' An uncertain look came into his eyes. "How sorry I am that I missed your humiliation. I only wish I understood how it came about. Was my father very disappointed in his protégé?''

"Only briefly. Afterward, he was as understanding as always.''

Roderick became very still. "I suppose I should offer my compliments. Sycophancy does not go unrewarded. Not ever, apparently.''

"What you regard as sycophancy,'' Max said acidly, "others would call affection.''

"Oh, yes?'' He raked Max's figure with bitter eyes. "Then what *you* would regard as a—what was it you said a moment ago?—woman, no, a *lady,* above reproach, *I* would call a lightskirt.''

Sir Hastings sprang like the uncoiling of a weighted rope, toppling Roderick to the carpet. Growling deep in his throat, Vaughan defended himself. For an interval there was only the speech of blows being exchanged, furniture crashing, bodies thudding against walls, and groans.

Gradually, above the din, the sound of frantic knocking could be heard. The combatants paid it no heed. But when the door was abruptly flung wide, the warriors froze into position; the baronet's arm pulled backward, ready to fire; Vaughan's hand clutching his opponent's cravat. Several people stood revealed in the hallway, their faces registering various stages of alarm, and, in the case of a pair of lads, delight. With a sinking of his heart, Max centered his gaze on Gwendolyn, who watched him in horror, her fingers covering her mouth.

"Sirs, stop it at once!" Henderson cried in a scandalized voice, clapping his hands commandingly. "Stop it right now!" He moved fussily toward them, plucking at Max's jacket sleeve, gently pushing Roderick back. "Look what you've done to this beautiful room! I cannot believe it. Oh, you are cut, Master Roderick. Let me—"

"Leave be," Vaughan commanded, brushing the hand away.

Turning his back to the small crowd, Max straightened his jacket and patted his face with his handkerchief. As he suspected, the corner of his mouth was bleeding. Burning with shame that Gwendolyn should find him this way, he hurriedly raked his fingers through his hair, then faced the threshold again.

She was nowhere to be seen.

Chapter Nine

By dinner, the sky had darkened to deep purple, and a light sprinkle of rain began to fall. Camille scanned the clouds worriedly as she stood before the French doors.

"You don't think it will pour, do you, Mama?"

Gwendolyn looked up from her writing. "It might," she said, glad of the interruption. She was not accomplishing anything anyway, only staring at the blank spaces and wondering how she could fill them when her mind could see only Max, his bruised face, his shocked eyes.

Camille clutched one side of the draperies. "Even if it does, we can still go, can't we?"

"Oh, darling, there will be other nights. There is no dancing tonight anyway, since it is Wednesday. Our gowns would be ruined, and you know how I feel about asking servants to carry us through the rain and mud."

"But I'm certain they don't mind it! Otherwise, why would they come to do the work?"

"They come because they'll lose their positions if they don't. You're aware of that, Camille. You know what it is to be poor."

"Then they should be glad for the wages. We are actually harming them by not making use of their services."

"Camille, this is not like you." Her eyes sharpened. "Why are you so intent on going to the Upper Rooms tonight?"

The girl's fingers loosened their hold on the drapes and trailed downward to settle gracefully at her side. She glided to the fireplace, her slippers making delicate padding noises on the carpet, and stared at the empty hearth, her expression pensive.

"No reason," she said, and sighed. "I'm bored, I suppose."

This dramatic performance did nothing to ease Gwendolyn. For the first time in her life, Camille was keeping something from her. She trembled with certainty as to the cause. There had been ample time that day for an assignation to be arranged between her daughter and the young and handsome Mr. Munroe.

Gwendolyn bit down the flaming desire to shake Camille until good sense returned to her. But nothing could be gained by violence, even were it gentled; she'd learned that much from her own mother. Instead, she changed the subject.

"Bored, are you?" she asked lightly. "After that unbelievable row next door?"

Something resembling the old Camille met her eyes. "I wonder they did not kill each other," she said with interest. "Such terrible sounds through my wall! What do you suppose it was about?"

Gwendolyn's gaze dropped. "I . . . could not venture to guess." She feared she knew the answer, though. Mr. Vaughan had probably told Sir Hastings of her request for money, and Max was infuriated. But why, then, had they fought? Shouldn't he be angry at *her* for disobeying his wishes? Surely Mr. Vaughan had not been foolish enough to tell Max he had propositioned her!

Perhaps she should have told Max what happened on the picnic. But she hadn't trusted herself to keep quiet about Vaughan's insult for dread of what the baronet would do. She was confident enough of his tender regard to know he would spring to her defense. But it seemed the very thing she had tried to avoid had happened.

Of course, the fight could have been about something else entirely. The formula. Some old unsettled argument.

It was difficult to find her thoughts so miserably occupied: *Maybe he meant this, maybe he thought that,* as though she were a schoolgirl again.

Camille interrupted her inner storm. "Do you think he still intends to fetch us for dinner?"

"I expect him." How the words shot pleasure through her! Dear God, what was happening to her? "Neither of the gentlemen appeared seriously injured," she added in a quavering voice. "I'm sure he'll send a note if he can't come."

Calm yourself, she instructed firmly. Even Camille had noticed her mother's distress, her expressive eyes clouding with puzzlement. Gwendolyn sent her a trembling smile and bent over the script.

She accomplished no work and had little peace during the next half-hour before Max arrived at their door. He had not changed clothes, though his coat had been smartly pressed; and his pantaloons looked damp, but clean, at the knees. His hair was combed into shining neatness, but there was little he could do to disguise the purple smudge beneath his eye or the red imprint of Roderick's knuckles on his chin.

"If you're ashamed to be seen with me, I'll understand," he said tentatively.

When Gwendoyn and Camille assured him nothing could be further from the truth, Max offered an arm to each lady, and they began making the winding trek downstairs. Their conversation consisted of stilted and formal spurts as all three avoided the obvious topic.

Gwendolyn's senses seemed heightened as they moved through the carpeted corridors and down the grand staircase. She nodded graciously to other residents passing by; she commented on the elegance of the statuary within the niches; even the beauty of the potted plants did not escape her notice. And all the while she was most aware of him: strength encased in broadcloth, the heady scent of soap and something indefinably masculine; the shock that thrilled her nerve endings every time his startling eyes met hers.

All of these feelings brought her joy and dismay in equal measure.

When Richard Hibbs had taken their orders, his eyes lingering curiously on the baronet's face as he walked off, Max smiled, then winced and touched his mouth gingerly. He dropped a hand to the edge of the table and clung to it unconsciously.

"I know an explanation is in order, but . . . The devil! I don't know what to say that won't make me look a bigger fool."

"You don't have to explain anything," Gwendolyn said. She stopped an impulse to caress his swollen knuckles only just in time.

"Did your fight have anything to do with the formula?" Camille asked.

"Camille," Gwendolyn murmured in censuring tones.

"No, it's all right. Yes, we did talk about it. As I suspected, Roderick wouldn't admit stealing it. He's not through playing his game yet."

Gwendolyn's heart sank. "Then . . . you don't really know if he's the one who took it."

"Oh, he has it all right," Max said with pleasure. "I'm absolutely certain. He gave himself away without meaning to. It's only a matter of time now."

"I'm glad." Gwendolyn hoped he was not deceiving himself, finding certainty because he wanted it so badly.

A crack of thunder sounded, heralding a sudden deluge from the skies. The roar of the rain brought a companionable, though unordinary, feel to the dining room. Diners spoke louder and with more excitement; the Hibbs brothers shouted orders to one another in order to be heard; dropped pans in the kitchen echoed to the farthest corners of the dining room; the candles glowed brighter in the increasing gloom. Gwendolyn would have found the change stimulating, if her daughter did not appear to be withering with disappointment before her eyes.

Dishes of mutton soon arrived, and the next moments were occupied with eating and inconsequential chatter. Camille said little and only stabbed at her food. Gwendolyn was weighing the value of trying to cajole her from her misery when the girl suddenly sat straighter, her startled gaze centered on the entrance. Gwendolyn glanced in the same direction and saw Albin Munroe heading stiffly toward them.

"Oh, dear," she said.

Max turned his head. He swerved back immediately. "Wonderful. My day only needed this."

Albin planted his feet within inches of the baronet's elbow. Keeping his head elevated, his gaze pinned on the far windows, he recited a stilted apology for his mistake with the baskets of food that afternoon. He had accidentally spilled a container of salt, he said, while trying to remove it from the pantry to sprinkle over birds' tails, as he'd heard that was the way to catch them. Unfortunately, the shaker had fallen over the baskets, and, fearing a scold from the hurrying footmen, he had not told anyone.

Gwendolyn tried to attend the boy, for it must be a dreadful blow for him to humble himself in this manner; but she could not prevent her eyes from watching Max, whose face was fluent with comical disbelief. As one unlikely sentence followed another, the baronet's eyebrows climbed higher, his eyes gleamed with more cynicism, and his lips moved with greater doubt. She could scarcely keep from laughing out loud, and had to bite her tongue to avoid doing so.

"Th—hank you," she told Albin, when he had finished. "I'm glad to know it was only an accident."

"Yes, indeed," Max said, his voice dripping with false sincerity. "You can be as sure of my gratitude for your apology as you are of its truth."

Albin's eyes narrowed to daggers as he stared at the baronet. "My sister would like to invite Miss Devane to take dessert with our family tonight," he announced spitefully. "We're having cheesecake, and it's too bad you're going to miss it, *Sir* Hastings."

Camille's ecstasy at this pronouncement shook Gwendolyn to the bone. "Oh, *may* I, Mama?" the girl asked eagerly. "Since it is raining, I have nothing to do." Persuasively, she added, "It would be rude to refuse."

With apprehension, Gwendolyn scanned her daughter's face, then Maxim's. His expression was suspiciously blank. As her eyes hardened on his, he rapidly looked aside. She could almost believe he was fighting a smile.

She turned a firm look upon Albin. "Your mother and father are present, I presume?" Receiving a positive answer, she said, "Very well, then, Camille. But you must return within the hour."

"Oh, thank you," the young lady said, and dropping a kiss on her mother's forehead, rose. "I adore cheesecake and always have! It is the very best sweet in the world!"

"But you haven't finished your dinner," Gwendolyn murmured hastily. "They will surely wait—"

Camille was already moving away. "Oh, I'm not hungry!" she called happily over her shoulder.

Forgetting for the moment that she had a dinner companion sitting attentively across from her, Gwendolyn set her fork on the plate and stared at the congealing gravy, imagining it looked like a dirty pool marring the pristine whiteness of the china. A great, shuddering sigh lifted, then lowered, her shoulders.

"It's the way of life," Max said gently. "You can't stop it."

Her gaze flew to his. "We've discussed this before, I think. My relationship with my daughter is none of your concern."

"As you say," he replied, his stiff posture conveying withdrawal.

Breathing in swiftly, she took fork in hand and began drawing patterns in the gravy. "It's not as though I'm an ogre. I didn't refuse to let her go upstairs."

"No," he said immediately, encouraging her. "And you allowed her to ride with Bryce today."

"I certainly did," she agreed. "She has quite a measure of freedom for a girl her age. There's no reason to skulk in the shadows planning secret meetings and the like. No reason at all.''

''Would that the young required logical reasons.''

She tilted a sharp look beneath her lashes. ''You still believe I'm overprotecting her.''

''As you said before, my opinion isn't really relevant. But since you asked, I'd say each situation merits individual consideration. Bryce Munroe appears the best sort of young man. I've questioned several of the most infallible references, the servants. Each one of them praised him to the heavens. I don't believe you need to fear for your daughter where he's concerned.''

She stared at him, transfixed. ''You've asked about him?''

His head lowered slightly, as if in apology. ''I hope you don't mind.''

She shook her head briefly, not trusting herself to speak. He could not know the riot of emotions he'd stirred within. It was as though her problems were as important to him as his own. He made her feel . . . *cherished*. No one had ever considered her concerns before, not her parents, not Harrison, and certainly not Arthur.

On the other hand, his protectiveness could be viewed as interference. He kept pushing at the gates of her resolve. Pushing and pushing and pushing. Like a wolf at the door, he was battering away her view of herself, her impregnable need to *not need*.

''I am a good mother,'' she said fiercely.

''The best I have ever seen,'' he said softly, his gaze stroking her face. So tender his eyes were; so warm, as though he understood her every thought. She could not look away from him. Tears, ridiculous, sentimental tears, pricked behind her eyelids.

With relief she saw Richard Hibbs approaching their table. Max moved slightly, breaking the tension. She squared her shoulders and straightened her knife to military precision beside the plate.

''What's for dessert tonight, Richard?'' Max asked grandly.

"Peach tarts, raspberry torte, and lemon ice," the waiter recited.

"No cheesecake?" Max inquired, with a wink for Gwendolyn.

"I could check in the kitchen, sir."

"The ice would be fine for me," she said quickly.

"And I prefer the tart. I only asked about the cheesecake for the lady. In case she wanted to see what she was missing."

The waiter glanced from Sir Hastings to Mrs. Devane. A twinkle came into his eyes. With lips turning upward, he promised to bring the desired treats, then walked away.

It was very quiet after he left. Quiet at their table only, for around them the sounds of genteel conversation, pounding rain, and silverware clinking against porcelain continued without pause, but sounding farther and farther away. They were an island of silence, but not of peace. She fingered her remaining silverware restlessly, conscious of Max's eyes upon her at every moment. She dared not look up. It grew harder to draw breath into her lungs; she could feel the blood pulsing through her veins, faster and faster. Images played against the stage of her mind; old images and desires she'd thought were long forgotten. Tangled young limbs; flesh against flesh; the heat of driving passion. But instead of Harrison's blond, slim youth, she dreamed of Maxim's dark, powerful presence. She was falling, falling, and nothing awaited her but disaster; if she met his gaze, he would be able to read everything in her mind; he could not miss it, he could not. But she felt him calling her as surely as if he'd vocalized her name, and she had no strength to resist.

Slowly, her eyes lifted to his, and her body instantly quivered, as if he had kissed her with bruising force. Though his gaze was as solemn as she knew hers must be, he smiled slightly. Her lips trembled upward in answer. For a space of time, they remained thus, a tableau in the center of a room flowing with movement.

Gradually, she became aware of someone watching. An older couple at a nearby table observed them with fond interest, as if remembering something inexpressibly sweet. People could see it, then. How could she deny her feelings when strangers recognized them? But she must, she must! She lowered her gaze, flushing. And saw Maxim's hand reaching for hers.

"I . . . seem to have lost my appetite," he said in a husky voice.

"I have as well," she said quietly. "Perhaps—perhaps I'd best return to my room."

They stood immediately, and he tucked her hand under his arm, passed a bewildered Robert Hibbs, who halted within a few paces of their table with desserts held aloft, and led her through the lobby and up the stairs, retracing their steps without speaking a word.

When they arrived at her suite, she could not fit the key in the lock, her hands were shaking so. He gently took the key from her and opened the door. She crossed into the room, then turned when he did not immediately follow. His strange, beautiful eyes locked with hers, a question in them, and barely restrained fire. How odd that she had always thought of green as a cool, calm color. She never would again.

Brazenly, she put her hand to his sleeve, pulled him into the room, and closed the door. Instantly he crushed her against his chest, his mouth finding hers with light, teasing kisses, then harder, more urgent ones.

"You are so beautiful," he whispered against her ear. "Oh, my love . . ."

Gwendolyn touched her mouth to his, silencing him, losing herself in pleasure as his lips explored her lips, her cheeks, her fluttering eyelids, the arch of her neck. She returned kiss for kiss, locking her arms around him, pressing closer, so close that nothing could ever come between them; her delighted fingers threading through his hair and down his neck and shoulders.

"I have never . . . known anyone . . . like you," he said between kisses. "You are the most—"

"Don't say anything, my dearest," she breathed. "There are . . . other ways of speaking."

He drew back suddenly, his eyes searing hers. An instant

later she was whisked into his arms. He carried her to the settee and sat with her across his lap, her head resting against the pillows at the end, his fiery gaze moving across her face and body.

"I love you," he said, before she could stop him, and, with trembling fingers, smoothed his hand down her neck, tugging aside the scrap of material covering her shoulder to bare the skin beneath. Slowly, he bent to press his lips to the tender spot above her collarbone. She felt his rapid breaths heating her flesh and closed her lids, every fiber of her being tingling in response.

Voices nagged at the back of her mind, little worry-ghosts flittering, cautioning, scolding, as his lips sought hers again. *This is wrong.* She would not heed them. For once she meant to obey impulse, to live completely for the present moment with this wonderful man who loved her.

Loved her. The voices jangled louder, more alarmed. Another man might declare love lightly, hoping to speed seduction. Not Max; she would stake her life on his sincerity. It followed that he would expect more from her than a brief interlude, no matter how sweet. Her pleasure began to diminish ever so slightly. No don't listen! she cried silently, and loosened her embrace in order to caress his face, to tug him closer.

But gradually she sensed him pulling back. *No, no!* she begged with her eyes, and raised herself to a sitting position to draw him toward one last, desperate kiss.

"We can't do this," he said, breaking away, sounding angry.

She opened her lids incredulously. A war was waging in him, she saw; but she felt more sympathy for her own frustration.

"We can't?" she cried.

"I have nothing to offer you."

"I haven't asked for anything, Max."

"No, but I won't take advantage of you in this manner. I love you too much."

It was over, then. She withdrew her legs from the settee to the floor. She felt as if her heart had melted and was leaking through her veins. "I don't expect declarations of love or offers for marriage. In fact, I don't want them."

He stared at her, his expression smoldering. "Speak like that and I will think Roderick was right." Standing abruptly, he walked to the door.

With a frown creasing her brow, she followed. "Right about what? What did he say?"

"Nothing. I'd like to leave for Halleydale at eight tomorrow morning. Can you be ready by then?"

"I'm not going anywhere until you tell me what your cousin said."

"Fine. I'll go alone."

Her anger rising to match his, she snapped, "Very well, do as you wish. Men always do! Though I'll be interested to know how you plan to find the estate or secure an introduction to my brother-in-law without me."

"I'll find it," he said with surety. "And him." His lips straightened into a tight, line. "Good night, Gwendolyn."

"Good night."

She closed the door firmly behind him, then stared at the crosspieces and fluted molding as if admiring its workmanship, though she really didn't see it at all. Her irritation melted almost instantly to disappointment, then sorrow. For several seconds she pressed her forehead to the wood. Blindly, she fumbled for the lock. Before her fingers could guide the metal into its track, the door opened and would have struck her had she moved less quickly.

"I need to ask you something," Max said.

Forcing the joy at his return from her eyes, Gwendolyn lengthened her face and waited.

The baronet viewed her sternly. "You said you don't want offers of marriage. What did you mean by that?"

"Simply what I said. I am happy alone."

"Really. What if we had finished what was started a moment ago and a child had been conceived. What would you say then?"

Her temples began to pound at the possibility. Where, indeed, had her mind been? The thought seemed ludicrous, tragic, and exciting, all at once. "I hardly think that would have happened," she said.

"Why are you smiling? I can't believe you've reached an age where it's not a consideration."

Her smile disappeared at once.

"I'm not nearly that old yet. It would have been my hope you'd realize that without asking."

"I did, of course; only you seem to have forgotten."

"You make it sound as though I were acting alone, Max. You were the one helping me forget."

"Yes, because I love you. But you don't feel the same, or you wouldn't be so set on remaining alone."

She looked away from the raw hurt in his eyes. "Max, I . . ." Desperately, she searched for words but could find none.

"You don't have to say anything." His voice was suddenly gentle. "I know that loving someone doesn't automatically mean the other person loves you. Life isn't always that fair."

"Max . . ." she began, one part of her fighting to say, *But I do love you!* and knowing it for the truth; while the other cautioned, You realize what happens when a woman gives her life to a man. While he waited with a sad, resigned look, she battled, detesting the whims of a fate that forced her to choose whether to hurt him or herself.

"That's all right, my dear," he said finally. "Don't distress yourself. I don't want you creating delicate speeches about how much you respect me and so forth. But I do want to warn you. You're a passionate, beautiful woman. Be more careful in the future. I don't want you to be hurt."

"Be more careful in the future?" she repeated in an annoyed voice. "I hope you don't think I make a habit of inviting gentlemen to my rooms. You are the first since . . ." *Since Harrison,* she had almost said. Deliberately, she relaxed her fingers, amazed that she could come so near giving up her shameful secret after all these years. "Since my marriage."

The relief she saw in his eyes both warmed and irritated her. Did he think she had no scruples, no morals?

"I'm glad," he said simply. "That's better for you. And Camille."

Camille. Dear, heavenly Father, her daughter had not once crossed her mind in the last half-hour. Her eyes grew wide. Fearfully, she cast a wild glance at the clock.

"The time! Max, you must go immediately; she'll be back any moment. How can I explain why we're alone together?"

She hurried him out the door.

In the corridor, Roderick was passing by on the way to his room. His steps halted for only an instant as he gazed knowingly at Maxim's wildly disarrayed hair and Gwendolyn's loosened clothing. Her cheeks blazed beneath that shrewd, assessing look. He bowed, the merest inclination of his head, and continued on with a faint, sardonic smile. None of them exchanged a word.

Max returned his eyes to hers, anger lingering. "Dismiss what I said earlier. I want you to come with me tomorrow. You must."

His protective urge had returned in force, she saw. With a multitude of conflicting emotions churning in her breast, she agreed.

Chapter Ten

Shortly before eight o'clock on the following morning, Max exited from The Allemande to wait beneath the portico. He gazed at the sky and spotted only a few wisps of white clouds. Last night's rain had washed the streets clean, and the mist rising from the ground felt like steam. The day promised to be a good one, though warm.

How unfortunate that it could not lift his spirits.

He eyed the muffin vendor across the street and fingered the handle of his cane. No one could be trusted, not the chubby, unkempt baker, nor the early morning pedestrians taking the air. Not even the grandfather wheeling his cart of dusty old books toward the inn.

He must remember to keep alert to Gwendolyn's danger instead of Gwendolyn herself. Never, never must he allow himself to forget as he did last night.

But when she exited from the inn wearing a violet plaid carriage dress and a matching bonnet, the shock of attraction was as strong as ever. He was not ordinarily moved by women's choice in clothing, but the deep color against her fairness made a lovely contrast. As they exchanged distant greetings, he schooled his features to show no pleasure in her appearance. Many of the previous evening's sleepless hours had been spent in coaching such restraint in himself.

"Where is Camille?" he asked as they waited for the carriage he'd hired to be brought around.

A line briefly creased Gwendolyn's forehead. "She wasn't feeling well this morning. She looked flushed and has a cough. Perhaps she caught your illness."

"I hope not." He began to relax. She was making an effort to appear as if nothing had happened between them. It made today's prospect easier. How he dreaded, yet anticipated, the exquisite torture of spending hours in a carriage with her. "You haven't left her alone?"

"No, of course not. I sent for Mrs. Merriweather. Did I mention her to you? She's an old friend who lives in Bath now. I've known her since I was a child."

"That's well, then. I imagine it was still difficult for you to leave her."

"She insisted. And since she did not appear to be feverish, I thought it would be all right."

The post chaise jingled around the corner, and a moment later he handed her inside. Following, he closed the door and tapped the ceiling with his cane. The carriage sprang into motion.

Conversation proved difficult. Subjects were introduced, commented upon, and dismissed. By the time the outskirts of Bath melted into open countryside, both had entered into an awkward silence. Max stared out one window, while she peered through the other. After long minutes of this, he heard her stir.

"Your eye looks painful this morning," she said softly.

He grunted and unconsciously touched the tender spot. "It's quite a horror, isn't it? I'm glad to say it looks worse than it feels. Sorry to appear so disreputable."

"No, you look very interesting." She smiled. "A little like a pirate, perhaps."

He returned her smile thinly. "So bad as that? Maybe I should purchase an eye patch."

"Or a schoolboy. I always think of schoolyard fights when I see black eyes on gentlemen."

"What about frustrated suitors?" he asked abruptly. "Do I remind you of one of those?"

Her lashes lowered uneasily, and he cursed himself for his bitter tongue. "I beg your pardon, Gwendolyn. I spoke without thinking."

For several seconds she remained quiet, then said, "Are you . . . is everything mended between you and Roderick? After your disagreement, I mean. I meant to ask you last night, but didn't." She blushed at making reference to what had become a painful memory for them both.

"No, but don't let it distress you. Things never have been right."

"I'm sorry," she murmured. "It's difficult when relationships are strained under the same roof."

"Very." He thought gloomily of how long that strain was apt to continue, then glanced at her with sudden attention. "You speak with the conviction of experience."

For an instant it seemed as though she would not answer. "Yes. I've had some experience with that."

She turned her head back to the window, apparently unwilling to say more. Her fingers moved restlessly across her knees, folding and unfolding wrinkles into her gown. He watched her with steadily growing compassion.

"Gwendolyn." At the sound of his voice, she swung her startled gaze to his. "What's troubling you?"

"Why, nothing." One hand fluttered to her collar, then settled back onto her lap. "I can't say I'm looking forward to this visit, but I'll be all right."

He had sworn to himself he would keep his distance today, but he could no more keep his eyes from her than he could stop breathing. Something was bothering her deeply, and to see her disturbed was worse than anything else that could happen to him.

"I hope you're not troubled about what occurred between us yesterday. I know you have a caring heart." He glanced out the window, then back to her again, and his lips quirked into a smile that as immediately died. "It occurs to me that you might be worried." He shrugged apologetically. "About me."

Her eyes grew wider and more luminous. He swallowed and hastened on. "I only want to say there's no need for us to be awkward with one another. I meant what I said last night. I don't hold it against you that you don't love me."

"Oh, Max," she said, and began to weep.

He was beside her in a heartbeat, one arm encircling her shoulders. She fumbled in her reticule, extracted a lacy bit of cloth, and turned her head against his chest. He could feel the dampness of her tears through his shirt. The ridiculous, perky feather in her bonnet tickled his nose. It was as though she belonged there, as if she had been designed to fit against him in precisely this way.

He stroked her back lightly. "Don't cry, my dear. It's for the best that you don't return my feelings." Hearing the lack of conviction in his voice, he gave a single chuckle. "It's not the best for me, of course; but I mean from the practical view of things. You know I have nothing. Without the formula, I've been set back ten years. No home, other than my uncle's. No occupation, other than what my uncle provides. Not a very enticing prospect, is it?"

"None of that would matter to the right woman," she said, struggling for composure, her breaths drifting from her in ragged little gasps.

You are the right woman, he told her silently. But he said nothing aloud, only squeezed her shoulder briefly.

She dabbed her nose with her handkerchief and tilted her head upward. The feather bobbed toward his eye. With a sad smile, he pushed it aside and stared down at her, thinking how kissable she looked.

"Don't disparage yourself, Max. You are too good, truly you are. If I had met you years ago—"

He pressed his fingers to her mouth, not able to bear it. "I told you last night I want no sentimental speeches."

To take the sting from his words, he caressed her cheek

with the back of his fingers. She gave him a shaky smile and straightened, leaving a cold place over his heart. He shifted slightly and brought his arm back to his side.

Moments passed wherein his ears filled with the sounds of the horses clopping along outside, the creak of leather overhead, occasional mutterings from the driver. He wanted to believe it was a companionable silence, but he could not fail to note that Gwendolyn's distressed air had returned. Her eyes scanned the window as if looking for highwaymen, her nervous fingers knitted together as though searching for something. His gaze dropped to her half-boots, which were making tiny scuffling noises against the wooden floor of the coach.

With dread his thoughts returned to Roderick's accusations. He tried to throw them from his mind but could not.

"Is there something else, Gwendolyn? You seem distraught."

"No, nothing," she said, so quietly he almost did not hear.

Suddenly, he was conscious of the heat pouring through the roof of the carriage, and he removed his handkerchief and wiped his forehead, then restored it to his pocket.

"If you did have a problem, you would come to me, wouldn't you? You do trust me to help, don't you?"

"Normally I would say that my problems are mine to solve," she said gently. "But not today or yesterday, not with this terrible threat hanging over my head, and Camille's. I'm most grateful for your help. Indeed, I wouldn't be here if I did not trust you." Her gaze became intense. "You keep asking me, as though . . . Max, you started to say something last night, something about Roderick. Does this have anything to do with him?"

"What makes you think that?" His voice rang with suspicion.

She spoke reluctantly. "Because your cousin and I had an uncomfortable time of it yesterday, and now I'm wondering what he told you."

The heat was becoming unbearable. He loosened his cravat and opened both windows. The pounding of hooves grew louder. Scents of hay-filled meadow flowed through the carriage. After wiping his forehead with his handkerchief again, he stretched his legs as best he could. Gwendolyn observed his activities steadily.

"Yesterday you said nothing was wrong," he said at last.

"That's because I was afraid of what you would do. And in spite of my keeping quiet, the two of you still fought."

"Then he was rude to you. What did he say?"

"What did he say to *you?*"

After an instant of a mutual examination, Max spoke, hating every word that fell from his lips. "He told me you needed a loan for ten thousand pounds."

She nodded, the corners of her eyes beginning to crinkle. "I was afraid of that."

He heard thunder in his ears. "You mean to say you aren't denying it?"

"Oh, I asked him for the money all right," she said merrily.

He could not keep disappointment from his expression. If this much was true, what did that say to the rest? "But why didn't you come to me if you were so desperate? I would have raised the funds for you somehow. I still can."

She broke into laughter. "I'm not desperate, Max. I only told him that to help you."

With twinkling eyes, she explained her plan to coerce Roderick into revealing the formula. Max listened, the knot of tension in his stomach gradually dissolving. He had not doubted her for an instant—well, an instant only. Thank God he'd not voiced the remainder of what his cousin had said about her.

"Don't dare scold me again for trying," she concluded. "I know you didn't wish it, but I thought it worth one last chance."

He briefly touched his hands to hers. "And I thank you for the effort. Only promise not to do it again."

"You have my pledge, sir. He has proved too stubborn for me, so I must leave him to your persuasion." Her merriment faded. "I wish I could have done that one thing for you."

"It means a great deal to me that you tried."

The glances they exchanged this time were soft, regretful

ones, as though they were old lovers remembering fonder days without pain. He could only look forward to the day when that would be true. The freshness of his loss was like a tearing wound.

The hours moved on with occasional, inconsequential conversation passing between them. When they were within a half-hour of Halleydale, they stopped for brief refreshment at a small inn set in a glade. The tea was strong and bracing, and the warm, freshly baked bread flavorful of butter and cinnamon. Max ate with good appetite, but Gwendolyn stopped after a few bites.

"I can't taste anything," she said when she noticed his concerned look. "Not now."

"You really are anxious about this meeting, aren't you?"

Gwendolyn's gaze drifted aside. Their server, a large-boned, heavy woman with frowsy yellow hair and a ready laugh, was taking orders from a group of gentlemen at a nearby table and exchanging good-natured jibes with them.

"There is no way to express how I feel about it," she said, her eyes wandering from one member of the jocular company to the other. "I never intended to return to Devane Place. I believe I had rather visit the gates of Hades."

He set down his cup of tea. "This is what you've been worried about all morning. You should have told me." One corner of his mouth lifted. "Instead of letting me go on and on about last night."

"Both, Max," she said, her hands reaching for his. "I'm troubled by both. I cannot forget last evening, and today is likely to drive me mad. My mind is a complete muddle. I keep wondering what we shall do when we arrive. Shall we walk in and demand if Bernard has tried to murder me? He would never confess to such a thing." Her eyes settled on him. "You know how certain you were of Roderick's reactions? That's how well I understand Bernard. I can't imagine we will learn anything from him."

He stared at her for a moment. "Only one thing is certain, Gwendolyn. We won't learn anything if we don't try. And I've been planning a way to approach him. See what you think of this.''

He leaned forward. As he spoke, a faint sparkle returned to her eyes.

Devane Place had hardly changed in the past two years, Gwendolyn thought as the coach slowed to traverse the pitted, gravel drive. She leaned back against the seat. There was no need to stare through the window as Max was doing. The low, rambling Tudor house with its creeping vines darkening the windows, the ancient, spreading oak set squarely in front would be imprinted on her mind forever.

Twelve years she had lived here. Twelve agonizing years. She had thought that stifling life would never draw to a close, that she would walk through her remaining days as one blind and numb, until death brought an ending. And death finally had, but she'd thought it would be her own.

When the chaise stopped, Max opened the door and guided her from the carriage. She paused for an instant when her feet touched the ground, scenting the smell of faint decay from rotting timbers. To her it was the odor of loneliness. The dogs barked furiously in their pens behind the house. There were few signs of life: no grooms rushing toward the horses, no butler flinging wide the door. Nothing had changed.

Taking courage from Maxim's glance, she nodded, and they walked forward. The door had not been painted since she left; streaks of grey and yellow marred what remained of the white, and the panels were beginning to warp. Max lifted the boar's head knocker and gave three sharp raps. Long seconds later, she heard footsteps approaching, a familiar step; rapid, decisive boots meeting the oak floor. Before the door parted to a crack, she knew who would be standing on the other side.

The woman who met her eyes scarcely looked a day older, though she had reached the years when a month could make a great difference in the depth and number of wrinkles in thin, fair skin. Her black dress hung just as loosely over a slight, curveless body; her short grey hair curled in the same, rigid rows beneath a black cap.

"Hello, Anderson," Gwendolyn said.

"Mrs. Devane." The housekeeper's round, nearly black eyes, flicked over her, then Max, without a hint of emotion. "What may I do for you?"

"We've come to see Lord Devane, if we may."

"He's not well enough for visitors."

This was one contingency for which she had not planned, and she shot a worried gaze at Max. He was already stepping closer to Anderson, his considerable presence making even her withdraw the slightest amount.

"We've driven a long way, my fiancée and I, to see Lord Devane," he said in commanding tones. "Even though the connection is distant, he's the only surviving male in Mrs. Devane's family, and she wishes to receive his blessing upon our marriage. Surely you won't deny her this simple request." He pulled a card from his pocket and handed it to the housekeeper. "You may tell him Sir Maxim Hastings calls."

Anderson studied the card, then opened the door wide. This was the authority that came with a title, Gwendolyn thought, her mouth twisting ironically. She wouldn't dream Max could sound so arrogant and demanding. But they were inside, so she couldn't deny there were some advantages.

"Come with me," Anderson said, and began walking toward the familiar old Gothic staircase that made several sharp angles leading to the upper two floors.

"Should you not announce us first?" Gwendolyn asked, following more slowly. She had forgotten how loudly boots could echo in the cavernous hall. Such a lost sound.

"It won't make any difference," replied the housekeeper without turning.

Gwendolyn darted a look at Max, who appeared as surprised as she; but they both continued to follow without pause, Gwendolyn trailing her hand along the wooden rail as she had done so many times in the past. The banners, proud tapestries from long-ago Devane victories, still hung from the balcony. Several of the paintings were missing from the walls; lighter rectangles marked their passing like tombstones.

At the top of the stairs, Anderson led them down the main corridor to the last room on the right.

"This was my husband's room," Gwendolyn said.

Anderson nodded, one brief jerk of the head. "He always wanted it for himself."

The servant entered the bedchamber and stood beside the door. Gwendolyn reluctantly walked past, her eyes flashing over the ancient, heavily carved furnishings, the whitewashed walls and dreary curtains, the plain bedspread covering a small mound of humanity.

Her gaze fixated on the face sunken against the pillows. The countenance sagged like an empty membrane, its tiny, restless eyes set midway into the skull. This could not be Bernard. Bernard had never been a tall man, but he was stout. Robust. This man appeared to be an empty hull, as though his inner body had been sucked dry. Her incredulous gaze flew to Anderson.

"It's best if you just go over to him. Maybe he'll recognize you."

Gwendolyn moved forward slowly. She was conscious of Max flanking her side, but her eyes were only for Bernard, who watched her approach with a look of frenzied glee.

"Tell Bumble to get the horses," he chattered. "I'm riding to Chelsea today. Get the horses ready. Now!"

Fear cast long shadows through Gwendolyn's heart. Her eyes swerved to Max, then back to the man in the bed.

Devane's head turned from side to side, rustling the pillowcase. "Who is this, who is this? Hallo, my beauty, and what is it you have for me, what?" His words were breathy and so rapid she could scarcely make them out. "Oh, you, I know you, you are my pretty one, ain't you? Come closer, come, I tell you!"

"Bernard," she said, her voice trembling. "Do you recognize me?"

"What? Recognize you, recognize you, of course, of course

I do. You've come to me at last, you have, you have! I knew you would.''

"I've brought a friend with me," she interjected quickly, and introduced Max.

The old man's eyes switched to the baronet. "You can go away. This is my house. Mine. You do as I say; I don't have to put up with you. Now, go!''

"If he leaves, I go with him," Gwendolyn said firmly.

"Do you, now? Do you?" He laughed wheezily. "I can do for you what *he* can't, and what my brother never could, the old *pretender,* he had all this. It should have been mine.''

"Lord Devane," Max said loudly. "Have you—''

"It should have been *mine!''* the invalid cried, ignoring him, holding Gwendolyn with his eyes, his face suffusing with blood. "You should have been *mine! We* would have had boys, fine boys to continue the line, but no, Arthur must come first. *Arthur!* Always Arthur. The useless old ...'' His gaze searched the chamber. "And where is the girl? The pretty little girl? Did you not bring her? Where is she? All of this is *mine.* Everything—''

Gwendolyn closed her fingers over her ears and ran from the room. She did not stop running until she reached the head of the stairs and Max caught her, wrapping his arms around her, murmuring comforts into her hair.

"I'm sorry, Gwen—''

"He is so horrible," she sobbed. "He was always after one or the other of us, and now he has gone mad with his evil.''

"I know, my darling; hush now.''

"I could never leave Camille alone for an instant!''

"Oh, God. I didn't know. I wouldn't have put you through this again for the world.''

"Arthur was no protection," she went on, hearing herself chatter but not able to stop now that she had begun. "He was always in a drunken stupor! Our marriage was only a pretense, a sham! He never once—he could not ...''

His arms tightened around her. She closed her eyes, trying to blot out the awful memories of her husband's fumbling attempts to consummate their marriage.

"We shouldn't have come," Max said. "This is my fault."

Gwendolyn dashed the tears from her eyes and stepped away from him. "No. I'm—I'm glad I came." She drew in a shuddering breath. "In a way, seeing him like this makes me feel . . . oh, relieved, I suppose. After we left, I was always afraid he would try to find us." She touched her handkerchief to her nose. "At least now I know he can't."

Speaking the words brought a measure of peace. By the time Anderson approached them from the hallway, Gwendolyn was able to summon an almost normal expression, though tear-stained.

"What happened to him?" she asked.

"An attack of apoplexy," the housekeeper said. "He can't walk. But he never stops talking. He talks about all the things he used to keep hidden. Day after day, he talks and talks and talks."

Max turned to her. "Who inherits this place when he's gone?"

"Everything is entailed. The estate goes to a distant cousin, what there is left of it. I keep having to sell the silver and things to buy food."

"What will you do, Anderson?" Gwendolyn asked, suddenly concerned for this strange woman. "When Bernard dies?"

"I don't know," she said. "Perhaps there will still be a place for me here." Her eyes seemed to soften. "How is your daughter?"

"She's well, thank you. Grown more beautiful than ever."

The woman regarded her with an unblinking stare. "I'm glad you made a life for yourself."

"Thank you, Anderson," Gwendolyn said softly, wishing there was a chance for the servant to do the same.

Moments later, the two travelers returned to the chaise.

"She seems an unusual woman," Max said, when the horses dashed forward. "But a good servant. I saw no signs of dust or filth in the house, though she looked to be alone. And she's obviously caring for Bernard as well as possible."

"Anderson always was exceptional in that way. She was

never unkind to Camille or me.'' Memories of many long days riffled through her mind. ''But she never showed understanding, either. She was one of the few adult females whom I saw on a regular basis, and I tried to make a connection with her but never could.''

''You must have been incredibly lonely.''

''I believe she was, too, and still is. I feel sorry for her. It's as though she isn't really here, as if she dwells in some faraway place while her body goes through the motions of living.'' She lowered her lashes. ''I suppose I was much the same for a long time. If it had not been for my daughter, perhaps I could not have broken away either.''

''You would have. I believe we make our own happiness or misery.'' He swept his hat from his head and put it on the seat, then ruffled his fingers through his hair. ''I'm sorry about today, Gwendolyn. You were absolutely right. We've discovered nothing that will help our investigation.''

''That's not entirely true. I've learned a very great thing, that there can be sadness in the defeat of one's enemy.''

His stare was so expressive of admiration and warmth that she glanced down uncomfortably. ''You're a woman of remarkable courage, Gwendolyn.''

''I am not.''

''You are. You've endured two unhappy marriages that would have sent many ladies to their graves, or at least their sickbeds. It's no wonder that . . .''

Crossing her arms over her bosom, she waited with an intense look in her eyes.

''Nothing,'' he said. ''That's all.''

''No, I won't let you off so easily. Now that you've put me to the blush telling me I'm brave—when I know very well I'm not—you must finish.''

''I was only going to say it's no wonder you're prejudiced by your past.'' When her brows lowered ominously, he hurried on, ''I'd be surprised if you didn't hate every man on earth.''

''Would you?'' She was jolted by a rush of anger. ''Then you are doubly wrong. You say I am brave for enduring my unhappy marriages. Call me *stalwart,* or *enduring,* but don't label me brave for existing through what could not be changed.''

''There are many kinds of bravery.''

She continued as if he had not spoken. ''And as for hating men, it's true my years with Arthur were dry and loveless ones, and the days so long that if Camille had not been there, I should have gone mad with tedium. But I did know some happiness with Harrison, though it was the love of overgrown children.'' Her face relaxed as she reflected with some fondness on the past. ''We bickered constantly over trifles. Neither of us trusted the other not to run off with someone better. But there was goodness in him. Camille could not be the person she is otherwise; she is much like her father.''

Her reverie was interrupted by a fleeting look of pain on Max's face. She regretted it, but now that he knew a portion of the truth, he must know the rest. So he could understand why she refused him.

''There was laughter among the tears,'' she continued. ''But more tears than not.'' She tilted her head, studying him. ''Can you imagine for a moment what it is, Max, to have no power of decision over your life? That if your husband takes it in his head to move from a village you've only begun to know well, where perhaps you've been able to save a small amount of money from minding the innkeeper's children, then you must go? What if everything you earned must be turned over to your husband's keeping to gamble away if he wanted, and not to pay the rent or buy food for his baby? How would such a life make you feel?''

He shook his head slowly. She wondered if it was because of a lack of empathy or because he perceived her hurt.

''This is the way I expected my life to be with Arthur, though his title made him too proud to allow me to work to alleviate our suffering. But that it should be the same with Harrison, who proclaimed he loved me . . . Do you see, Max? This is how it is for all married women, and most single ones. A life of dependence on the generosity of the men in their lives. Well, now it is different for me. By trickery and effort, I am able to provide a comfortable existence for my daughter and myself. I never intend to give up my independence again.''

For a space of time, he watched her in silence. When he spoke, his words were measured and slow.

''So you're saying it's not that you can't love another man, but that you *won't.*''

She hesitated briefly. ''I suppose that's what I'm saying, yes.''

His lips widened in a humorless smile. He glanced away, then back. ''You have disappointed me for the first time.''

Her mouth went suddenly dry. She could not countenance how hard his words struck her. ''Have I indeed?''

''I suppose you were right. You do lack courage.''

''*Do* I?'' she asked, making the words a challenge. She didn't disagree; but she had liked it better when he had thought she possessed that quality.

''I fear so. Last night I could have sworn your reaction to me was that of a woman in love. And when I declared myself to you and you failed to respond, I thought it meant I was mistaken, that you were a lonely, passionate woman and simply vulnerable to a man you found somewhat pleasant. But now it occurs that you never *denied* loving me, and I'm wondering if perhaps I was right the first time, only you're too afraid to admit it.''

Gwendolyn's pulse pounded in her neck, her temples, her wrists. She longed to rip the door from the coach and run away, but it was impossible to move, impossible to tear her eyes from his.

''Well, Gwendolyn? Is every man cut from the same cloth? You've been hurt twice. Does that mean no man alive can be trusted to put your welfare above his own?''

''He might not mean to treat me unfairly,'' she said, bending toward him, gesturing earnestly. ''And during the first stages of love, he probably wouldn't. But gradually, as that bloom fades as everything does in time, what happens then? Society decrees his mastery, don't you see? Little by little, people fall into their roles no matter how much they intend to do otherwise!''

"You have not answered my question," he said demandingly. *"Do* you love me, Gwendolyn?"

She would not be tricked into answering. There was too much warring within her for her to give in to what she wanted, which was to fall into his arms and declare, *Yes! Yes, I do love you, more than I have loved anyone in my life!* For therein lay a greater danger than she had faced before. Yes, she was afraid. Terrified. And she would not trade her nice, steady, painless life for one that lacked certainty.

"And what would you do about it if I did?" she parried, forcing lightness into her tone.

That settled him back into his seat again, she saw cynically, watching his lashes lower to veil flaming eyes. It might be a low blow, reminding him of his financial distress, but he had pushed her to it.

She grabbed his cane and tapped the ceiling. The coach began to slow. "Here is that little inn again," she said, "and I am suddenly famished."

Max's eyes narrowed further. As the driver drew the horses from the road, she was relieved to see a glint of humor in her companion's expression. If she also saw a look of determination, she refused to worry about it.

Chapter Eleven

"We can't dismiss it so easily," Max said as they neared Bath later that afternoon. "Just because we haven't been successful in finding the source yet doesn't mean there's no danger."

Gwendolyn stared at him stubbornly. "I'm still inclined to think the incident was a fluke. It's been days since anything happened. Why would my hypothetical enemy wait so long?"

"If someone was determined to make murder look like an accident, he would take time to be careful. We've been together most of the time, and there's been no opportunity."

"Well, we cannot stay together forever," she said in brisk tones, and shifted her gaze to the window. He wanted to protest, but he remained silent, knowing she was right. "Your uncle will want you back at the business," she added.

"I'd like you to think about something, Gwendolyn," he said uncomfortably. "I've avoided mentioning this until now because I didn't want to worry you unnecessarily; but if you're contemplating letting down your guard, I believe I must. There's a good chance that the serpent was not the first attempt on your life." When she frowned furiously, he continued, "On the day

we met you said something about a recent carriage accident . . .''

Her brow cleared immediately. "Oh, no. There was nothing
to that. Camille and I were only shaken a little; our lives were
never in danger. And the coach was hired. How would a villain
know which one we would take? Or if he did know, how could
he find time to tamper with the wheel when it was in the care
of the driver the whole time?''

"There are always ways if a man is determined enough,
though you do present convincing arguments against it." He
took his hat from the seat and rotated it in his hands. "Have
you given any more thought to possible suspects?''

She regarded him critically for a moment. "Are you back
to my scripts again?''

"We should consider every avenue.''

"It would take a madman to react so extremely to my little
efforts, and I haven't parodied anyone insane to my knowledge.''

The carriage slowed. They were crossing shop-lined Pulteney
Bridge, and pedestrian traffic was increasing. Max leaned back
and stretched one arm across the seat, eyeing the woman across
from him with impatience. "Why do you refuse to even think
about it?''

"Why?" Her gaze roamed the carriage, then returned to his.
"As I've said before, I don't think I've hurt anyone to that
extent, and I've been very careful to keep my identity secret.
But most of all, I believe the true reason you insist on this line
of thinking is your disapproval of what I do.''

"It is not," he shot back. "I admire what you've been able
to accomplish for yourself and Camille with your talent.''

"You just wish I'd use different subject matter.''

"I do, yes.''

"Well, it may surprise you, but I'd like to write other things
as well. Unfortunately, my banker prefers the sound of gold to
the voicing of high ideals.''

Abruptly, an old memory seized him. Mr. Evans stood before
one of the last paintings Max had ever done. His father was

still alive and, unbeknowst to them, waylaying mail coaches and demanding gentlemen's purses with an unloaded pistol. The painting was, as most of them were, fanciful: a crumbling castle half-hidden in the mist; a tattered knight approaching it on a proud horse, his lance pointed downward. The sense of story in it was strong, as he recalled, though he'd had little conscious awareness of its origins as he'd painted; his fingers had always seemed to find their own way. Mr. Evans had studied it a long time, then startled Max by viewing him with glistening eyes. "You have surpassed my ability to teach you," he said. "I don't know whether to embrace you or slit your throat. Yours will be the future I always wanted for myself."

He wondered what his old tutor would think of him now, if he was still alive. He could not dispute Gwendolyn's practicality. He had sold his own gift as cheaply as she. Perhaps it happened to everyone. Perhaps life meant constant compromise between beauty and hunger. Perhaps everyone sold their souls every day in the marketplace, bit by bloody bit.

"I'm no judge to cast blame at your door," he said, as much to himself as to her. "No blame."

Exchanging frequent, searching glances, they remained silent for the small distance to The Allemande. After disembarking, Max escorted Gwendolyn upstairs. When they arrived at the door to her suite, she bid him farewell softly and extended her hand. He bowed over it sadly, wishing he dared take her in his arms again. He could not resist touching her forehead with a kiss before turning to go to his room.

Behind him, he heard her knock, then murmur worriedly when no one answered. His steps slowed. She fumbled the key into the lock, and the door creaked open.

"Camille?" she said, her voice sounding muffled as she entered the room. "Mrs. Merriweather?"

The hairs at the nape of his neck bristled at the anxiety in her tone. He swerved, reaching her suite just as she emerged from Camille's room, her face compressed with tension. "She's gone! There's no sign of her anywhere! Oh, God, Max, what shall I do?"

"Don't panic," he said, as much to himself as to her. They should never have left the child; he should have known better. He tucked Gwendolyn's arm in his and closed the door behind them. "We'll go downstairs and ask the desk clerk if he knows anything."

"What if he doesn't?" she queried, hastening to keep up with his larger strides.

"Then we'll search for her," he said simply.

The clerk was the same sleepy-eyed fellow he'd met on the first day of his stay, but the man looked less sullen when he saw Gwendolyn. "Sorry," he told her, "I only came on duty last hour. Haven't seen Miss Devane at all."

"Are you certain?" Gwendolyn cried.

"Yes, ma'am. I always notice her." He glanced at Max and flushed.

"Oh, Max," she said miserably, then spun back to the clerk. "Call the magistrate at once!"

"Wait," the baronet said distantly, his attention riveted on something beyond the glass doors.

"We can't wait! Every moment is essential. That man must have—"

"I believe I see her now," Max said.

Gwendolyn whirled toward the glass. Three young people were scurrying toward the inn: Bryce, Lucy, and Camille. They were laughing and talking loudly enough to be heard within the lobby.

Max looked at Gwendolyn. Terror was fading to incredulity, and little blotches of color stained her ashen features. He glanced away uneasily.

"Camille?" she queried in tones of disbelief as her daughter entered the building.

The girl stopped instantly, her cheeks blooming like pink rosebuds. "Oh, Mama, you are early! You said it would be nightfall when you returned!"

"When I left this morning, you were ill." Gwendolyn's

words extended thinly into the hall. Max imagined a great rift opening wider with each syllable.

"Ill?" Bryce looked from mother to daughter, then exchanged a troubled glance with Lucy.

"I felt so much better after you left that I told Mrs. Merriweather I didn't need her anymore," Camille said rapidly, her eyes overbright. "Could we—could we speak about this upstairs? Please?"

"You cannot know how worried I was," Gwendolyn said, her voice gaining strength. "We almost called the authorities." She turned to Bryce. "Surely you could have left a message with the clerk, or you, Lucy. Both of you are old enough to realize—"

"They didn't know!" Camille said loudly, her tears beginning to fall. "This is all my fault, and Mr. Munroe had nothing to do with it!" Her voice trailed off as she fled toward the stairs.

Gwendolyn's lips parted in shock. "I'm sorry," she said in flustered tones. "I had better . . ." She hurried after her daughter.

Bryce moved to follow, but Max held him back.

"I don't believe we dare," he said.

Lucy fluttered to one of the mirrors mounted on the wall and began to adjust her bonnet and hair. "My mother is happy for me to do as I wish. I've never found it necessary to lie in order to enjoy activities. The more suitors I have, the more pleased she is." Her reflected eyes raked over Max disdainfully. "As long as they do not make a habit of pretending they are more than they *are,* of course. My mother wants only the best for me. She says that I deserve to have a soft life because I am fragile, isn't that so, Bryce?"

After a brief hesitation. Bryce asked worriedly, "Do you think Camille will be all right?"

"Mrs. Devane is a fair woman," Max answered, and prayed it would hold true, that she wouldn't allow her lack of trust in men to extend to her daughter.

*   *   *

Heavy sobs escaped through the closed door of Camille's room. Gwendolyn treaded the carpet awhile, wondering how best to handle this unknown and unwanted situation. In the end, anger overshadowed empathy, and she decided to do nothing at all for the moment. She swept into her own bedroom and shut the door. Sitting at her desk, she pulled the unfinished script from its drawer and prepared to focus on work. After staring at the pointless words for many long minutes, she finally fell into the rhythm of the characters and began to scratch her quill across the paper.

The duke was on the point of declaring himself to a chambermaid when the sound of knocking drifted across Gwendolyn's consciousness. Fighting down fond irritation—for she could not doubt Max was intruding yet again, and she would have to put him straight, though she felt a secret delight at his solicitousness—she set down the quill and went to the entrance. From the corner of her eye she saw Camille open her bedroom door a crack, sight her mother, then close the door soundlessly.

Feeling a wave of ire at this fresh insult, she twisted the knob and pulled recklessly, beginning, "Now, Max—"

"Now I'm not Max," said Roderick with a disarming smile, his shoulders lifting in a shrug, his hands stretching outward. A deep bruise darkened his left cheek.

"Oh," she said.

"I've come to apologize."

"Really?" She hoped her tone would convey how little that meant to her.

"Please, may I come in? I won't stay long, beautiful lady."

"I don't know, Mr. Vaughan. This is really not the best time."

"Oh, please, I beg you to be kind to one who deserves no kindness, but who can't sleep at night for counting his sins. Won't you have pity on me?" When she still hesitated, he added fetchingly, "It's my intention to mend fences with everyone I've offended, including Max. But I must begin with you."

She waved him in with a suspicious look. From everything she knew about this man, there could be no relying on him. Yet he had a decidedly contrite expression . . . If things were to be right in Max's life, she would not be the one to stand in the way.

"Thank you, ma'am," he said, walking to one of the chairs without invitation and sitting. "I want us to be friends, and after yesterday, I'm beginning to wonder if I have any in this entire city." He laughed briefly.

Following him grudgingly, she stationed herself behind the opposite chair and rested her hands on its back. "You mentioned something about making amends to Max."

"Yes. I said some things to you yesterday that I'm ashamed of. And others to him that were worse." He patted his cheek with his fingertips and chuckled self-deprecatingly. "You can see how much worse."

She said nothing, but shifted her weight from one foot to the other. He hurried on. "Anyhow, I want to start over. I didn't understand how it is between you and Max—"

"There is nothing to understand," she said immediately. "We're good friends only." Her cheeks grew warm as she remembered how Roderick had seen them last night, her lips red with Max's kisses, her hair flying loose about her shoulders.

"Truly?" His tone was mild, as if he had noticed nothing as he'd passed by her room. "That's what he said, too. Well, no matter. I want us *all* to be good friends. Therefore, I suggest we spend tomorrow evening together at my expense: you and your daughter and Max and myself."

"That's kind of you but entirely unnecessary."

"Come now, Mrs. Devane," he said persuasively. "You're not still worried that I will press unwanted attentions upon you any longer, are you? Because I swear I won't. Truly. Upon my honor. No, you may not trust that. I swear upon my life!"

She smiled faintly. His exaggerated charm had little effect upon her, but she sensed strong emotion behind his begging eyes and roguish grin. If it were true, if he really *did* intend to call a truce, then refusing his invitation would be a cold act.

While she debated, Roderick added, "I know my cousin. He won't come unless you do, and you don't want to stall a family reconciliation, do you? I thought we might see that play again, *Lydia's Secret,* unless you are tired of it. Several people have told me how amusing it is, and since I only saw the first half last week, I wanted to give it another try."

Gwendolyn instantly softened. He could not have suggested anything that would please her more. She was susceptible to compliments for her creations from any source, she acknowledged to herself with rueful insight. And the prospect of exposing Max to one of her works was decidedly enticing. Perhaps he would modify his opinion if he saw her words in action.

"I would be pleased to accept," she said, "but first I must speak with my daughter. Camille hasn't been feeling well." *And might not want to go anywhere with her mother right now.* When he nodded and continued to wait expectantly, she added, "If you will give us a few moments, I'll send word to your room."

"I understand," he said, rising. "I'll be waiting anxiously."

When Roderick was safely in the hall, she walked to Camille's chamber, took a deep breath, and tapped on the wood.

"Go away," said a muffled, tear-choked voice. "Please."

"We need to talk," Gwendolyn replied firmly. "May I come in?"

Reluctantly, the girl gave her assent, and Gwendolyn entered. As she did, Camille scooted herself against the headboard and pressed her eyes with the heels of her hands. Gwendolyn sat on the bedside chair, viewing her child's wrinkled muslin and swollen face with equal measures of compassion and pain.

"Were you ill this morning at all?" she asked softly.

Resentment boiled in Camille's eyes for an instant, but her lashes quickly covered the expression. "No."

"You lied to me." Gwendolyn's gentle voice throbbed. "You've never done that before." Horrible seconds passed. "Have you?"

"Oh, no, Mama," she said quickly, sounding much like her old daughter again.

"But why have you done so now? Did you want to be with Mr. Munroe so badly that you would risk violating our trust in one another?"

"Yes!" Camille burst out resentfully. "Last night at dinner he invited me to see the watermill and Bathwick today, and I knew you expected me to go to awful old Halleydale and wouldn't let me do what I wanted, even though Miss Munroe was to walk with us, and no one could ever think anything was amiss except you!"

Gwendolyn recoiled as if she had been slapped. "What have I done to warrant this opinion? Did I not let you dine with him last evening or travel with him to the picnic?"

"Yes, but only because his entire family was present at dinner. And as for the picnic! You wanted to refuse, but everyone pressed you into it. Then last night you wouldn't permit me to attend the Upper Rooms, and I believe it was because you thought he might come, too."

"The skies were pouring rain, Camille! We *were* planning to go; you know Sir Hastings was to accompany us. How can you imagine I was trying to keep you from Mr. Munroe?" She stared tensely at her daughter. *"Was* he planning to be attend? Had you arranged an assignation?"

"There, you see?" Camille declared. "I knew you didn't want me to spend time with him. You treat me like an infant!"

"You are only sixteen," Gwendolyn reminded sternly.

"Sixteen, sixteen, *sixteen!* As if I don't know it, as if that's all that matters! I don't believe you would feel differently if I were twenty, would you?" Camille's voice began to tremble. "You want me beside you forever so that you won't be alone!"

Gwendolyn rose slowly, tears stinging her eyes. Had anyone told her yesterday that Camille could be so unjust, so hurtful, she would have laughed. A part of her wanted to lash back, to deny all; but there was enough truth in her daughter's speech to make that impossible. And more was at stake here than her own wounds. Every instinct shouted that the future of their bond depended on what she said during the next few moments. In her most secret depths, she had known this day would come in spite of her years of warnings, her careful teaching and guidance; but she'd never dreamed it would be so soon. She felt as though she stood on land while her daughter peered downward from a ship's deck, the boat slowly edging out to sea.

"You're being unfair," she said quietly. "You are the center of everything I do, but that doesn't mean I won't let you go when . . . when you are old enough and find someone deserving."

Saying the words made them true, she knew that, though her heart leaped and quivered like a frightened rabbit at the saying. She had never wanted to voice such sentiments. Still, it was that or watch the ship disappear over the horizon. Camille had too much of her father, and far, far too much of her mother in her to make it otherwise.

The girl was watching her with doubtful eyes. "What if I don't find someone deserving?" Seconds passed as tension built between them. "What if I only find someone I can't live without, as you did with Papa?"

As she crossed her arms, Gwendolyn's nails dug hidden creases into the tender flesh above her elbows. "I would advise you against it, because a mother never wants her child to be hurt. But if you were determined to go ahead . . . then I would give you my love as I always have," she said, the future yawning bleak and empty before her, a bottomless well of lonely years stretching into forever.

The girl's lips moved soundlessly for a moment. "You would?"

"What did you think—that I would banish you like some overwrought character I might create for the stage?" When Camille's face brightened, Gwendolyn managed a tremulous smile. "That doesn't mean you may run off tonight, mind."

"Even if I wanted to do that, Mr. Munroe would not. He is much too sensible and steady, truly he is, Mama. He is the most grown-up young man and says the most amusing things! And of course he's very nice to look upon, which I'm sure you've noticed already, for who could not? I think you will like him when you know him better!''

''I already like him, my dear,'' Gwendolyn said, her mood lifting slightly at her daughter's enthusiasm. ''But you are still too young to see him without a group present. You must never to do things in secret again.''

''Yes, ma'am,'' the girl said with a drastically chastened expression. ''I never shall.''

Gwendolyn could not help smiling at this, a genuine smile. ''All right, miss; that's going it too strong.'' They embraced briefly, and she smoothed a loose strand of Camille's hair behind her ear. ''Now, to show you my good faith, here is an idea. We've been invited to attend *Lydia's Secret* tomorrow night with Mr. Vaughan and Sir Hastings. But what would you say to attending the Upper Rooms tonight? They hold the Fancy Ball on Thursdays, you know. I could send a note down to Max—I mean, Sir Hastings, to escort us—and also tell Bryce that you are going. Perhaps he would like to accompany us.'' As joy leaped into Camille's face, Gwendolyn added jestingly, ''Only if you feel sufficiently recovered from your illness now. I wouldn't want you to suffer a relapse.''

When Max opened the door and saw his cousin, he immediately moved to close it. Roderick lunged against the wood and struggled to keep the narrowing crack open, laughing as he did so.

''Not so fast, old boy. I've come to apologize.''

''Get your boot out of the doorway if you want to keep that foot. I'm not interested in your apologies.''

''Really? Mrs. Devane was. *She* accepted them and is even accompanying me to the theatre tomorrow night. Are you going to let her go alone with me, or will you allow me to come in and invite you to join us?''

Max eyed his cousin narrowly, but after a second's hesitation, he stepped back. Roderick entered, adjusting his lapels and sleeves with a flourish as he surveyed the bedroom.

"This room is not bad at all. I'll have to request it when I return to Bath."

"You sound as if you're thinking of leaving."

"Yes," Roderick said airily, as though it were a small matter. "I'm growing bored."

Maxim's stomach knotted into what felt like a fist. If Roderick left, he had no excuse to remain, either. Or none that Uncle Harry would understand. All this time squandered, and he had nothing to show for it except a hole in his heart the size of London. Certainly he had come no closer to finding the formula.

And worse, he was hardly nearer finding Gwendolyn's attempted killer, either. Perhaps she was right; perhaps all of it had been a wild mistake. But he wasn't willing to take a chance on her life by making suppositions. He *had* to remain until something was resolved. His uncle would have to be patient.

But the old man wouldn't be, Max knew. A letter from his mother had been awaiting him when he returned from Halleydale. When did Max plan to come home? she asked. Harold was growing anxious with both his nephew and son gone. Gently she reminded him of the disappointment her brother experienced daily concerning Roderick. Now his eyes clouded whenever Maxim's name was mentioned. "Return soon, son," she had concluded. "Hurry."

None of this would have the slightest effect on Roderick, however, and Max feigned a mask of indifference, striving to match his cousin's bland expression. "I'm sorry to hear it. What's wrong? Has your legendary prowess with the ladies proved ineffective?"

For a fraction of an instant, a glacial look entered Roderick's eyes. He glanced away quickly and ambled to the center of the room, his gaze continuing to move restlessly.

"It happens sometimes. Not often, but enough to keep me humble."

Max gave a single grunt of laughter. "If this is humble, my mind boggles to imagine proud."

Roderick cocked an eyebrow and viewed him with good

humor. "You had a hand in that failure, I think. Mrs. Devane prefers you. Oh, but I forget. You are only friends, which explains your presence in her room last night."

The baronet's arms fell to his sides. "I think you had best tell me what you came to say and get out."

"All right." A faint smile played at Roderick's lips. "I was off the mark yesterday with my comments about your *friend,* and I beg your pardon for it. *And* for that colorful eye you have there."

"Very nice, Roderick. It's a pity I don't put any value in your remorse. I've heard your prattle before and know how much you mean it."

"You're too hard, cousin." He walked to the window and looked out. "We're not getting any younger, either of us. I'm tired of all this . . . bickering, or whatever it is between us. I want to start fresh."

"Do you have a handkerchief on you? I need to wipe my tears."

"Oh, you may laugh," Roderick said lightly, still not looking at Max but keeping the countryside square in his vision. "But then you will miss an opportunity to heal the breach in this family. Isn't that what you've always wanted?"

Max hesitated, wondering if he detected a new note of sincerity in his relative's tone. But then he thought, *No.* "I've always wanted it, but you haven't. And I don't believe you do now."

"You cut me to the quick. Let me prove it to you by making the first move." He issued his invitation formally, emphasizing again that Mrs. Devane and her daughter had already accepted, and that he planned to accompany them to *Lydia's Secret.*

The baronet could not disguise his interest. He had intended to see Gwendolyn's play before leaving Bath. He could hardly allow Roderick to escort them alone.

When Max assented, Vaughan expressed his satisfaction and breezed to the door. Max followed more slowly, measuring him with shrewd eyes. This invitation to make a truce was unlike his cousin. Something was afoot with him.

"I'll have Henderson spruce up my Weston jacket for you

tomorrow,'' Roderick said as he entered the hall. ''I say, just where the devil *is* your man? He should have been here days ago.''

''I've been wondering that myself.''

''Well, now you know the real reason why I'm leaving Bath: to have an exclusive wardrobe again.'' His interest quickened as a young woman wearing a green and white uniform approached them. ''And what lovely vision is this?''

Max recognized the maid, Betty. She grinned widely and bobbed a curtsy, nearly dislodging her cap. The fingers of one hand flew upward to rescue it, and, giggling delightedly, she extended a letter toward him with the other.

''The note's from Mrs. Devane, sir,'' she said. ''I'm to wait for a reply.''

''How interesting,'' Roderick commented, his appreciative gaze running over the maid from head to toe. ''A letter from a *friend,* Max. What does your kind friend want, do you imagine?''

Max glared at Roderick as he accepted the missive, keeping it folded.

''But then, it's not my business, is it?'' Roderick said agreeably, easing back a step while exchanging a long, friendly glance with the pretty maid. ''I have never seen such glorious hair,'' he told her.

She blushed and smiled. ''Oh, sir, it's only brown.''

''Only brown?'' He cast an incredulous look at Max. ''Did you hear that, cousin? She calls that brilliant shade of chestnut *only brown.* I had sooner call Buckingham Palace only a cottage.''

Betty gave a peal of laughter.

''Roderick,'' Max ground between his teeth.

''All right, I'm leaving. I have some business to attend to overnight, but I'll see you tomorrow evening.'' And with a deep bow for the maid, who responded with an elegant curtsy marred only by waves of laughter, he walked away.

Max watched him with a knowing look, imagining the kind of business his cousin planned. Now Roderick's sudden generosity became understandable. Someone new had entered his life. Turning his attention to the note, Max read it within seconds.

"Come in," he said to the maid, leaving the door wide. "It will only take a moment to write an answer." He hurried to the desk. "Sit down if you like."

While he wrote, she strolled toward the chairs, but stopped when she neared him. Her breath drew inward as she reached for one of the many scattered sheets of paper on his desk.

"Oh, Sir Hastings," she said in an awe-filled voice. "This . . . these are beautiful." She began to shuffle through the others. "All of your drawings are of Mrs. Devane, aren't they? You've made her look like a fairy queen, you have. And ooh! This one I really like! The woods are all around her, and the little animals are hiding behind the trees! It looks like she's lost! How did you learn to—"

He clamped a hand over her wrist. "My sketches are for me alone," he said with a penetrating stare, though he was secretly pleased that she admired them. He liked to imagine they were good. It had been years since he'd had the will to draw anything, and he had feared his skill might be lost.

She immediately restored the sketches to the desk. "Pardon me, sir, I shouldn't do such things, I know. Everybody tells me I'm too curious, but I never saw such drawing, never in all my life!"

"Thank you. Now sit down, will you?"

She obeyed, though he saw from the corner of his eye that she perched restlessly on the edge of the seat, repinning her cap in place, then drumming rhythms on her knees. What a storehouse of energy she was; enough restless distraction to cause him to make an error in his writing and to have to start again. Finally, he finished writing his acceptance of Gwendolyn's invitation, and, standing with a satisfied air, he handed the note to her.

She almost leaped for it. "I'll take it right down."

"Thank you, Betty." He walked her to the door. "I hope I didn't sound gruff a moment ago."

"Oh, you didn't bother me," she assured him, her dimples

appearing and disappearing like magic. "You're a nice gentleman, you are." Bobbing, she started to move down the corridor, then paused abruptly. "Oh, sir? Did that man ever find you the other day?"

He had almost closed the door when he heard her question. Now he swung it open again and stepped into the corridor.

"What man?"

"The one who was looking for you." She made a florid gesture. "You know, that little man." Her eyes grew wide as Max paced forward to tower over her.

"When was this?"

She pressed one hand to her heart. "Why, it was the morning after you first came, I think. He asked what room you was resting in, and . . . I . . ."

He grabbed her shoulders. "Yes? And you what? Tell me, woman!"

"You're affrightening me, sir! Did I do wrong?"

"No, no." He cursed himself for his excitement and released her, then begged her pardon in a calmer voice. "Where did you tell him I was?"

"Why, in Mrs. Devane's room, which is where I thought you was staying. I thought you might be her brother or something. I didn't know you'd taken a room close to Miss Lucy. Not then, I didn't. I been worried about it ever since, that I sent him to the wrong place and he might've missed you. He did, didn't he?"

Her skin flared pink, and she put her hands to her cheeks. "And now I've made you miss something important, haven't I? There you go again, Betty, making a mess of things like always! Though he didn't look important, so I don't know how I could be expected to . . . Are you very angry with me, Sir Hastings? Sir?"

Chapter Twelve

As she stepped from the sedan chair beneath the portico of the Upper Rooms, Gwendolyn braced herself for an evening that promised to bring a headache. There were far too many people present for it to be otherwise, even if the month was an off-season one. But her spirits lifted nevertheless; the gaiety of the attendees, the sheer richness of their fine clothes and jewels, would buoy even the most ill-tempered of old mothers, and she hoped she was not that yet.

It was hard to know for certain, though. The day had been a wrenching one, the kind that signaled change for all time and held the potential of turning her into a shrew.

Her relationship with Camille had seemed so secure. For the past decade, her whole perception of life had narrowed to the two of them; just the two of them, standing alone against all Society. What a pretty dream it had been, but the dream had flown away, altered forever, and against her will, because it was not what her daughter wanted.

On the other hand, as if to balance that fissure, Gwendolyn had gone a long way toward making peace with her past.

Though she doubted she could ever forget Bernard's pathetic, evil face.

But it was Max who caused the greatest portion of her disquiet.

Eyeing his lean, virile frame as he stepped next to her, she experienced a rush of longing that nearly made her groan. Almost, almost she could give in and admit her love. But how much of that sentiment was caused by her newfound certainty that Camille would leave her one day? She could not cling to someone merely because she feared being alone. Such a reaction would cheat both him and her. It was better, much better, to hang onto her long-held ideas of independence.

She could always get a dog for company. Or a cat. Cats were nice; at least they did not slobber over one.

The thought did not amuse her in the least. She seized Max's arm and shuffled closely behind Camille and Bryce through the octagon and then into the magnificent blue and yellow ballroom. As always, she was struck by the vast proportions of the palace: over one hundred feet long and almost half that in width and heighth. The upper level was lined with Corinthian columns, and from the ceiling hung five of Mr. Parker's breathtaking chandeliers.

She could never admire them without thinking of the ones which had formerly hung there, fashioned by another designer. During a ball, a section of one of the chandeliers had fallen upon the dancers. The offending creations had quickly been replaced. Even so, she could not help breathing a prayer that nothing of the like would happen tonight. Or that the pressure of the crowd would not cause the walls themselves to collapse. There must be more than a thousand people filling the ballroom, card and tea rooms. Many entire villages housed fewer people.

Perhaps it was the mother in her that caused such worry, she thought, her eyes moving restlessly to find empty seats among the tiers lining the walls. Or mayhap she was reaching an age when hearing chatter and music from every quarter no longer appealed. That was a quelling idea, but reinforced by her infrequent sightings of her daughter's face, which had an expression as near ecstasy as seemed possible for this side of sainthood. Certainly she didn't mind the noise, and neither did young Bryce, apparently.

"There's a spot," Max said, gesturing toward one of the higher tiers. "We'll have to climb, but you'll be able to see the dancers from there."

She heard a flat note in his voice and glanced at him curiously. He had not seemed his usual self since he'd rejoined them an hour ago. Perhaps he was only tired as she was after their long drive and the draining events that had taken place. She nodded and touched Camille's arm, and the party made their way through the throng to take their seats.

"This is wonderful, isn't it?" her daughter said happily, and Gwendolyn smiled in reply.

The girl looked like a vision in her white embroidered muslin with its simple train. From the way Bryce's eyes constantly swept over her, he thought so, too, Gwendolyn saw with less pleasure. But that was normal, utterly normal. She would not let Bryce's roaming gaze spoil her evening. This was the first test of her new resolve.

Loosen the strings, Gwendolyn. Let go!

A new set was forming, and Camille and Bryce bubbled past them to join the dancers, Gwendolyn removing her knees from their path only just in time. She gave Max a rueful look.

"Would you like to dance?" he asked, leaning closely so she could hear.

"Perhaps the next one."

She exchanged waves with a pair of older ladies of her acquaintance sitting in the row beneath them.

"Keeping an eye on your daughter," he said with a thin smile.

"No, not at all. Just . . . catching my breath."

"As you say." A pensive look came into his eyes as he watched the dancers begin their movements. "I'm pleased you were able to work through matters with Camille. I know it was a shock, finding out she only pretended to be sick. But after learning how things were for the two of you at Devane Place, I can't blame her for not wanting to go.''

"It wasn't that so much as her desire to spend time with Bryce,'' Gwendolyn said in ironic tones. "I don't think she was ever aware of her danger from Bernard. I tried to protect her from that.''

"As you've protected her from so many things. She's a fortunate girl to have a mother like you.''

The words fell from his lips like the tolling of a funeral bell. She gazed at his profile searchingly. Alarm began to trickle through her veins.

"What's wrong, Max?''

For a moment she thought he meant to deny that anything was the matter. But when he turned hollow eyes to hers, she knew with jolting certainty that something *was* terribly wrong. And suddenly she was afraid to find out what.

"I'm leaving Bath,'' he said.

She felt as if he had plunged a knife into her heart. The music, the loud conversations surrounding her, faded to a dim buzz; she could hear only him, see only him.

"You *are?* But I thought—''

"That I meant to stay until I found the man who tried to murder you?''

She nodded, wondering at the bitter tone in his voice.

He laughed humorlessly. "For days I've pressured you to think of potential enemies. I've made you imagine your writing could have caused great harm, enough to drive someone to murder. Today I even coerced you into revisiting a devil who hurt you deeply in the past. And all along you've said you had no enemies, that Deevers must have made a mistake when he put the serpent in your room.''

"If you think I'm upset because we haven't found the villain yet, I am. But I don't blame you in the least.''

"I should have listened to you. Maybe you were correct when you talked about men falling into their roles. I guess I'm no different from everyone else. I thought I was supposed to be right. I wasn't.'' He scanned her face with tender regret. ''You were.''

''I don't care who was right or wrong,'' she said breathlessly. ''We've both been conducting our search blindly and doing the best we can. What have you learned?''

He stared at her for a moment, then averted his eyes to the dancers again. ''I'm the one who was supposed to die.''

''What?'' she cried, so loudly that the gentleman nearest her turned curiously.

''Deevers approached the maid that morning and asked where I was staying. She had seen me in your room the previous afternoon and assumed I was still there.''

''He wanted to know where *you* were?'' she repeated, still unable to believe it. He nodded silently. ''But . . . but who would want to''—she glanced aside and lowered her voice, moving closer to him—''who could possibly want to harm *you?*''

Max's mouth tightened into a grim line. ''I'm finding that as difficult to consider as you did.''

''Oh, I cannot believe this, Max. Perhaps the maid misunderstood—''

''I don't think so.''

A gentleman of middle years was climbing determinedly toward them, and Gwendolyn forced down exasperation as he blundered his way past.

''But how could you have offended anyone so deeply?'' she continued when the man was a safe distance away. ''Do you have any ideas at all?''

''My contact with the outside world is limited,'' Max said slowly, seeming to pull the words from some deep place inside. ''I seldom see anyone. Other than my family.'' His jaw set.

She studied him anxiously, a horrible conviction growing. ''Oh, no. No, Max. You can't be thinking . . .''

''Can't I? We've been rivals for half a lifetime. He resents my relationship with his father. Maybe he thinks the old man means to change his will in my favor. I don't know. Who can say what goes on in Roderick's mind?''

"But it could not be," she said with sudden hope. "Why would Roderick instruct Deevers to place the serpent in my room? He knew where you were staying."

"For a while, that settled my suspicions as well. Then I remembered that Deevers is a complete sot by all accounts. Roderick must have told him my room number, and he forgot. Which explains why he asked the maid."

Her thoughts churned desperately. There had to be another solution than this terrible one. "Didn't the man at the circus say the stranger had an accent?"

"Another of his games. Roderick has enjoyed imitating foreigners from boyhood. His Italian accent is his best."

Pressing her fingers to her cheeks, she blinked rapidly, trying to keep tears at bay. *Please God, let him be wrong.* This was too awful too contemplate; that a family could become so irretrievably divided that one of its members would try to kill another. And that it should happen to Max, the most caring, thoughtful, and honorable man she had ever met! It was unthinkable. This would kill him without the necessity of an assassin. He held deep affection for his cousin; she knew he did, had seen the humorous light and swiftly masked disappointment that came into his expression whenever he spoke of him. She could not guess at the grief he must be feeling at this moment. Would that there were something, anything she could do to alleviate it. But he looked beyond comfort, as if he had retreated into a dark, inner region that no one could touch.

"Is it possible, Max?" She linked her arm through his, wanting to fling both arms around his neck and draw him next to her heart. "Roderick is not the man you are." Striving hard, she injected hopefulness into her voice. "He doesn't possess your integrity and loyalty, and goodness knows he's one of the most outrageous flirts I've ever met; but do you really believe he could hate you so much? I don't think so. Why, that grey jacket you are wearing is proof alone. I know it is his; he wore it the first night he approached Camille and me."

"It's not so hard to conceive, that such a long rivalry could grow into hate. Though God knows there's no reason for him to be jealous of me.''

"Yes, there is," she said immediately. "You are everything he is not."

This brought a brief smile. "Well, I won't say you're wrong about Roderick. I've learned that much—not to cast aside your judgments simply because . . .''

"I am a woman," she finished for him, as he seemed unwilling. She could hear traces of resentment in her tone even now.

"You are that," he said, stroking her face with a glance that suddenly grew several degrees warmer. "The rarest of women. I've never met anyone so strong yet so soft." Looking down at her arm resting within his, he placed his other hand over her fingers. "You are knowledgeable, but not haughty about it." His throat worked, and the aching look in his eyes brought her tears closer to the surface. "Refined, yet not proud." His voice lowered to a whisper, and she leaned nearer to hear him, her temple touching his shoulder, her eyes stinging. "Poised, but never, never cold."

"Oh, Max," she said in a broken voice.

He was telling her goodbye. Here in the middle of the largest room in Bath, with a thousand people swirling around them, he was pouring out his heart to her and knowing there could be no happy ending, no resolution to anything.

"But now I have to leave," he continued relentlessly. "My remaining might put you and Camille in jeopardy."

There was truth in what he said. The mistake with the serpent was ample evidence. Were it only herself she had to worry over, she would beg him to stay. But she could never, ever put her daughter in danger.

"When?" she cried. "How soon must you go?"

"Saturday morning. I'm staying long enough to see your play."

"But your cousin is to accompany us. Perhaps he means to—"

"He won't attempt anything in a crowd. We'll be safer there

than anywhere. He's not that mad. If he tries again, he'll wait until we're alone.''

"Oh, don't travel back with him. Promise you won't!"

The set had ended. Camille and Bryce were returning, looking flushed, innocent, and heartbreakingly young.

One of Max's eyebrows crept upward. "I thought you didn't believe he was my enemy."

Ignoring his attempt at a bantering tone, she said quickly, "And you will be returning to live in the same house with him. Can you not go somewhere else? Just for a while?"

"What, and leave my mother to fend for herself? And what reason could I possibly give my uncle?" He looked ill suddenly. "He mustn't know what I suspect."

"But, Max, you will be in constant danger!"

"I'll be careful, my dear."

"You can't do anything else, can you?" she said miserably. "You wouldn't be yourself if you did."

"Gwendolyn. Let's forget all of this. I want to—"

"Mama!" Camille swished into the seat beside her mother, and Bryce squeezed past to sit on the girl's other side. "Did you see how I was almost tripped by that girl in the yellow dress? Have you ever seen anyone so clumsy? Though I felt sorry for her; she didn't mean it and kept apologizing. Do you think it will be all right if Mr. Munroe and I dance another set?"

With effort she returned to her daughter's world. "I see no harm in it in this crowd; who will be counting how many times you stand up together? But rest a while and save our seats. Sir Hastings and I are going to dance."

The baronet escorted her willingly. "You must have known what I wanted to say," he told her as they approached the dance floor. "I want to hold you in my arms tonight. I want to hear you laugh."

"Making memories," she murmured.

He did not hear her. "Pardon?"

She summoned all the fortitude in her being and produced a grand smile. "And I want to see your drawings of me."

He gazed at her with surprise, then irritated certainty. "Betty."

"Who else?" The music began, a country dance. She looked expectantly.

"The little chatterbox," he said with a measure of strained amusement, then took her hand in his.

By half-past twelve, Gwendolyn looked ready to dissolve. Max suspected her weariness did not stem from their long day so much as the emotional toll it had extracted. After a whispered consultation with her, he suggested they depart early. She agreed readily, and though the younger couple's disappointment could not be missed, they were gracious enough to acquiesce without complaint.

As the ball remained in full swing, chairs were easily hired, and the gentlemen began the long walk back to The Allemande beside the porters, speaking now and then to their ladies, their voices dropping hollowly into the darkness like stones in a well.

Once within the walls of the Allemande, Bryce invited them to a midnight supper in his parents' apartment. They never slept before two, he declared, and had requested he bring them up. Gwendolyn pled fatigue, but gave her permission for Camille to join the Munroes for a half-hour only. After seeing the young couple disappear up the stairs, she turned to Max.

"Those drawings," she said, her voice wobbling. "There might not be a chance tomorrow to see them."

Max looked at her steadily, then took her hand and led the way to his room, saying nothing, but intently aware of her gentle breaths coming faster. He opened the door and lit the lamps while she waited, then motioned her to his desk, his heart drumming.

"I wanted them to be better," he said, while she paged through them silently pausing at one, then the other.

"They are beautiful!"

Pleasure bolted through him. "They are not, but the subject of them is."

"No, really, Max," she said with excitement. "I recall your telling me that you once liked to paint. Have you done anything recently?"

"Not in years."

"But whyever not? You're obviously very talented."

It was absurd how her compliments pleased him. Yet there was pain as well. "I haven't had time."

She gave him a searching look that set off uncomfortable echoes inside. You have been given a great gift. To waste it seems . . ."

"Well, go on," he said, feeling scorched at her disapproval. "Scold away; I can bear it."

A small smile flickered at her lips, then died. "To not use your talent seems a crime to me."

"I use it, never fear. Every day at the factory, designing glassware."

Her head tilted as she appraised him. "You speak with bitterness. Do you not like your work?" She frowned suddenly. "Oh, you don't! I can see it from your face. Oh, Max! You believe you must do this work for your uncle, is that it? I know how obliged to him you feel for his taking you into his home."

As she reached for his hands, he felt something give within him, and, suddenly, he gave voice to emotions he seldom spoke about: his old desire to paint; his longing to restore Hastings Hall to his mother. Words flowed from him, swept along by Gwendolyn's sympathetic eyes, for what seemed forever; but it could not have been longer than a moment or two that he spoke. Every second that passed brought him closer to his companion. She understood as no one ever had. He saw it in her glistening eyes; he felt it through the warmth of her hands.

When he finished, she leaned closer to him as though drawn by a tide of eagerness. "You think you cannot support your mother and yourself with your art, but I believe otherwise. Oh, I understand that it's difficult to make a name for oneself and have patrons lining up for portraits or the like, though I won't say that's beyond you. But there are many other ways to be creative and successful, too.'' Her brow creased in that adorable manner she had when thinking deeply. He loved that expression, he realized abruptly. ''For an example, have you thought of illustrating books? Your drawings are better than many I've seen in print. I mean, not because they are of me, but . . .'' She released his fingers and held one of the sketches closer to the light, the one of her offering a crust of bread to a deer. ''Your style captures a sense of wonder. If I write a storybook for children sometime, would you consider—''

Max closed his lips over hers. The drawing slipped to the floor as she lifted her arms around his neck. Slowly, slowly, his hands made their way down her body and circled her waist, pulling her so closely that nothing could divide them; not responsibilities, not lack of trust, and especially not fear.

He was so lost in bittersweet pleasure that he did not hear the tapping at the door, which stood slightly ajar, nor the sound of it swinging open. But he could not miss the sound of Carleton's embarrassed cough or his uncle's scandalized, ''Maxim!''

With Gwendolyn's gasp ringing in his ears, Max veered toward the doorway, one hand lingering at her waist, his astonishment beyond measure. Had Bonaparte himself appeared in the hall, he would have been less surprised.

''Uncle Harry? What are you—?'' And now, worse; behind his uncle's large frame he saw two female figures. He moved toward them with the slowness of nightmare, unconsciously abandoning Gwendolyn and forcing a welcoming smile while his mind raced to imagine reasons for this inexplicable visit. ''Why, Mother . . . Felicity; why are you—? What is this, another family holiday?''

''Hardly,'' said his uncle in strangely condemning tones. ''We've come to see you. After riding hard for two days and waiting nearly three hours for your return, I might add.''

While he spoke, Max enfolded his mother in an embrace, sharply aware of her distressed look and the air of desperation of Felicity, who hovered beside her. When he moved to greet her, she turned away mysteriously, her face whitening, her freckles standing out like dots of ink on cream.

"I'm sorry you had to wait; had I known you were coming, I wouldn't have gone out."

Max heard a tremble in his voice he didn't like, but his uncle's scarcely contained rage was as tangible as Felicity's perfume and a hundred times less comprehensible. Swiftly he returned to Gwendolyn, who was in effect trapped in the center of the room and looking lost. Protectively, he put a hand to her back and brought her forward.

"Forgive my manners," he said to her, and was rewarded with a tiny, anxious smile. From the glassy expression in her eyes, he knew she worried about his family's perception of her presence in his room. He made hasty introductions, explaining pointedly that they had just returned from the ball, that he'd been showing her some sketches he'd made; that she would be meeting her daughter momentarily.

His mother greeted her warmly, Felicity murmured something he could not hear, and Harry viewed Gwendolyn with hard eyes.

"Sketches, eh?" he said. "That's one way of putting it."

Max bridled. "Mrs. Devane is a very dear friend of mine—"

"So I saw," Vaughan said bitingly.

"—and I won't permit you to speak like that—"

"*You* won't permit!"

"—to a lady, sir."

"Well, you'd best tell her your days with ladies are done," Vaughan growled, "as you're getting married."

Max stared at Harry, too stunned to speak. Beside him, Gwendolyn stiffened, her fingers drawing into a fist against the fabric of his sleeve. And then she sagged, ever so slightly, against his shoulder. Lady Hastings hurried forward to clasp her son's other arm in a gesture of support.

"Harry, calm yourself. You're behaving like an old lion."

"With good reason," he replied.

"What's this all about?" Max said, his voice growing strong with indignation. "Whom am I supposed to be marrying?"

"As if you didn't know!" cried Harry. "Dear God, could I have nourished such an animal beneath my own roof?"

"Hush, brother! You are speaking of my son. You can't doubt what a fine man he is. He's never done anything like this before."

"That we know of!"

The baronet felt as if his face was on fire. Surely the world had turned inside out. Or maybe he was dreaming. None of this made the slightest measure of sense. And then a sudden, horrifying conviction seized him, and it was confirmed by Felicity's continued silence, her refusal to meet his eyes.

"Felicity? Does this have anything to do with you?"

As an indignant sound burst from Harry's lips, Felicity's gaze slid to Max's, then fell. At the same instant, Carleton, who had been fluttering from bed to desk to window behind them, squawked and weaved a path to the door through the company.

"Well now, you've found him right and good, Mr. Vaughan, sir, so I'll be off until you need me, Sir Hastings; up in the servant's quarters, just send word, sir; I've brought your clothes as you ordered. Thank you, sir. Good night." And was gone.

Gwendolyn cleared her throat. "I—I'd better be going as well. My daughter will be wondering where I am."

Max looked at her, saw her eyes were bright with unshed tears. "I don't know what this is about," he said softly. "I don't."

She appeared to be on the verge of saying something, but Harry interrupted.

"You don't know what this is about, Max? Well, let me educate you. It's about making right a terrible wrong—"

"Don't, Harry," Anne Hastings said swiftly. "Think of Felicity."

"I am, but it's important for this woman to know before she's caught in his snare. If it's not already too late." He eyed Gwendolyn doubtfully. "I'll ask your discretion, madam, but

I'm guessing you'd like to know what kind of man is standing beside you. He has seduced an innocent young woman living beneath his own roof—a girl I'd promised to look after and keep safe from such shame as this. And now that she is with child, he thinks he can escape. Well, I'm here to show him he cannot!''

Chapter Thirteen

With a little cry, Gwendolyn broke away from Max and ran for the door. He moved after her, but was slowed by Harry's firm grip on his shoulders.

"Don't go after her. You've done enough damage."

"No, *you've* done the damage." Max ripped free and raced after Gwendolyn, catching her at the stairs.

"Let me go!"

She struggled to release herself from his hands, but he held onto her arms heedlessly. He had never seen anyone look so crushed. Her distress struck him like a blow, magnifying until he almost cried out.

"It's not true. None of it is true."

"Oh, Max, why would she lie about a thing like that?"

"I don't know, but you have to believe me. I've never touched her."

The force of hurt wrath that whipped from her eyes nearly made him stagger. "The deed is bad enough, but to deny it is beyond all reckoning! If you don't release me, I'll scream the house down!"

He straightened slowly, his hands falling to his sides, and stepped back a pace.

"There's nothing I can say that will make you believe me." He heard the wondering note in his voice without surprise. Something told him that wonderment would be the last thing he felt for a long while.

She shook her head and fled up the stairs. He watched until the hem of her skirt disappeared past the landing.

The brief walk to his room passed without awareness.

Harry waited outside his door. Max glanced at him stonily and entered. His mother was seated on the edge of the bed. Felicity had braced one hand on the desktop as she paged through his drawings. She bent to retrieve the one that had fallen to the floor when he'd kissed Gwendolyn a lifetime ago. In the act of placing it with the others, her eyes met his. He marked a brief flare of some indefinable emotion followed by, he was certain, shame.

"Felicity," he said softly, entreatingly.

"Don't try to condemn her for telling the truth." Harry closed the door and walked near, looking less frail than he'd seemed in recent months; looking quite belligerent and strong, in fact. Though age had bowed his shoulders to a small degree, he was almost as tall as Max. "Billings caught her trying to sneak off three nights ago while he was patrolling the grounds. Would have missed her if he hadn't varied his routine because of that poacher who's been thieving us blind. Foolish, silly lass, thinking she knew best, that leaving home was the answer. She didn't want to tell, wanted to protect you 'til the end. But I got her to admit it at last."

Felicity cast a look of desperation at Max, then collapsed into the chair, huddling sideways, her eyes averted from his steady glare.

Harry looked at her with pity. "I don't want details about how this came about under my roof. I'd just like to know why you abandoned her. I thought I knew you. I thought of you as a son, Max."

Max's heart twisted with the disappointment he heard in his

uncle's voice. Then rage. Did Felicity think he would go meekly, like a pig, to the slaughter?

"I have not touched her, Uncle, other than as a brother would. Tell him, Felicity."

As he turned toward her, Vaughan slapped him so violently that involuntary tears sprang to Max's eyes. He recoiled, his hand flying to his cheek, his lips parting in shock.

"Harry!" cried Lady Hastings, rushing to her son's aid. Max gently moved her aside, keeping his uncle in sight.

Vaughan scowled fiercely. "I won't listen to him while he tries to deny it, Anne. And I'm more let down than ever, sorry to say. Be a man about it, Max, for pity's sake."

"You said you think of me as a son," the baronet declared acidly. "I thought fathers had at least enough faith in their children to hear them." Still feeling the sting of his uncle's blow, Max stepped back and lashed out. "Why are you so silent, Felicity?"

Vaughan sighed wearily, suddenly looking his age. "Leave her alone. You'll have to marry her anyway, unless you plan to lose your home and position, and God forgive you for making me put it like that. You're not to leave this city until we've posted the banns and made my ward respectable. In that manner, no one in Blackpool need ever know. You'll simply come back married. We'll let on we knew about the wedding, that you wanted to keep it secret to avoid fuss."

"This cannot be happening," Max whispered, and went blindly to sit on the bed. When Lady Hastings nestled beside him, he asked, "Is it possible you don't believe me, either?"

He watched his mother's elegant face struggle through a variety of emotions. She cared deeply for Felicity, he knew. "Darling, I—I've always trusted your word. But Felicity is in very great trouble."

What was she saying? Did she expect him to marry as an act of kindness? The urge to run shafted through him. To run and keep running, for he didn't know anyone anymore.

"I need to be alone," he said.

"That I can understand." Harry said. "We're all tired.

Tomorrow we can speak about the details. Just give me your word of honor you won't run off in the night.''

"You trust my word?" he asked bitterly.

"Now that you understand how the land lies."

"I won't run," he said quietly, looking at Felicity with frigid, glittering eyes.

"Don't be thinking of bothering the poor girl, either," Harry warned, pausing in the doorway. "I've put your mother and her together."

Felicity was the last to file past him. "Why didn't you bring me to Bath when I asked you?" she whispered.

This must be what it feels like to know the hangman's noose awaits.

Shortly after daybreak the next morning, Max rose from the chair beside the French doors, went to the wash basin, and splashed water over his face, then ran his fingers through his hair. Good enough, he decided, glancing at the haggard, stubbled features in the mirror without emotion. With a persistent, dreamlike sensation, he walked through the halls, down the stairs, and to the dining room, which had just opened. Moving numbly through the unpopulated room, he sat at a small table beside one of the large windows. A sleepy-looking Andrew Hibbs brought him coffee but could not persuade him to partake of the sideboard's fragrant offerings.

As he sipped, he idly admired the workmanship of the mullioned windows and wondered who had crafted them. The thought was only a fleeting respite from the agonizing conflict tearing at his mind. A night of staring into the dark fields behind The Allemande had yielded no answers. Felicity had him tight in her net, that much was certain. The only solution he could imagine was a conference with her. He would force her to tell him the identity of the child's true father. And if she did not . . . He could not think beyond that.

"I hoped I would find you here," said a soft voice at his elbow.

Max sprang to his feet. "Gwendolyn!"

Surprised joy coursed through him. Unlike himself, she had dressed carefully, and the apricot color of her morning gown set off her shining, golden hair. Only the paleness of her complexion and a certain puffiness about the eyes gave evidence of the night's toll.

"May I join you?" she asked, her voice shaking the slightest amount. "I'll understand if you say no."

"Of course! Always." He rapidly pulled out the chair nearest him. She sat gracefully and, when Andrew hastened to their table and replenished Max's cup, ordered tea. This flurry of activity over, she lifted dark eyes to his wondering ones, giving him a look so piercingly direct that he felt his stomach clench with unbearable tension.

"You look tired," she said.

"I've been awake all night. Thinking."

"I can imagine. I've been awake most of the night, too."

"I'm sorry."

"I'm the one who is sorry, Max. I should never have left you as I did last evening. I behaved abominably, and I'm ashamed of myself. After all we've been through together and . . . meant to one another, my very first reaction was to doubt you."

After all we've meant to one another. He felt weak as a spring colt at her words. She did love him. Though she might deny it thirty times a day, he would still believe it. It seemed a window had opened inside him to admit a sunrise streaming with light.

Andrew bounded over with a tray containing a small pitcher of tea, cream, sugar cubes, and a plain white cup and saucer. She leaned back slightly while he poured her first cup and hurried away, as if he knew he intruded and wished to give them privacy.

"What changed your mind?"

Her brow creased briefly. "The memory of your face. The way you looked when you told me it was all a lie, and your disappointment when I failed to believe you . . . it haunted me the entire night long." She poured a wisp of cream into her tea, took spoon in hand, and stirred slowly. "This is not a justification, but when your uncle made his accusations, the very first thing I thought was: How could all of them be mistaken? What kind of woman would name the wrong man as father of her child?"

"I can't blame you for wondering that."

"But then, something else occurred to me. I've often railed against Society for its strictures on females, and sometimes for gentlemen as well, in the area of work and class consciousness and the like. But gentlemen enjoy such an unequal measure of freedom in their social lives that I'd never considered how vulnerable they are to something like this."

"Neither had I," he said with feeling.

She smiled briefly. "And there was one other incident that convinced me, when I calmed myself enough to think of it."

"What was that?"

Color stained her cheeks. "If the seduction of females was your goal, you missed an opportunity with me the other night." She lowered her glance to her cup, cradling the china in her hands. "And I hope I don't flatter myself when I say I believe your restrainment was due to honor and not lack of desire."

His fingers sought hers across the table. "There was no shortage of desire, my dear, I assure you."

"I didn't think I was mistaken." She pressed his hand, then removed hers slowly to her lap.

"So," he said expansively, leaning back in his chair, "you've made up your mind to believe me?"

"You spoke truth last night, didn't you?"

"I did."

"Then I believe you."

His eyes shone bright as a new leaf. How much had that leap of faith cost her? he wondered. Was she beginning to trust again? The possibilities brightened before him, then as quickly dimmed. Felicity's lies must be dealt with. The loss of his money . . . he had to come to terms with that. Gwendolyn had hinted that his penniless condition would not be a problem for her, but it was for him.

Downward, downward spiraled his thoughts.

Early risers were beginning to trickle into the dining room. A young couple sat nearby with two small children who appeared unusually quiet. Gwendolyn leaned closer.

"I'm very concerned about you, Max. What are you going to do about this tangle?"

"I don't know. I mean to speak with Felicity privately, if it can be arranged. She simply must tell me the truth."

"But if she doesn't? What will you do?"

"I wish I knew."

"You won't let her force you into something that will make you unhappy, will you? Don't ruin your life."

"You sound very concerned," he said, a smile playing at his lips. "One would almost think you care."

"You know I care deeply. Don't tease, Max."

"Should you continue in this vein, one might almost believe your feelings match mine," he said lightly. "I might even begin to think you love me."

Very, very slowly, her gaze lifted from her teacup to meet his. She blinked once, then looked away. "I think I'm going to visit the sideboard and see if they have muffins this morning," she said. "I'm quite hungry all of a sudden."

After breakfast, Gwendolyn and Max parted, promising to meet for the play no matter what happened. The baronet went on with the next order of business, marching to the clerk to learn his mother's room number, then taking the stairs two and three at a time in his eagerness to remove the noose tightening around his throat.

Lady Hastings was dressed and readying herself for breakfast when he knocked, but Felicity still lay in bed. She was awake, though, her head supported by a tower of cushions, and she watched him warily as he spoke to his mother.

"I need to speak with Felicity alone for a few minutes."

"I don't think so, Max," she said hesitantly. "It wouldn't be proper."

Her pronouncement wavered indecisively. It worried him, her lack of decision, of confidence. He remembered a different sort of mother from his childhood, one who laughed often and was unafraid to express her opinions. Their long-held dependence on her brother was at the heart of her insecurity, he was certain, and it formed the major reason for his desire to cut the tie.

"Proper?" he said gently. "I don't think we need worry about that at this point."

"I'm not well," Felicity said in strong voice. "Go away, Max. I have nothing to say to you."

"I think you do."

Lady Hastings' hands moved helplessly. "You see how it is, son. I can change nothing. Perhaps if you spoke to Harry. Though you will have to wait until tomorrow; he has gone to Brighton to talk with a man about a cheaper source of coal for firing the glass, I think it was."

He inhaled deeply. "That's all right, dear. I'll speak with her another time."

The relief on his mother's face wrung his heart. Turning, he walked to the end of the hall, slid into an alcove and prepared to wait. No more than five minutes passed before he heard the door open and close. Dashing a look, he saw Lady Hastings heading for the stairs. When she descended out of sight, he returned to the room and knocked.

"Who is it?" Felicity called.

"Room service, miss," he answered in a high, piercing voice. "I have a dozen red roses from an admirer."

The silence stretched for several seconds. Finally she said, "Come in and put them on the table. The door is open."

Max entered, lifting his brows. "Sorry, no bouquet. You really should tell my mother to lock the door."

She snorted. "I was afraid it was you, but I'm too sick to move."

He searched his heart for pity and found none. Stalking forward, he grabbed the desk's chair and dragged it to her bedside.

"Who is the father of your baby, Felicity?" he demanded.

"It doesn't matter," she said bitterly. "He won't admit it."

"I see. And your answer to this is: Accuse Max, he'll take care of things. Easy target there."

Her tongue caught between her teeth as she smiled. "You'd make a better father than he would, anyway."

"Am I supposed to be flattered by that? I won't let you do this to me."

"Oh, really? It seems I *am* doing it, and your precious uncle is helping. Did you see how easily he was duped? When he caught me trying to escape, I had to come up with a story quickly. He believed me in an instant and never gave you a chance to defend yourself. What does that say to your life of toil and sacrifice?"

"I suppose he never dreamed you'd lie about something like this."

"Hmmm. His problem. But *your* problem is worse. I tell you, Max, you'd do better to live your life as it pleases *you* rather than trying to please someone else. This is something I've always known. I can't fathom why it's so hard for you to understand."

"You'd better be careful how you advise me, Felicity. If I followed my real impulses, I'd be halfway to the Orient by now. Marrying you is *not* what I want."

"Oh, how bad could it be, Max?" She flashed a coquettish look at him. "Surely you remember all those stolen kisses beneath the hickory tree. Don't tell me you aren't the least bit interested."

"I'm not. Not in the least."

Her hands clasped over her heart. "How you wound me! What's wrong? That Devane woman?" Her voice throbbed with drama. "Another case of doomed love for Sir Maxim Hastings, to follow in the tradition of Lucy Munroe. And before her, the vicar's niece and the foreman's twin daughters."

"Your memory is too long. Everyone has a name or two in their past."

"You are such a romantic—never satisfied unless the female

provides a merry chase. You'd never know what to do with a real woman who desired you. *That* sort of relationship is too mundane for your high-blown ideals.''

He did not trouble himself to answer this. ''Why were you trying to escape, Felicity? Were you running off to join your lover? Because if you were, I'll be glad to drive you there, wherever it is. No village or continent is too far.''

Her lips turned downward in a pout. ''No, I was not trying to join my lover. I told you he will never admit what he's done. I was simply . . . running away.''

''To what?''

''A new life,'' she said stubbornly.

''What kind of new life?'' For the first time, he did feel a twinge of pity for her plight. ''You would have starved, idiot. You never have more than two or three pound notes to rub together.''

Averting her face, she mumbled, ''I would have done something. Something better than living at that house forever and ever.''

''But if you marry me, that's exactly what will happen.''

''How do you know? Are you a prophet? Things can change.''

''What things?'' he asked scornfully. ''The only changes occurring in my life recently seem to be moving from bad to worse. And that's what marriage to me will be like for you.''

''Oooh, so frightening. What will you do? Lock me in a closet? Beat me? Uncle Harry won't let you.''

''No, nothing so Gothic. Let's simply say you'd best find fulfillment in your one child, for you won't be getting any more from me.''

She regarded him in silence for a moment. ''That is only anger talking.''

''Have you ever known me to go back on my word?''

''Oh, you'll change your mind eventually,'' she said with a sudden catlike sensuousness, her body moving beneath the sheets. ''I won't let you remain a monk. But even so, I'm not changing my story, so you had best accept it.''

A flash of rage shook him. "This isn't a trick to gain a bridegroom, is it? You truly *are* with child?"

She pulled a face. "Do you really think I'd humiliate myself like this if I weren't? If you don't believe me, ask my maid. She knows I'm sick at least once every morning. Otherwise, I wouldn't have to go to such lengths. If only I could get out of Blackpool, if only I were not as I am ..." She stroked her still-flat stomach sadly through the bedspread. "I could have made a really good match, given the opportunity. But what chances have I had? None. There is no one to choose from. Or hardly anyone." Her glance flickered over Max. "Except you, of course."

Slowly, the baronet squared his shoulders. There was a high degree of truth in what she said; few men swung through their rather dull circle at Vaughan Manor, and most of them were married. Not that that necessarily excluded them, but surely Felicity was not *that* foolish. All life, everyday and social, centered around glassmaking. Which narrowed the field of prospective papas quite nicely.

"Who's the father, Felicity? Is he the new head groom? The gardener?"

She pursed her lips disdainfully. "Thank you so much for guessing the servants first. You don't credit me with much taste, do you?"

"You wouldn't be the first to be attracted by a square jaw and steady eye."

"I'm looking for a little more than jaws and eyes, Maxim."

"What else, then? Wealth? You certainly won't find that with me."

He watched as she started to say something, then closed her pretty mouth as if thinking better of it. Going to make some comment about his not being able to force Roderick into restoring the formula, he guessed; that would be a typical response, to dig and dig at him for his failure.

And suddenly he knew why she didn't voice her bantering criticism, why she didn't dare speak Roderick's name. Certainty tided through him, dead-on certainty, and along with it a fresh dose of disillusionment and crushing sorrow; for with all of his good-natured and not-so-good-natured competitiveness with his cousin, he admired and, he supposed, loved him. Moreover, to see the ruin of any man with talent and potential was hard to behold. And ruined he was, if Roderick had fallen to such depths: the deflowering of one in the protection of his own household, the failure to assume his responsibility. Not to mention the attempted murder of another. Max had almost forgotten his own danger during the past mad twelve hours.

He directed a grave look at Felicity. "I should have known."

"Known what?" she asked tensely.

"You wanted to come to Bath with me. Now it begins to make sense. You meant to gain a husband one way or the other. I'll wager you intended to start with the real father first, but failing that, I would have served."

"What *are* you talking about?"

"Say the name, Felicity. *Roderick.*"

"Roderick!" She gave a brittle laugh. "What a ridiculous notion! How do you manage to make up such things, Max?"

"Tell me who he is, then."

She turned her face away, her false merriment dying. "I don't have to tell you anything."

"You were afraid to accuse him in front of his father; that's why you didn't name him, isn't it?" He waited a moment. "All right, don't answer. I'll make certain he fulfills his obligation to you, never fear." He stood. "You know, chit, if my heart wasn't already taken, I'd consider getting you out of this spot of trouble. Truly I would. But I can't do it now. You were right about Gwendolyn Devane. I love her. What I feel for her makes those other relationships you mentioned seem like rehearsals for the true event. I've never known anything so powerful as this, and I pray to God it's what you feel for Roderick."

He moved quickly toward the door, turning away as swiftly as possible from her look of burning disappointment.

"No, no, Max, please stay away from him!" she begged, gesturing imploringly. "You don't understand anything."

With his hand resting on the doorknob, he paused. "Why don't you explain it to me, then."

Shaking her head, she covered her face with her hands. Max nodded grimly and left.

Chapter Fourteen

Shortly before eight that evening, Gwendolyn had nearly finished threading the silver bandeau through her hair when she glanced at the clock on her desk. "Are you almost ready, Camille?" she called. "Sir Hastings will be here any moment."

A waiflike figure padded into Gwendolyn's bedroom. Arms still raised, Gwendolyn spun toward the girl and viewed her with surprise. Although Camille was dressed in one of her finest gowns, a pale pink satin trimmed with Irish lace, her hair trailed over her shoulders in wild disarray.

"Don't say anything, Mama," Camille said mournfully. "No matter what I do, this frazzled mess won't obey me."

Quickly, Gwendolyn tied the ends of her bandeau, hid them among her sleek curls, and rose from her dressing table. "Sit and let me try."

Camille complied with a pronounced lack of enthusiasm. While Gwendolyn's fingers flew through her hair, she watched her mother's work in the mirror with a dead expression so uncharacteristic of her that Gwendolyn could not fail to notice.

"You look as though you were given a dose of sour medicine."

"I don't really feel like going tonight, Mama," Camille said, and sighed.

"Why not? Oh, don't tell me. It's because Mr. Munroe is not accompanying us. Sweetheart, you can't expect to spend every day with him."

"That's not it. Well, not precisely. It's only that he's returning to Oxford on Sunday." Her shoulders drooped.

"I see." Twirling a curl around her finger, Gwendolyn pinned it with the expertise of long practice. She had never felt the need for a personal maid, not that she could have afforded one before the past year. Arranging hair was a particular joy of hers, especially when the hair was Camille's, not only because the golden strands were silky and pliant, but because she could relive their history as she labored. How many times had she stood thus, brushing and grooming her daughter's hair? She could look into the mirror and almost see the layers behind that maturing face; misty, beloved images growing younger and younger: Camille at thirteen years, at ten, five, three. Would this child ever be able to imagine how precious she was in her mother's eyes?

Probably not; at least not until she dandled *her* daughter or son on her knees.

Gwendolyn's hands stilled as she imagined, for absolutely the first time, the sight of Camille holding her very own infant. Perhaps it was Felicity Warren's terrible fix which planted the notion in her brain, but it wouldn't be like that for *her* daughter. No, Camille would marry—in a few years' time: certainly no less than two—a fine young man who could make his way in the world, and who would of course be entirely besotted with her. And then they would have babies, perhaps two or three. No more than four, certainly, for childbirth took its toll on a woman's body and health.

With so many children, they would need help, naturally.

A quite ridiculous smile widened across her face.

"Mama?" Camille queried.

"Hm? Oh." Gwendolyn rapidly returned to her work. "I

don't think you should worry about Bryce. He'll come back, never fear.''

"Not for at least a month, maybe longer.''

"Then we shall have to find something worthwhile to fill the time.''

"I don't want to do anything.''

Gwendolyn gave her an assessing look. "You know what, darling? We've never really begun to gather your trousseau. I think we should start preparing the linens, at least, for it will take awhile to embroider your initials—''

"Really, Mama? Oh, *could* we?''

There certainly appeared to be nothing wrong with her daughter now, Gwendolyn thought with a lifting of her brows. She was tying the ends of the pink ribbon in the girl's hair when she heard a knock. "You look beautiful,'' she told Camille, and went to answer the door.

Max stood there alone, holding a bouquet of red roses and looking heartachingly handsome in his formal black attire, his silver embroidered vest an astonishing match to her own silvery-white gown. She had not seen these clothes before; Carleton must have brought them.

His eyes were moving across her with equal appreciation. "You're breathtaking,'' he whispered. Abruptly, his vision caught at the single satin rose that decorated her gown's high waist. With a small grin, he said, "How daring, Madame Rose. Are you not afraid?''

"That someone will make the connection?'' She motioned him inside. "The easiest way to keep a secret is to pretend everyone knows. Only subterfuge and clandestine acts give rise to questions.''

"I'm sure you're right,'' he said, handing the bouquet to her. "And here is the lovely Camille. I'm glad I didn't bring corsages. The flowers wouldn't have been able to hold their own against such beauty.''

"You sound like Mr. Vaughan,'' Camille said, but looked pleased.

"He can't be wrong all the time,'' Max replied, with admirable pleasantness Gwendolyn thought, and she looked at him intently.

"Speaking of Mr. Vaughan . . ."

"He's not in his room and hasn't been all day. I've spent the entire afternoon searching for him." He appeared to be on the point of saying more, but, after a brief glance at Camille, stopped.

"It seems odd that he hasn't returned," Gwendolyn commented. Opening the door of the credenza, she found a vase, hastened into the bedroom, and filled it with water from the porcelain pitcher on her bedside table. Returning, she set the vase on the credenza and dropped the roses in it, making a distracted attempt at arranging them nicely. "I wonder if he'll make it in time. The curtain rises in a half-hour."

"It *is* strange. Henderson is gone, too. But it doesn't really matter. I'll be delighted to escort both of you myself. I'll be the envy of every man at the theatre."

"Now you really *do* sound like Mr. Vaughan," Camille teased. "Mama told me your family was here. Shall we meet them?"

"Not tonight, but perhaps tomorrow. My uncle's ward is not feeling well, and my mother is staying with her. Uncle Harry has traveled to Brighton overnight to conduct some business."

Reading the relief in his eyes, Gwendolyn felt her own heart lighten. She had wondered if the old gentleman might insist on accompanying them to the theatre, or at the minimum make a scene about their going at all. His presence would have cast a pall over the evening for her and probably everyone else.

Only a trace of guilt followed this admission. In her brief contact with Harold Vaughan, she had sensed the heart of a despot. And while Max seemed of the opinion that his uncle was benevolent, she could not manufacture any fondness for a person who could so readily turn against a trusted member of his family. Especially when the victim was Max.

Gwendolyn gathered her gloves and fan from the table, then caught Max's reflected eyes in the mirror. With a studied neutral tone, she asked, "Have you spoken with Miss Warren today?"

"At some length," he said significantly. Gwendolyn immediately thought she would die from curiosity but knew he could say no more with her daughter present.

"I hope whatever she has isn't catching," Camille said idly. When both her mother and the baronet regarded her in shock, she looked confused and added, "Sir Hastings said she was ill . . . I merely hoped he wouldn't take sick again."

Max coughed into his fist. "I believe there's no danger of that. Shall we go? I think we've given Roderick fair time."

Tonight the baronet had ordered a carriage, and as they waited in The Allemande's lobby, talking softly as guests came and went past them, Roderick burst through the doors with Henderson flurrying after him.

"Glad I didn't miss you," Roderick said. "Forgive me for being late, but I had important business to attend that took longer than I thought." His gaze skimmed over both ladies "I'm *very* glad I found you in time. To have missed such beauty would have been a shame."

All the while he spoke, Henderson fidgeted with Roderick's jacket, pulling the sleeves just so, adjusting his cravat precisely over his collar in back. "All *right,* Henderson." he snapped. "That will do." As the valet puffed out his cheeks and glided away, Roderick explained. "The fellow gets on my nerves, but he's the best at what he does. Had to take him with me because I thought I might end up dressing in the coach, and so I did." He shot a look at Max for the first time. "Well, cousin, how have you occupied yourself today?"

Such brass, thought Gwendolyn. What a cool monster this was; not a single hint to cry *Murderer!* in any of his actions. Though his eyes sparked with a dangerous excitement that shadowed her with foreboding.

"Looking for you, among other things," the baronet said tightly.

"Well, now you've found me. Your eye is looking better, but"—he peered closer—"what's that bruise there? Did I do that?"

Gwendolyn's eyes sharpened. Yes, she could see the faint

outline of fingers on his cheek. She had not noticed it in the dim lighting upstairs.

"No." Max glanced through the glass, remarked that their carriage had arrived, and guided both Gwendolyn and Camille forward. An expectant silence fell as they filed through the doors, but the baronet did not burst into explanation.

The evening was stifling warm, Gwendolyn noticed unhappily, but the scent of the nearby meadow was sweet. She enjoyed the proximity of nature and the convenience of town. This section of Bath was comparatively undeveloped thus far, and she was thankful for it. She had chosen The Allemande as her dwelling place for that precise reason.

Camille asked the question she wanted answered. "What did happen to your cheek, Sir Hastings?"

"Just a little accident with a door. Here. Watch your step now."

While she waited for Camille to climb aboard, Gwendolyn's glance happened to snag Roderick's. The look of doubt in his eyes matched her own. Doors did not have fingers. Could Felicity have slapped him? She must be very wicked. And quite strong.

Gwendolyn reminded herself she was a lady and that her growing desire to throttle Miss Warren was entirely inappropriate.

Once the party had boarded and the horses lunged forward, an uncomfortable quiet filled the coach. Max glowered like a hot coal beside her, his arms folded, his eyes fixated on Roderick. She snapped her fan open and fluttered it before her face.

"This is the first time you've returned today?" Max asked in cold tones.

"The very first," Roderick returned. "Why, did you miss me?"

"You don't know about our visitors, then."

"Visitors?"

"Your father—"

"He's here? Why on earth?"

"Right now he's at Brighton."

"Oh, seeing Durfhausen, I'll warrant. He'd travel five hundred miles to save ten shillings. But why did he stop at Bath? Is he coming back?"

"He's coming back all right. My mother traveled with him and is staying here." There was a slight pause. "Felicity came with them, too."

Roderick fell silent for the duration of several seconds, his eyes pinned to Max's.

"Felicity?"

The baronet gave a single nod, but said nothing.

"Oh." Something resembling a smile flitted across Roderick's face, then disappeared. "How . . . interesting. I wonder what brings her here. Oh, but she is always looking for adventure."

Gwendolyn glanced from Max to Roderick and back again, her fan stilling. The tension building between the two men, the spaces in between the words, spelled only one thing to her. Max believed Roderick to be guilty of fathering Felicity's child. She could not prevent the scorn which filled her eyes as she, too, stared at him. Was there no end to his villainy? The man must desire to destroy everyone.

Slowly, Roderick tore his gaze from Max's to meet hers. He smiled faintly, insincerely, his eyes as expressionless as wood. She interpreted that look as a full acknowledgment of guilt. It took all her courage not to grab Camille's hand and Max's and leap from the coach.

Camille apparently felt none of this, for she sighed faintly; her bored sigh, Gwendolyn recognized. "Could we speak of something else? *Lydia's Secret* has a new actress in the lead role, did you know that? Miss Sturbridge has returned home to nurse her sick mother."

Thereafter, the subject veered to less uncomfortable areas for the remainder of the way to the theatre. This did not take long, for the distance was not far; the greatest delay being caused by traffic in front of the Vagabond. Gwendolyn fought impatience as their driver jockeyed the carriage into line; she was as eager as a child to hear Max's opinion of her work.

She could not prevent a sigh of relief when the driver finally let them off.

The Vagabond might not bask beneath the endorsement of the royal charter as the Theatre Royal did, Gwendolyn thought as she almost pulled Max through the lobby, but it formed a perfect jewel box of its kind. With an opulence bordering on the overdone—gilted walls, glimmering chandeliers, crimson carpet, and splendid mirrors throwing back the colorful reflections of the well-dressed crowd—the theatre's decor magnified the excitement of an evening spent in fantasy. Nothing was real here, the walls declared; therefore, *enjoy!*

Or perhaps it was all in her mind, Gwendolyn suspected. Her heart was laden with dread and anxieties, yet the energy of the theatregoers and the atmosphere of the room seeped traitorously into her pores.

She could not stop thinking of the danger surrounding Max, not only the physical threat offered by Roderick Vaughan, but the life-destroying lies of Felicity Warren. And overshadowing every thought was the inescapable fact that this would be their last evening together; for while it appeared he would not be leaving on Saturday after all, Max could hardly spend time with her if he was preparing to wed Felicity.

But that would never happen now, surely. Not if Roderick was truly the baby's father. How he might be made to accept responsibility for it was another matter. The important thing was for Max to be kept free from shouldering an undeserved burden. Knowing the strength of his honor and loyalty to family, she could well imagine him stepping into the breach to save Miss Warren and his uncle from further shame. It would be like him. Any man willing to sacrifice his own desires to serve his family for so many years might do anything.

Such an honorable man, she mused as they made their way upstairs, finding it difficult to keep her eyes from him. A noble gentleman, unlike anyone she had ever known. A sudden vision sprang into her mind: a play, a serious play—or perhaps a novel—about a young man whose life was almost ruined by his high ideals; a gentleman willing to stand alone for what he believed amid a decadent society and demanding relatives. She would call it . . . *An Honorable Man,* or perhaps the *The Noble Gentleman.* This work would not be a parody but would capture the essence of Maxim's character and life without disclosing him. For that reason, she could not make him an artist; perhaps he should be . . . a vicar? No, that did not feel right. A teacher? Well, she could not worry about that now; the details of the story would come later. She might not possess the plot, but she was looking at the theme.

She was so preoccupied that Max watched her with concern as she stumbled into her box seat. He sat on her far side, and Camille took the seat to her right. Gwendolyn hardly noticed; she was too busy promising herself never to disappear from his life until she was certain he was all right. If necessary, *she* would prevent this mockery of a marriage. Somehow. Max must be protected from himself. Her feelings crested; she could keep silent no longer. She leaned very close to his ear.

"Have you discovered the true father of Felicity's baby?" she whispered, almost soundlessly.

"I believe so," he whispered back.

"Is he Roderick?"

After an instant's hesitation. he said, "She has all but admitted it to me."

"Will your cousin own up to it, do you think?"

"God alone knows. He still hasn't confessed to throwing away her best pair of slippers when she was twelve."

Putting all the authority of her thirty-two years into a look, she whispered fiercely, *"Promise* me you will not marry her."

Though his eyes glimmered strangely in the darkening auditorium, she could intuit how well her remark sat with him. "I appreciate your concern, Gwendolyn, but lately I've begun to feel lonely." He spoke so ponderously that she knew he teased her. "I've been thinking more about marriage in spite of my circumstances. Felicity is very willing. If I don't wed her, what shall I do? Have you any other suggestions for me?"

How he could make light of the situation mystified her. Perhaps he'd caught the impetuous spirit of the theatre as she had. She shook her head at his nonsense, then became aware of Roderick as he leaned forward, looking past Camille to Max and herself.

"What are you two whispering about over there? Camille and I are beginning to feel left out."

The lights plunged all the way into darkness now, and Gwendolyn hushed him, saying the play was about to begin and they must be quiet.

"Sorry," Roderick whispered heavily. "We certainly don't want to miss a word."

The curtains rolled apart, and the familiar fall scene came into view. The man playing Nevin scurried to the bench, looking eagerly for his love. Seconds later, Lydia joined him with a furtive air. They began to speak, and Gwendolyn settled back in her chair, the better to observe Maxim's reaction, though the hard pounding in her chest made it difficult.

She was not very pleased with the actress who had replaced Miss Sturbridge; the girl's performance did not contribute the necessary lightness to the lines, and the first jest was approaching. Yet Max smiled obligingly at the critical moment, and as the act progressed, he leaned forward with lively eyes and even laughed aloud or four separate occasions. Slowly, she began to relax and enjoy the play. Perhaps the new Lydia was not so bad after all. She certainly was pretty.

When the first act ended, the baronet clapped enthusiastically. Sending her a look of vigorous approval, he said, "I'm enjoying this. I hope you'll pardon me for saying I didn't expect to, but I've been pleasantly surprised. One doesn't get a feeling of mean-spiritedness behind it."

Though her emotions buoyed upward, she pretended to be offended. "Mean-spirited, indeed. Everything you've said has a negative ring to it. Why don't you say what you *do* like?"

With concern, he took her hand. "I didn't . . . Oh, you little minx. You're only fishing for compliments."

"And if I were, what would you say?" She fluttered her fan with a flirtatious air, sparing a lightning glance for her daughter, who was conversing with Roderick.

"What would I say?" His eyes glittered with warmth. "That the humor is sophisticated, the pacing adept, the acting tolerable, and the playwright extremely gifted. Bordering on genius, in fact."

She laughed lightly. "Oh, what pudding talk. If only it were true."

"I think it could be," he said, suddenly serious. "Given a subject worthy of your talent."

A portion of her merriment faded. "Not again, Max." Just as quickly, she lightened. "But I do plan to write other things, and I'm not going to postpone doing so much longer."

"I'm pleased to hear it. May I offer you refreshment?" When she shook her head, he leaned past her. "Camille? Would you like something to drink?"

"Yes, please; a strawberry ice. I'm terribly thirsty."

"I'll get it for you," Roderick said quickly. "You stay and watch, Max. I've seen most of the play before. You want something?"

Gwendolyn saw the look of surprise on the baronet's face as he declined. Roderick hastened from the box like one fleeing a fire.

The between-acts skit had begun, and, since it was one of her newer ones, Gwendolyn became preoccupied in watching. Taking her cue, Max turned toward the stage. A young couple waltzed in front of the curtains to the center, then stopped. The girl cried out that she was too dizzy to continue, while the young man declared they could not cease dancing in the middle of the ballroom floor. The argument continued. Gwendolyn was disappointed in the audience's reaction, but she could hardly blame their inattention; it was not one of her more amusing efforts.

As the skit drew to a close, Roderick returned, burdened with four drinks which he distributed to each member of the party. Max accepted his reluctantly, saying he hadn't asked for anything and wasn't thirsty.

"But you will be," Roderick said. "What have I missed?"

"Nothing much," Gwendolyn said in tones of discouragement. "The second act is about to begin, though."

"Look, Mama!" Camille nodded to the floor below. "There is Lucy Munroe. See? She's waving at us. I wonder if Bryce came with her? No, I don't see him. But Lucy's escort is very handsome, isn't he?"

Gwendolyn agreed and sipped her unwanted ice, then set it carefully on the floor beside her chair. The second act began and the audience grew quiet.

Characters were developed more fully in this section, and the groundwork was laid for the uproarious activities of the third. It was a necessary act, but leaned toward dullness. She was glad when it was over and the next skit began.

Camille began to chatter speculatively about Lucy's gentleman, and Gwendolyn listened distractedly as stage hands brought a ladder and a tall, rectangular box decorated as a balcony to center stage. She could not imagine what this was; had Mr. Alferton been so displeased with her work that he'd ordered something from another writer? What a dampening thought.

The curtains parted briefly as someone exited, then climbed the ladder to emerge at the top; a beautiful young lady who trailed a comb through her long hair with an attitude of boredom. A flamboyantly dressed actor sauntered from offstage, followed by a pair of guitar-strumming musicians. With the dignity of a bride, the suitor carried a nosegay before him, then ceremoniously extended it upward to the woman. When she could not reach it, he threw it at her, striking her on the nose.

A dreadful certainty struck Gwendolyn. Her body stiffened.

"Ouch!" the actress cried. "You simpleton, what are you trying to do, kill me?"

"Kill you!" he shouted indignantly. "I've come to declare myself."

"Declare yourself mad? I heartily endorse that!"

Chuckles rippled through the audience. Gwendolyn slid forward and gripped the rail, her lips parting. This was not possible. There simply must be a mistake.

"No," she whispered.

"No!" cried the extravagant young man. He swept a look behind him at the musicians. "Carlos, Pedro! Begin a melody of love, I command you! Something that will prepare my lady's heart!" Immediately the minstrels launched into a rollicking sea chanty. "Not that! Something soft!" The same melody continued, though at a slower tempo and somewhat quieter.

As the actor clutched his hair and pulled a face, laughter came from various corners of the audience. The between-acts conversation began to die as more and more patrons attended the stage.

"Thank you for preparing my heart," the girl pronounced sarcastically. "I now feel ready for a long sail!"

Gwendolyn could not breathe. Without daring to turn her head, she slid a glance toward Max. He had gone perfectly still, his glassy eyes centered on the actors.

"Oh, Lucianna, Lucianna," called the suitor. "Wherefore art thou, my Lucianna?"

"I'm right here! Are you blind? You must be. Here, perhaps this will help!" With a swooping gesture, she poured a bucket-ful of confetti over the gentleman's head, causing great hilarity in the audience.

Of course the director would order confetti, Gwendolyn told herself, her stunned thoughts fracturing like glass. Water is not good for the stage.

In the audience below, Lucy's red-cheeked face turned upward toward them, her expression wavering between merriment and embarrassment, her tinkling giggles audible even here in the box seats.

"See how she leans her cheek upon her hand!" said the suitor, pulling off a piece of confetti clinging to his lips. "Would that I were a glove—"

"You want gloves, you say?" the actress challenged. "Far be it from me to deny you!" A second bucket rained upon the hapless fellow, gloves this time.

From the corner of her vision, Gwendolyn saw Max slowly

pivot toward her, his eyes like scorching flames. She could not look at him.

The actor began to press his suit once more, his tones even more dramatic. In one swift motion, Max stood and made his way past their knees to the exit behind the curtain. Camille's shocked eyes met Gwendolyn's as he moved by.

"Mama, did you . . . ?" she began, then glanced at Roderick and back again. "I think Sir Hastings believes it is about him."

Gwendolyn was already on her feet. "I know," she whispered, and stumbled past her daughter and Roderick as quickly as she could, conscious that both of them were watching her intently.

The baronet was well down the corridor by the time she swept beyond the curtains. When she called his name, he continued without pause.

"Max!" she cried louder, causing the few patrons ambling through the halls to look at her curiously. Oh, curse her gown! Its circumference was too narrow to allow long strides. "Please wait, please!" He could not have failed to hear her. Oh dear God, she prayed, make him stop!

He was at the stairs now. Without looking at her, he leaned indecisively with one hand on the banister. But then he began his descent. She broke into a mincing run. By the time she reached him, he was halfway down the stairs.

"I don't know what happened, Max," she said in a pleading voice. "I really don't. It's not what you think, I promise you!"

"You mean you didn't write the piece?" he asked in clipped tones, still not meeting her eyes.

"No. I mean, yes, I did write it. But then I threw the sketch away. Someone must have stolen it from the rubbish container. I never gave it to Mr. Alferton, I vow I did not!"

At the third step from the bottom, he finally looked at her. When she saw the devastation in his eyes, she had to lower her own.

"But you admit writing it."

"Yes, but only as an exercise; there was never any intention of using it."

"An exercise," he said with disbelief. "Your life is so void of activity that you have time to practice writing things you will never use." He had reached the bottom of the stairs, and now he began to stride through the lobby toward the doors.

"There was a purpose to it, Max," she said, tripping along beside him, reaching for his arm to slow him down.

He gazed at her fingers disdainfully, then stopped. "I'm listening."

"I wrote it because I was afraid of my feelings for you," Gwendolyn said, her heart twisting. She had never wanted to admit this to anyone. "I thought if I made . . . fun . . . it would diminish my growing attachment."

A quick glance upward revealed only scorn. Oh, she had not dreamed he could be so cold. But she had hurt him in the worst way—humiliated him. He would never forgive her, never. And she could not blame him for it.

"And did it work?" he asked icily.

"No," she moaned. "I've had no success in forgetting you at all."

There was little satisfaction in his eyes. "You expect me to believe that, just as I'm to believe that by some wild coincidence, someone merely happened to be passing by your room and found your skit during the small fraction of time the trash is collected. Then, by another stunning quirk of fate, he or she decided to bring it to the very theatre where your other works are being performed. I'll admit to many shortcomings in my character and intellect, but I'm not *that* gullible."

For the space of several pounding heartbeats, she stared at him with wide eyes. "The thief would have had to know my identity and pretend to be me," she said in a husky, speculative voice. "Mr. Alferton has come to expect my contributions anonymously. I cannot imagine him accepting something so quickly from a stranger."

"No more, Gwendolyn," he commented, suddenly sounding very tired. "I have no further taste for plays or questions; I'm going to my room. Roderick will take you home."

"Don't you understand?" she asked with a desperate excitement. "It must have been Roderick who took it. I never mentioned it to you, but one evening after you left my suite, I opened the door afterward and saw *his* closing! We had been talking about trying to find your formula, do you recall? I don't remember our exact words, but what if he'd heard us plotting?" Her words fell faster as conviction grew. "He would have become angry beyond measure, I'll warrant! It would explain many of his actions since!"

"I'm beginning to think we put too much blame on my cousin," he said grimly. "I never thought I'd hear myself say that," he added, more to himself than her.

The few remaining people in the lobby began filing toward the auditorium, and a couple of the vendors shot curious glances their way from the stalls lining one of the walls. Max made as if to move off, but she tightened her grip on his arm. She would not allow him to leave until he believed her, she vowed to herself.

"The very next day was the picnic. He began to act strangely toward me then."

"There is no beginning or ending to Roderick's strangeness. Everything he does fits that designation."

"But don't you see? He might have searched my room; obviously it was easy enough to do, or Deevers could not have done it. What if he discovered the skit and found out about me?"

A sorrowful look came into the baronet's eyes, and he gently removed her fingers from his sleeve. With tears springing beneath her lids, she looked slowly from his hand to his face.

"Enough, Gwendolyn. Enough fabrication, enough explanation. I can't listen anymore."

As he turned his back to her and walked away, it seemed her heart shattered into a million pieces. The rest of her life stretched forward as a bleak, endless, empty landscape.

"You cannot walk out of my life," she said loudly, the words tearing from her soul, "I won't let you."

He did not turn or break his stride.

"What will you do?" she cried through her tears. "Marry

someone you don't love? Destroy your future, all because of this stupid misunderstanding? Don't you do it, Maxim Hastings! I love you too much to let you go!"

He stopped abruptly, his back stiffening. Around her, the inhabitants of the lobby became very still. Everyone was watching them as if *they* were the actors in a play. But she didn't care. All that mattered was that Max believe her. And not stop loving her.

With elegant slowness, he turned. She saw light gleaming in his eyes.

"Would you say that again?"

Nervously, Gwendolyn darted a quicksilver glance at the workers, all of whom continued to watch with keen interest. One short, portly man nodded encouragingly. She cleared her throat and moistened her lips.

"I said . . . I love you too much . . . to let you go . . ."

In the space between heartbeats, Max crossed the lobby and lifted her into a swirling embrace. He began to laugh, and she laughed with him. The ushers standing against the wall burst into laughter, too, and one or two of them applauded. Her awareness of them faded as Max gave her a resounding kiss that nearly curled the bandeau on her hair.

She had never been happier in her life. Never.

"What a tender scene," Roderick said as he descended the stairs.

Chapter Fifteen

Gwendolyn could feel the tension in Max's arms as he swung her toward the voice. Roderick's unwanted presence was like a cloud blocking the sun, she thought as her slippers touched the floor.

Vaughan's eyes were unreadable as he looked from Max to herself.

"Camille begged me to look for you. We were afraid you'd both abandoned us. Are you all right?"

"We're perfectly well," Max said sternly. "Now."

"You don't know how relieved that makes me. When you left, you looked ill. Or disturbed. For a moment I worried the intermission drama might have offended you. Strange how closely it paralleled what happened between you and Lucy Munroe last summer."

"Did it? I hadn't noticed."

Gwendolyn could remain silent no longer. "You wouldn't know anything about how the piece came to be performed, would you?"

"I?" He laughed in amazement. "Surely you're not suggesting that I wrote that paltry bit of nonsense."

Max stepped forward angrily. Gwendolyn clung to his sleeve, afraid of what he might do should she let go.

"Stop playing, Roderick. I know you gave the skit to the theatre manager. The question is, *why?* Was it to embarrass me or to estrange Gwendolyn and myself? Or both?" To Gwendolyn's surprise, Vaughan denied nothing; although cold lights flickered in his eyes. Max turned from him scornfully and gave her a swift, fond look that sent her pulse tripping. "Your plan has failed. In a way, I have you to thank for that."

"I live to serve you, cousin, though you do astonish me. Your lady is all elegance and beauty, but her occupation is—"

"Careful," Max warned.

"Shall I just say I'm surprised at your . . . friendship? You've always been the one with the ideals. That you can ignore her rather . . . Well, politeness forbids that I—"

"Say another word and I'll feed your tongue to the river rats," Max bristled.

"Lud, Max, so violent! I was only trying to make the point that Mrs. Devane seems more suited to my nature than yours, but fate has not decreed it; therefore, I shall step aside. What else can a gentleman do when an old friend is willing to sacrifice his staid, upright existence for a more . . . shall we say, unconventional one? Oh, but I had forgotten; no one knows the truth about your scandalous lady."

"If you're thinking of divulging her true identity, you'll live to regret it."

"Why would I do that? What an opinion you hold of me, Max. You of all people should know I'm discreet. Your powers of reasoning have always lacked a certain . . . rationality. I've been meaning to tell you that for years."

He had recovered completely, Gwendolyn saw. The realization filled her with uneasiness.

"However," Roderick continued, "knowing about your warm relationship makes the news I have to give you even more unfortunate."

One of the workers dropped a glass, and Gwendolyn almost cried out. Max was watching Roderick intently, his hostility as apparent to her as flames at a hearth. She longed suddenly for the strawberry ice she had left upstairs. Her mouth was so dry she could hardly swallow.

Folding his arms and pulling at his chin, Roderick gave Max a look colored with sadness. "First, I have to admit something that shames me a bit, though my intentions were all to the good, I assure you. Your formula . . ."

"You *do* have it!"

After a dramatic hesitation, Roderick said, "I can deny it no longer."

Max sprung forward, clutching his cousin's lapels.

"No, Max!" Gwendolyn cried.

" 'Ere, 'ere, none 'o that!" shouted a tall, husky man who paused in his wiping of the refreshment tables to take a step toward them.

Max turned furious eyes upon him, then released Roderick with a little push. "All the time I knew you lied! Where is it?"

Roderick straightened and smoothed his jacket meticulously. "Remember what I told you. I only borrowed it for your own good." At an explosion of disbelief from his companion, his lips turned downward. "Well, I did. It all came about because of the poacher. I tell you this because I don't want you to think I was following you. I've often noticed a tendency you have to suspect me of such things, as though I have nothing better to do—"

"Would you get on with it?" Max demanded.

"I will if you'll stop interrupting me," Roderick returned in offended tones. "As I was saying . . . you recall how the poacher has been stealing game the past couple of months in our wood? About three weeks ago, I decided to stop him. I began leaving the house after dark, hoping to catch him at it. I never had any success, but on the third night, I found you."

Comprehension flooded the baronet's face. "Are you speaking of the evening I met with Soufrière?"

Roderick gestured carelessly. "Whatever his name was, I neither knew nor cared. But when I watched you walking so furtively through the wood, my interest was caught. I followed you to the pavilion and took cover behind a tree while you talked with him. To say truth, I was hoping you were on your way to a romantic rendezvous, for that would mean you were bending a little, becoming a trifle more human, perhaps. I should have known it had something to do with the factory.''

"Spare me the nursery tales, Roderick; you were spying and might as well admit it.''

"Oh, believe what you like; you always do. Which goes a long way in explaining why you allowed him to mislead you. Still, you should have seen him for what he was. A child could have.'' He shivered with exaggerated distaste. "I'll carry the memory of you handing that money pouch to him forever. Especially after hearing the amount. How my heart sank at your foolishness! I know it must have been all you had, or nearly. And just to please my father, yes? That's a never-ending occupation, in case you haven't discovered it. Which is the reason I've chosen to live my own life as I please.''

An expression of such loss came into Max's eyes that Gwendolyn's heart contracted. "Your father has nothing to do with this.''

Roderick looked amused. "I think he has everything to do with it. But even that doesn't explain your idiotic faith in the Frenchman. He didn't trust *you,* did he? Do you recall how he opened that pouch and looked to see if the payment was truly there? That should have been a clue, Max. You should not have believed him without evidence of some kind—''

"I did have evidence: a piece of ruby-red glass that he had manufactured.''

"But did you see him *make* it? The man was a liar. Standing behind a tree many yards away and in the dark, I saw that.''

"Of course you did. You were so convinced of his deceit that you stole the formula for yourself. What did you hope to gain, Roderick? Did you plan to give it to your father and claim you discovered it?''

"Here we are again!'' Vaughan threw his hands into the air hopelessly. "Always, *always,* you must think the worst of me.

What truly happened is that I waited a few days, wondering what you planned to do. For all I knew, you could be nourishing a scheme to open your own glass company; one never knows with you. When you did nothing, I admit my curiosity got the better of me. I wanted to know if the receipt might actually be genuine in spite of my instincts. So I borrowed it, hoping my substitute was near enough that you wouldn't notice should you glance at it during the next few days. My intention was to have it examined at another firm—privately, of course. By so doing, I hoped to save you from embarrassment.''

Max's lips curled scornfully. "How altruistic you are. Thanks to your *selfless* act, I became the fool of my own birthday celebration and lost a great measure of your father's respect.''

"Max, think a moment. How could I guess what you planned to do at your birthday?'' He chuckled. "Besides, do you actually believe I would have missed that occasion had I known?'' When the baronet maintained a seething silence, Roderick continued, "Unfortunately, my plans were delayed after I met a young lady who eventually led me to Bath. Quite frankly, I forgot about the formula until you appeared.''

"But he asked you for it,'' Gwendolyn said, "and you denied having it.''

With an apologetic shrug, Roderick grinned. "You must forgive me that. I didn't want to release it until I knew it was genuine—''

"At which time you would have claimed it as your own.''

"Faith, you try me, cousin! No matter what I say to defend myself, you must accuse. Well, none of it matters now. I ordered a trial run at the factory of an acquaintance of mine in Gloucester, and the test was completed this afternoon. That's why I left last night and was so late getting back today.'' Roderick paused dramatically. "All is as I expected. The formula is false.''

For a timeless interval, Gwendolyn could not breathe. She dared not look at Max. Surely, surely this was another of Roderick's fabrications. *Please God.*

"You lie,'' Max whispered finally, hopefully.

"I wish I did," Roderick said slowly, lifting a hand toward the baronet's sleeve. His features lengthened, looking so sympathetic that for an instant Gwendolyn thought he truly was sorry. But Max did not; he stepped out of reach. "The paper is in my room, inside the jacket I wore today. I'll give it to you when we return to The Allemande."

"You would rather lie than say truth. It's always been that way with you."

Roderick shook his head, as if hopeless before his persistence. "You can test it for yourself. I'd recommend you do so before trying to give it to my father a second time."

"Do you think I can believe you so easily? I've come to think you're capable of anything. Your conduct with Felicity proves my point."

Roderick frowned. "What? Explain yourself."

"As if you didn't know. You never stop, do you?"

"No, I'm truly at a loss. I thought you were insinuating *something* on the ride here, but I can't guess what it is."

Gwendolyn caught her breath as Max swept dangerously close to Roderick. "I will not take responsibility for your child," he said in a heavy whisper. "Felicity has accused me, and your father believes her."

Roderick gave a surprised burst of laughter. "Lud, what a droll sense of humor you have!"

Max's fingers tightened into fists. At that moment, a swirl of pink at the top of the stairs drew his eyes upward: Camille. Relief flooded Gwendolyn when the baronet stepped back a pace, his stance relaxing slightly.

"We'll continue this later," he ground out *sotto voce* to Roderick.

"There you are!" Camille said gladly, beginning to descend. "I'd begun to think you'd all forgotten me!"

Gwendolyn directed what she hoped was a calming look at Max, then rushed forward. "Never, darling. We were merely talking."

"Is everything all right, Sir Hastings?" the girl asked concernedly as she joined Gwendolyn, then approached the gentlemen. "I was worried that you might have"—her eyes flicked in Roderick's direction—"might have been, um, bored with the play."

Max managed to smile at her. "No, my dear. Everything is all right."

Strong laughter came from the auditorium, and Gwendolyn knew the play would soon be over. She could not imagine returning to their box seats, not with lightning crackling between her masculine companions.

"I should like to return home, if no one objects," she said. "I'm feeling weary, and we won't have to wait in line for our carriage if we leave now."

As no one voiced dissension to this plan, the foursome exited from the building. All the while, Gwendolyn's fingers signaled restraint through Max's sleeve. She had sensed his wrath growing to the breaking point, and now, passing through the doors and into the humid heat of the night, she was certain only the tightest control prevented him from seizing Roderick and throwing him against the wall.

During the ride back to The Allemande, Camille was the only member of the party to attempt conversation; and after a few minutes of receiving taut, distracted replies to her comments, she, too, fell silent. Max distantly assumed the blame for this failure of civility, but he knew he could not act otherwise. Roderick's crimes occupied his thoughts to the exclusion of all others, even the sweet memory of Gwendolyn's lips.

Repeatedly his eyes haunted Roderick's until his cousin closed his own, his face a stony mask. His previous amusement had dissipated entirely, and he appeared no more willing to exchange pleasantries than Max himself.

As the driver pulled his team beneath the inn's portico, the baronet slid a guilty look toward Gwendolyn. She offered him a shaky smile, her eyes communicating understanding but warning. He held her hand unduly long as he helped her descend the steps of the coach.

"I promise to make amends for this evening," he whispered to her. "Will you meet me in the dining room for an early breakfast tomorrow?"

"We are like to make a habit of it," she said, her voice attempting lightness.

"That would be my hope," he returned with feeling.

Camille emerged next, and Gwendolyn linked arms with her, pulling her slightly ahead of the gentlemen. Like an arrow seeking its target, Roderick seized the moment to draw close to Max, and it took all the baronet's self-restraint not to shrink away.

"What you said about Felicity; that was not a jest?" Vaughan asked quietly.

Max slowed. "Is this an inquiry you really need to make?"

"You mean she truly *is* with child?" Roderick persisted, his face pale beneath the lanterns flanking the doors. "This is not one of her melodramas?"

"If so, she's convincing enough for the stage."

"Oh, my God," Roderick said simply. "It was only the one time, I swear. I was foxed, and she came to my room looking like . . . Oh . . . my . . . God."

In that instant of admission, Max became aware of several things at once. He saw the Devanes enter the building and Gwendolyn turn to watch him anxiously. He heard a cluster of guests approaching from behind. And in his heart, he became convinced that Roderick was telling the truth about everything. No one could look so devastated and lie. He felt shame he had suspected him of attempting murder. He was grateful he'd resisted the urge to accuse him.

Maybe he was too trusting, as Roderick had insinuated earlier; but he'd rather believe in his cousin than not. He could not imagine what kind of person he would become if he were capable of thinking otherwise.

Glancing again at Gwendolyn's beautiful face through the glass further soothed his ravaged soul. Roderick had told him the formula was worthless. He had given ten years of his life

like our crystal in that country. We will make the fortune there, we think. But you!'' His mouth twisted as he turned bulging eyes upon the baronet. ''You gave him a packetful of paper, and he was too much the innocent to see! When he learned the truth, his heart gave out. And now you must forfeit your life in return!''

''If he told you that, *he's* the one who lied. I gave him everything I had for a formula that was false!''

''Of course it was false!'' Soufrière cried. ''I am the one who made him do that, for Paul Soufrière is not the innocent babe his brother Jules was! 'Do not give him the true receipt,' I told him. 'When we are safely in America; when no one stops us at the ship to claim we have stolen an English gentleman's money, you may send it to him,' I said.''

''My, such integrity,'' Roderick said, his voice heavy with sarcasm. ''Do you have any other entertaining stories? The night is long and I'm easily bored.''

Soufrière spat on the ground. ''Jules did not like it, but that is what I made him to do. And it is a good thing, no? Now you have no receipt, and I have no money. But someone must pay for my brother's death!''

Several men were trotting toward them across the field. Behind them came Gwendolyn, running as quickly as her gown and strength would allow, and Max experienced a surge of pride at her brave foolhardiness. Returning his attention to the captive, he gave him a shake.

''You could have killed two ladies who have nothing whatsoever to do with this.''

''Bah! It was not my doing but that of Deevers, which is why I dismiss him to do it myself. But me, I study and watch for the best opportunity. When my brother died, I came to Blackpool, but you are already gone. Then I follow you here, where you are seldom alone, and I want to make no mistakes.''

''But you have,'' Roderick said with satisfaction. ''However, if you give us the receipt for red, perhaps we'll forgive you.''

''Roderick,'' Max said gratingly, then stopped, feeling an

irrational sense of excitement. If he did possess the true formula . . .

But the man between them suddenly seemed to grow small. "I do not have it. In our family, only one possesses the secret for the most rare receipts. The one for true copper red passed with Jules." A fresh wave of fury shuddered through him. "Which is another reason you should die!"

"Listen to me!" Max grabbed the Frenchman with both hands and glared into his eyes. "I gave your brother fifteen thousand pounds in good faith. What he did with it I can't say."

"I will never believe your filthy English lies!"

He was impossible. The men coming to their rescue were almost upon them, all but one of them dressed in footmen's livery. Gwendolyn had slowed to a rapid walk, looking out of place in her elegant gracefulness in the tall grass, but a welcome dream nevertheless. Max nodded at Roderick, and they tugged the prisoner toward them.

Questions swam through Max's mind. If the Frenchman told the truth and his purse had been stuffed with paper, what had happened to his savings?

As the footmen bundled Soufrière toward the inn to await the authorities, Gwendolyn rushed tearfully into Max's arms. "I understand everything now," he said, kissing the top of her head and promising to explain all later. "Except for the little matter of my fortune."

Vaughan caught the implication immediately and raised defensive hands. "Don't look to me for your money. In the past week, you've blamed me for everything except the war, and I'd be surprised if you don't get around to that, too. I just saved your life, I blush to remind you. That ought to account for something; though given your usual sense of gratitude, I won't strain myself waiting for rewards."

With laughter rippling inside, Max felt the final barrier break down between him and his most irritating enemy—but his friend still. "If I have accused you in the past, it's because you make such a worthy villain. Still, I do thank you for your aid, so I won't lay the theft at your door, not if you're willing to take on Felicity. Jules Soufrière must have lied to his brother; maybe given the fortune to a woman or lost it, God forbid. But you couldn't have my fifteen thousand. If you did, I believe you'd disappear."

A wildly speculative look flew into Vaughan's eyes.

"Don't even begin to consider it," Max said.

Chapter Sixteen

The night had brought a bewildering but satisfying array of answers, Gwendolyn thought as she waited for Max to arrive at breakfast the next morning, but it had offered them little time to be alone. Having admitted her love to him in the middle of a theatre lobby—a terribly public arena, contrary to everything natural to her—she now longed for a quiet time wherein they could discuss their future.

Their future. Oh, she could not believe this was happening, that her life was changing again. But this time, *this time,* she held no doubt that future would be a bright one. And yet it was frightening. Her life had seemed so set, so perfect in its orderliness, before. She needed Max, needed to hear his reassurances.

Of course, he had not asked her to marry him. The problem of his fortune still remained. She wondered if his pride would keep them apart.

Andrew Hibbs hurried over and poured a second cup of coffee. After telling him she would wait awhile lo~~~ eating, he withdrew, his shoulders set in disappr~ tardy suitor.

There were only a few diners in the large room, and the small noises of scraping forks and rattling cups sounded unwarrantedly loud. She blew little waves across her coffee, then set down her cup gladly as Max rounded the entrance at a half-run. He appeared well groomed except for a few strands of hair falling across his forehead and making him look boyish. For one wild moment she considered jumping to her feet to smooth back his hair, then kiss him boldly. She was too well bred for that, but if she had him alone . . .

"My pardon for being late," Max said as he breezed into the seat beside her. "Both Carleton and I overslept. The night went on forever. I wasn't done with the magistrate until nearly four."

"I forgive you," she said lightly, "but I'm not sure Andrew will."

"Oh, bosh Andrew." He took her hands across the table. "You look fresh and beautiful as a new rose this morning. How do you manage it? I know you were up late as well."

"Not so late as you, though I did have a nice conversation with your mother."

One side of his mouth lifted in a grin. "She's quite fond of you. She told me so."

"Did she? I like her as well."

Andrew returned with a cup and a pitcher of coffee. "Your usual, I presume?" he asked haughtily.

"Yes, give me coffee as dark as your soul, my man."

"Sorry, this brew is as black as yours," Andrew returned. "So you shouldn't complain it's too pale."

"Ouch," Max said as he huffed away.

Gwendolyn laughed merrily. "Since you were late, he thinks you don't deserve me."

"He's right, of course."

She thanked him with a lingering, flirtatious look, then grew solemn. "What will happen to the Frenchman, do you know?"

" re will be tried and imprisoned. I'll do all I can to om hanging, but deportation isn't likely. He still blames me and could pose a threat. He did at least tell where his accomplice is hiding out, so Deevers should be apprehended by now.''

"I'm so relieved to have the mystery solved at last. And speaking of mysteries . . . have you forgiven me for penning that terrible skit? Even though it was the *mysterious* Roderick who had it performed?''

"There's nothing to forgive. Not after you finally admitted so prettily to loving me.''

"Oh, finally, is it? It couldn't be that the process of love took awhile longer for me, and that I might have discovered it only last night.''

"Is that how it was? You only found out the very moment you blurted it for all the world to hear?''

"You're very proud, Sir Hastings,'' she said, pretending to be offended. "We have hardly known one another a week. Must a woman fall at your feet *immediately* before you are happy?''

"I suppose not, so long as she does fall in the end.''

Both of her eyebrows arched upward. "A very ambiguous statement, sir.''

"Then allow me to modify. I don't care when you decided to love me. All that matters is you do. And that you promise to be my wife.''

Twice before she had heard similar proposals, and her life had veered downward because of them. Yet she did not hesitate an instant before answering.

"Yes, dearest Max. Oh, yes.''

Leaning toward her, he kissed her so thoroughly that her heart nearly escaped from her body, so ecstatic was she. Finally, she edged away, smiling and protesting that Andrew would throw them from the dining room in shame did they not stop.

With a rascally smile, Max said, "It's well that Blackpool is so far from Bath or I would go mad with the waiting. But it will be worth it, no matter how long.''

Her gaze moved searchingly across his face. Now that she had finally committed herself, she had no interest in delays.

"How long are you speaking about?''

"Only until I've saved a little. A year, maybe two. Just until I have enough to begin refurbishing my estate. Once the farms are running again, that should provide enough income to finish it over the years. It's not what I'd like, but better than nothing."

"The money I've been saving has been for a dwelling place for Camille and me. You may use that."

"No, I can't. You've worked too hard for your earnings. If you want to use a portion of it to decorate one or two of the rooms once we're married, that will be your decision."

"It's so unfortunate about your savings," she said desperately. "To never know what happened ..." His expression became so carefully neutral that she knew she must not pursue this topic. "I cannot bear that its loss should affect our lives so."

"I feel as you do, Gwendolyn. But I also believe I must provide the home."

She had not fallen for a perfect man but a stubborn one, it seemed. Well, there were worse things. Yet it perplexed that there must be this sense of heaviness amidst all her happiness. Could nothing ever be uncomplicated?

But their marriage was worth the wait, as Max had said. And perhaps as time went along, she would be able to persuade him to accept her contribution. Other men had no compunction in taking dowries and their wives' entire fortunes.

But then, Max was not other men. Which was the very reason she loved him so.

He stiffened abruptly, his features becoming guarded as he looked toward the door. Harold Vaughan was approaching them. A flare of irritation rose in Gwendolyn then dampened. This was not the proud, vindictive man she had seen two nights ago. His shoulders drooped slightly, and his stride was hesitant.

When he drew near their table, Max stood politely.

"My pardon for interrupting," Mr. Vaughan said. "May I join you for a moment?"

"Of course." Max pulled out a chair, and the older man settled into it slowly. "When did you arrive?"

"Around daybreak this morning," groaned Vaughan. "Too

much travel over too few days. Age deprives a man of what he feels he should be able to accomplish.'' Glancing from one to the other, he added, ''But you don't want to hear about old age. Young folk never do. I didn't either.''

He grew silent for a moment, and in that interval, Andrew returned. Gwendolyn knew a guilty leap of hope when Vaughan ordered only a cup of tea. She truly wanted Max to herself for a while, even if it were in a public dining room.

''No, there's no sense in complaining about aches and pains,'' Mr. Vaughan said, fingering the silverware as if afraid to meet their eyes. ''I've come to apologize to both of you for my conduct the other evening. I was unkind to you, Mrs. Devane, for my insinuations about your character. Anne straightened me out on that score this morning.''

''Thank you, sir,'' Gwendolyn said. ''There was no harm done, I assure you.''

''You're kind for saying so.'' His face reddened alarmingly as he slowly turned his eyes upon Max. ''I *have* done harm, though; if not to you, then to this young man so dear to me. The things I accused you of, Max . . . they rise in my craw like stones to choke me. God forgive me that I should have trusted Felicity's word over yours. Perhaps God can, but I don't know if you will.''

Max was greatly moved by this speech, Gwendolyn saw, and tears of empathy came to her eyes. He stared downward at his cup.

''I won't deny that your lack of belief in me hurt—''

''It will never happen again.''

''—but I cannot hold it against you. Not after all you've done for my mother and me.''

''Anything I've offered you've repaid in full, my boy.''

The gentlemen shook hands across the table. Mr. Vaughan clapped his other hand over Max's, and the baronet same. They both smiled, and Gwendolyn smiled wi

''I suppose my mother told you the truth,'' Max he could speak, bringing his hands back to cradle hi was it Roderick or Felicity?''

"No. Well, Anne told me some of it, after I awakened her. When I returned, I found a note from Roderick explaining most of it to me."

"A note!" Max exclaimed, exchanging a disturbed look with Gwendolyn, who felt a similar panic rising. "Has he left?"

"Yes, he's run off with Felicity to get married."

Gwendolyn was so relieved that, for a fraction of a second, she felt faint. Max visibly relaxed, sinking back into his chair with a sigh.

Mr. Vaughan continued as if unaware of his companions' reactions. "He knew I was returning and wasn't man enough to face me. I guarantee we won't see either of them for a month at least. It would be like him to think I'd cool my wrath by that time, but he'll be wrong! His actions could have separated our affection for one another irretrievably, Max." He paused to remove a handkerchief from his pocket, then wiped his eyes and blew his nose. "I hope you won't allow this to change your feelings for me or the company. My home is your home always, you know that." His gaze shifted rapidly to Gwendolyn. "And as your family grows, they will be welcome as well."

"Thank you, uncle. I'm glad to hear it, for I plan to continue working with you for an appreciable while. Although my dream remains the same—to one day restore my mother's home."

"I know, son," he said affectionately. "I know. It's good to have dreams."

A horrific thought struck Gwendolyn. Harold Vaughan held a fierce attachment for Max. What if *he* had taken the money in order to prolong his nephew's stay—to make it last, perhaps, forever? Could such villainy be possible?

While Andrew served Mr. Vaughan's tea and replenished ‥r coffee, the older man settled back comfortably, his compo‥ ‥eturning. Gwendolyn, hovering on the rim of anxiety, ‥‥ ‥ a lump of sugar into her cup and stirred it around and ‥‥ ‥ ‥‥ ‥

‥‥ ‥‥ not, Harold Vaughan was at the very least guilty ‥‥ ‥‥ ‥her hopes for a tête-à-tête with Max.

‥‥ older man took several healthy sips of his brew. "Would

that you could have been my true son as well as the one I'm cursed with. He should have been here to meet me today. I've raised a coward.''

''No, you haven't. He saved my life last evening, did he tell you that?''

Mr. Vaughan's faded blue eyes sharpened, and Gwendolyn's suspicions dissipated. The old gentleman might love Max, but this news of his offspring filled his heart with a delight he could not keep secret.

''*Did* he now? Well, don't hesitate, son; give me details! I need something to brighten my days!''

Uncle Harry stayed with them throughout breakfast, then insisted upon walking Gwendolyn to her room himself. Max fought a fond but helpless resentment as he entered his own chamber. His uncle had agreed to remain two days further in Bath, but insisted they must all go home then. Max understood the need to return to the factory. Yet from the look of things, every moment with Gwendolyn would hereafter be shadowed with relatives.

Carleton was tidying his room and now bustled toward the door with an armload of clothes. ''Off to the wash,'' he said unnecessarily. ''There's a letter and package for you on the bed, sir. One of the footmen delivered it while you were at breakfast.''

Max thanked him idly and walked to his desk. His drawings of Gwendolyn had been stacked into a neat pile; his valet's work, no doubt. He paged through them thoughtfully. Did he possess talent? Would it someday be possible to leave his vile— no, no, not vile, only distasteful—work at the factory and earn a small living doing what he truly enjoyed? Could such things happen in an imperfect world?

He had found love, hadn't he? Anything was possible.

Smiling a little, he replaced the sketches and turned to the bed. The package was the standard size of a gift containing a shirt or cravat, though its paper was plain and tied with household string. The missive caught within the string was written by a surprisingly familiar hand that immediately captured his curiosity. He pulled the letter free, broke its seal and sat on the edge of the bed to read.

Dearest Max,

I have a terrible confession to make, and I am too ashamed to render it in person. Besides, it is late, and by the time this is delivered, you will know Roderick and I have run away to Gretna to avoid all the horrid details his father would impose upon a more formal wedding.

It was I who took your fifteen thousand. Before you condemn me rashly, please know that I only meant to borrow it. What choice did I have? I was in the worst kind of trouble for a woman, and I didn't believe Roderick would marry me. You certainly weren't willing, either: that much was evident to me, for you responded to nothing I said or did. There was no one to rescue me but myself!

I never planned to be a thief. I've never stolen anything before. But one day, very soon after I discovered I was with child, I wandered into Roderick's room. I meant to take something from him to support me, but he never has anything, or if he does, he must carry it on his person.

I was very angry. Angry not only with him, but with you, Max, who used to favor me but couldn't be persuaded to any longer, as if I were an old, discarded shoe. Therefore, I searched your room as well as his when you were working. When I came upon your horde, all tidy in pound notes as though waiting for me, I believed Providence had heard my prayers at last. Now I can go to Italy, I thought. I can afford to pass myself off as a widow, rent a villa, perhaps meet a dashing Italian who will support my child and myself. Then I would return your money anonymously. But I kept waiting, hoping either you or Roderick would rescue me.

I would have restored your money eventually, Max, no matter what happened. That is the vow I pledged as I

*made the false notes and banded them into groups with
a true one on the top of each stack, so that you would
think your money was still there if you glanced inside.*

I had no idea you planned to use it so soon.

*And now Roderick has agreed to marry me, and I am
happier than I can say. I cannot take your money, for
my need is no longer desperate. You will discover all of
it, or almost all, inside the package. I hope you will find
happiness with it, you and your lady. I am not jealous
of you any longer, for jealousy has no room to breathe
when there is love. But I beg you, beg you, never to speak
of this. Roderick, Harry, everyone would be so angry
with me. Could this not be our secret, Maxim dearest?*

*Remember the first girl you kissed with fondness, will
you? And forgive me.*

Felicity

Max's hands were shaking as he lowered the letter. The tide
of rage that had coursed through him as he read the first lines
had eased to a trickle. Hardly feeling his legs beneath him as
he walked to the desk, he took the letter opener in hand and
slit the strings binding the parcel. The money was all there,
just as Felicity had said.

The rivulet of animosity slowed, then stopped. How could
he hold a grudge when his future—*their* future—had been so
happily restored? Had the little vixen done nothing, he might
never have known his one true love. No, he had no room for
resentment.

A knock sounded at the door. "A moment, please," he said,
and quickly slammed the letter within the desk drawer, then
lay the package with studied casualness on its top. After his
visitor left, he would put his savings in the inn's safe. No one
had to teach him twice.

He went to open the door.

"I hope you won't think it forward of me, Sir Hastings,"
Gwendolyn said with a playful smile, "but I was wondering if
you would like to walk with me at the Crescent this afternoon."

With a grin nearly splitting his face, Max wrapped his arms around her, pulling her as close to him as humanly possible without crushing her. Even so, she gave a little squeak of delighted protest.

"What a strange coincidence," he said, resting his chin on her hair. "I was wondering if you'd like to run with me to Gretna Greene right now."

Giving her no time to raise questions, he kissed her breathless.

AUTHOR'S NOTE

Although many advancements were made in glassmaking during the late eighteenth and early nineteenth centuries, the formula for a true copper red somehow eluded glassmakers until Georges Bontemps "rediscovered" it in 1826. When I stumbled upon this interesting fact while doing research for another novel, Maxim Hastings was born. I hope you enjoyed his search for the formula and weren't disappointed with what he found.

I love hearing from readers. Please write c/o Zebra Books.